# FIVE DAYS
# IN PARIS

★Published outside the UK under the title PASSION'S PROMISE

# FIVE DAYS
# IN PARIS

## Danielle Steel

**CORGI BOOKS**

# FIVE DAYS IN PARIS
## A CORGI BOOK : 0 552 14378 2

Originally published in Great Britain by Bantam Press,
a division of Transworld Publishers

PRINTING HISTORY
Bantam Press edition published 1995
Corgi edition published 1996

5 7 9 10 8 6

Set in 12½/14pt Monotype Bembo by
Phoenix Typesetting, Ilkley, West Yorkshire.

Corgi Books are published by Transworld Publishers Ltd,
61–63 Uxbridge Road, London W5 5SA,
a division of The Random House Group Ltd,
in Australia by Random House Australia (Pty) Ltd,
20 Alfred Street, Milsons Point, Sydney, NSW 2061, Australia,
in New Zealand by Random House New Zealand Ltd,
18 Poland Road, Glenfield, Auckland 10, New Zealand
and in South Africa by Random House (Pty) Ltd,
Endulini, 5a Jubilee Road, Parktown 2193, South Africa.

Reproduced, printed and bound in Germany by
Elsnerdruck, Berlin

*To Popeye,*
*with all my love,*
*Olive*

Five minutes . . . five days . . .
and a lifetime forever changed
in a single moment

# FIVE DAYS
# IN PARIS

# Chapter One

The weather in Paris was unusually warm as Peter Haskell's plane landed at Charles de Gaulle Airport. The plane taxied neatly to the gate, and a few minutes later, briefcase in hand, Peter was striding through the airport. He was almost smiling as he got on the customs line, despite the heat of the day and the number of people crowding ahead of him in line. Peter Haskell loved Paris.

He generally traveled to Europe four or five times a year. The pharmaceutical empire he ran had research centers in Germany, Switzerland, and France, and huge laboratories and factories in England. It was always interesting coming over here, exchanging ideas with their research teams, and exploring new

avenues of marketing, which was his real forte.
But this time it was far more than that, far more
than just a research trip, or the unveiling of a
new product. He was here for the birth of 'his
baby.' Vicotec. His life's dream. Vicotec was
going to change the lives and the outlook of
all people with cancer. It was going to dra-
matically alter maintenance programs, and the
very nature of chemotherapy the world over.
It would be Peter's one major contribution to
the human race. For the past four years, other
than his family, it was what he had lived for.
And undeniably, it was going to make Wilson-
Donovan millions. More than that, obviously,
their studies had already projected earnings in
the first five years to well over a billion dollars.
But that wasn't the point for Peter. The point
was life, and the quality of those lives, severely
dimmed, they were flickering candles in the
dark night of cancer. And Vicotec was going
to help them. At first, it had seemed like an
idealistic dream, but now they were just inches
from final victory, and it gave Peter a thrill
every time he thought of what was about
to happen.

And so far, their most recent results had
been perfect. Their meetings in Germany and
Switzerland had gone brilliantly. The testing
done in their laboratories there was even more

rigorous than what had been done in the States. They were sure now. It was safe. They could move ahead to Phase One Human Trials, as soon as the FDA approved it, which meant giving low doses of the medication to a select number of willing, well-informed subjects, and seeing how they fared.

Wilson–Donovan had already submitted their application to the FDA in January, months before, and based on the information they were developing now, they were going to ask for Vicotec to be put on the 'Fast Track,' pressing ahead with human trials of the drug, and eventually early release, once the FDA saw how safe it was and Wilson–Donovan proved it to them. The 'Fast Track' process was used in order to speed the various steps toward approval, in the case of drugs to be used in life-threatening diseases. Once they got approval from the FDA, they were going to start with a group of one hundred people who would sign informed consent agreements, acknowledging the potential dangers of the treatment. They were all so desperately ill, it would be their only hope, and they knew it. The people who signed up for experiments like this were grateful for any help available to them.

Wilson–Donovan wanted to move ahead as

quickly as possible to clinical trials on patients, which was why it was so important to test Vicotec's safety now before the FDA hearings in September, which would hopefully put it on the 'Fast Track.' Peter was absolutely sure that the testing being concluded by Paul-Louis Suchard, the head of the laboratory in Paris, would only confirm the good news he had just been given in Geneva.

'Holiday or business, Monsieur?' The customs officer looked unconcerned as he stamped Peter's passport, and barely glanced up at him after looking at the picture. He had blue eyes and dark hair and looked younger than his forty-four years. He had fine features, he was tall, and most people would have agreed that he was handsome.

'Business,' he said almost proudly. Vicotec. Victory. Salvation for every human being struggling with the agonies of chemotherapy and cancer.

The agent handed Peter his passport, and Peter picked up his bag and walked outside to find a taxi. It was a gloriously sunny June day, and with nothing left to do in Geneva, Peter had come to Paris a day early. He loved it here, and it would be easy to find something to do, even if it was just a long walk along the Seine. Or maybe Suchard would agree to meet him sooner than he'd planned, even though it was Sunday. It was still early in the day, and he hadn't had time to call Suchard yet. Although Suchard was very French, very serious, and more than a little rigid, Peter was going to call from the hotel and see if he was free, and willing to change their meeting.

Peter had learned to speak some French over the years, although he conducted all of his business with Suchard in English. Peter Haskell had learned a lot of things since he left the Midwest. It was obvious, even to the customs man at Charles de Gaulle, that Peter Haskell was an important man, of considerable intelligence and sophistication. He was cool and smooth and strong, and had an air of assurance about him. At forty-four, he was the president of one of the largest pharmaceutical companies in the world. He was not a scientist, but a marketing man, as was Frank Donovan, the chairman. And somewhat coincidentally, eighteen years before, Peter Haskell had married Frank's daughter. It hadn't been a 'smart move' on his part, or a calculated one. In Peter's eyes, it had been an accident, a quirk of fate, and one which he had fought against for the first six years he knew her.

Peter didn't want to marry Kate Donovan.

He didn't even know who she was when they met, when she was nineteen and he was twenty, at the University of Michigan. At first, she was just a pretty blonde sophomore he met at a mixer, but after two dates, he was crazy about her. They'd been going out for five months before someone made a crack, and suggested that he was a hell of a smart guy for going out with pretty little Katie. And then he'd explained it. She was the sole heiress to the Wilson–Donovan fortune, the biggest pharmaceutical firm in the country. Peter had been incensed, and he had raged at Katie for not telling him, with all the furor and naïveté of a boy of twenty.

'How *could* you? Why didn't you tell me?' he stormed at her.

'Tell you what? Was I supposed to warn you who my father was? I didn't think you'd care.' She'd been desperately hurt by his attack, and more than a little frightened he'd leave her. She knew how proud he was, and how poor his parents were. He had told her that only that year they'd finally bought the dairy farm where his father had worked all his life. It was mortgaged to the hilt, and Peter was constantly worried that the business would fail, and he'd have to give up school and go home to Wisconsin to help them.

16

'You knew perfectly well I'd "care." What am I supposed to do now?' He knew better than anyone that he couldn't compete in her world, that he didn't belong there, and never would, and Katie could never live on a farm in Wisconsin. She had seen too much of the world, and she was far too sophisticated even if she didn't seem to know it. The real trouble was that he felt he didn't belong in his own world most of the time either. No matter how hard he tried to be 'one of them' back home, there was always something different and much more big city about him. He had hated living on a farm when he was a kid, and dreamed of going to Chicago or New York, and being part of the business world. He hated milking cows, and stacking bales of hay, and endlessly cleaning manure out of the stables. For years, after school, he had helped his father at the dairy farm he ran, and now his father owned it. And Peter knew what that would mean. Eventually, he would have to go home, when he finished college, and help them. He dreaded it, but he wasn't looking for an easy out. He believed in doing what you were supposed to do, in living up to your responsibilities, and not trying to take any shortcuts. He had always been a good boy, his mother said, even if it meant doing things the hard way. He was willing to work for every-thing he wanted.

But once Peter knew who Katie was, being involved with her seemed wrong to him. No matter how sincere he was, it looked like an easy way out, a quick trip to the top, a shortcut. No matter how pretty she was, or how in love with her he thought he might have been, he knew he couldn't do anything about it. He was so adamant about not taking advantage of her that they broke up about two weeks after he found out who she was, and nothing she said to him changed that. She was distraught, and he was far more upset over losing her than he ever told her. It was his junior year, and in June he went home to help his father in Wisconsin. And by the end of the summer, he decided to take a year off to help him get the business off the ground. They'd had a hard winter the year before, and Peter thought he could turn it around, with some new ideas and new plans he'd learned in college.

He could have too, except that he got drafted and sent to Vietnam. He spent a year close to Da Nang, and when he re-upped for a second tour, they sent him to work for Intelligence in Saigon. It was a confusing time for him. He was twenty-two years old when he left Vietnam, and he had found none of the answers he wanted. He didn't know what to do with the rest of his life, he didn't want to go back to work on his father's farm, but he thought he should. His mother had died while he was in Vietnam, and he knew how hard that had been for his father.

He had another year of college left to do, but he didn't want to go back to the University of Michigan again, he somehow felt he had outgrown it. And he was confused about Vietnam too. The country he had wanted to hate, that had so tormented him, he had come to love instead, and he was actually sorry when he left it. He had a couple of minor romances there, mostly with American military personnel, and one very beautiful young Vietnamese girl, but everything was so complicated, and relationships were inevitably affected by the fact that no one expected to live much past tomorrow. He had never contacted Katie Donovan again, though he'd had a Christmas card from her that had been forwarded to him from Wisconsin. He had thought about her a lot at first in Da Nang, but it just seemed simpler not to write her. What could he possibly say to her? Sorry you're so rich and I'm so poor . . . have a great life in Connecticut, I'm going to be shoveling

19

manure in a dairy farm for the rest of my life . . . see ya . . .

But as soon as he got back, it was obvious to all of them in Wisconsin that once again he just didn't fit, and even his father urged him to look for a job in Chicago. He found one easily in a marketing firm, went to school at night, got his degree, and had just started his first job when he went to a party given by an old friend from Michigan, and ran into Katie. She had transferred and was living in Chicago by then too, and she was about to graduate from Northwestern. The first time he saw her again, she took his breath away. She was prettier than ever. It had been almost three years since he'd seen her. And it stunned him to realize that even after three years of forcing himself to stay away from her, seeing her could still make everything inside him tremble.

'What are you doing here?' he asked nervously, as though she were only supposed to exist in his memories of his school days. She had haunted him for months after he left college, and especially when he first went into the service. But he had long since relegated her to the past, and expected her to stay there. Seeing her suddenly catapulted her right back into the present.

'I'm finishing school,' she said, holding her

breath as she looked at him. He seemed taller and thinner, his eyes were bluer and his hair even darker than she remembered. Everything about him seemed sharper and more exciting than her endless memories of him. She had never forgotten. He was the only man who had ever walked away from her, because of who she was, and what he thought he could never give her. 'I hear you were in Vietnam,' she said softly, and he nodded. 'It must have been awful.' She was so afraid to scare him away again, to make some terrible wrong move. She knew how proud he was, and just looking at him, she knew that he would never come near her. And he watched her too. He was wondering what she had become, and what she wanted from him. But she seemed so innocent to him, and fairly harmless, despite her seemingly ominous background, and the threat he had convinced himself she presented. In his eyes, she had been a threat to his integrity, and an untenable link between a past he could no longer live, and a future he wanted, but had no idea how to accomplish. Having seen so much more of the world since they had last met, looking at her now, he could barely remember what he had once been so afraid of. She didn't seem so daunting to him now, she seemed very young, and very naïve, and irresistibly attractive.

They talked for hours that night, and he took her home eventually. And then, although he knew he shouldn't have, he called her. It seemed so easy at first, he even told himself they could just be friends, which neither of them believed. But all he knew was that he wanted to be near her. She was bright and fun, and she understood the crazy things he felt, about how he didn't fit anywhere, and what he wanted to do with his life. Eventually, far, far down the road, he wanted to change the world, or at the very least make a difference. She was the only person in his life then who understood that. He had had so many dreams back then, so many good intentions. And now, twenty years later, Vicotec was bringing all those old dreams to fruition.

Peter Haskell hailed a cab at Charles de Gaulle, and the driver put his bag in the trunk, and nodded when Peter told him where he was going. Everything about Peter Haskell suggested that he was a man in command, a man of impressive stature. And yet, if you looked in his eyes, you saw kindness, and strength, integrity, a warm heart, and a sense of humor. There was more to Peter Haskell than just well-tailored suits, the starched white shirt and Hermès tie he wore, and the expensive briefcase.

'Hot, isn't it?' Peter asked on the way into town, and the driver nodded. He could hear from the accent in his French that he was American, but he spoke it adequately, and the driver answered him in French, speaking slowly, so Peter could understand him.

'It's been nice for a week. Did you come from America?' the driver asked with interest. People responded to Peter that way, they were drawn to him, even if they normally wouldn't have been. But the fact that he spoke French to him impressed the driver.

'I came from Geneva,' Peter explained, and they fell silent again, as he smiled to himself, thinking of Katie. He always wished that she would travel with him, but she never did. At first, the children were young, and later she was too caught up in her own world and her myriad obligations. She hadn't taken more than one or two business trips with him over the years. Once to London, and the other time to Switzerland, and never to Paris.

Paris was special to him, it was the culmination of everything he had always dreamed, and never even knew he wanted. He had worked so hard for what he had, over the years, even if some of it seemed to have come

23

easily to him. He knew better than anyone, it hadn't. There were no freebies in life. You worked for what you got, or you wound up with nothing.

He had gone out with Katie for two years, once he'd found her again. She stayed in Chicago after she graduated, and she got a job in an art gallery, just so she could be near Peter. She was crazy about him, but he was adamant that they would never be married. And he kept insisting that eventually they'd have to stop seeing each other and she should go back to New York and start dating other men. But he could never bring himself to break off with her and actually make her do it. They were too attached by then, and even Katie knew he really loved her. And ultimately, her father stepped in. He was a smart man. He said nothing about their relationship to Peter, only about his business. He sensed instinctively that it was the one way to get Peter to let down his guard. Frank Donovan wanted Peter and his daughter back in New York, and he did what he could to help Katie woo him.

Like Peter, Frank Donovan was a marketing man, and a great one. He talked to Peter about his career, his life's plan, his future, and liking what he heard, he offered him a job at Wilson-

Donovan. He said nothing about Katie. In fact, he insisted the job had nothing to do with her whatsoever. He reassured Peter that working for Wilson-Donovan would do wonders for his career, and promised him no one would ever think it had anything to do with Katie. Their relationship, according to Frank, was an entirely separate issue. But it was a job worth thinking about, and Peter knew it. In spite of all his fears at the time, a job with a major corporation in New York was exactly what he wanted, and so was Katie.

He agonized over it, debated endlessly, and even his father thought it was a good move when Peter called him to discuss it. Peter went home to Wisconsin to talk to him about it over a long weekend. His father wanted the moon for him, and encouraged him to take Donovan's offer. He saw something in Peter that even Peter himself hadn't yet understood. He had qualities of leadership that few men had, a quiet strength, and an unusual courage. His father knew that whatever Peter did, he would be good at. And he sensed that the job with Wilson-Donovan was only the beginning for him. He used to tease Peter's mother when Peter was only a small boy, and tell her that he would be president one day, or at least governor of Wisconsin. And sometimes, she believed him. It was easy to believe great things about Peter.

His sister Muriel said the same things about him too. To her, her brother Peter had always been a hero, long before Chicago or Vietnam, or even before he went off to college. There was something special about him. Everyone knew it. And she told him the same thing as their father: Go to New York, reach for the brass ring. She even asked him if he thought he'd marry Katie, but he insisted he wouldn't, and she seemed sorry to hear it. She thought Katie sounded glamorous and exciting, and Muriel thought Katie looked beautiful in the pictures Peter carried with him.

Peter's father had invited him to bring her home long since, but Peter always insisted that he didn't want to give her false hopes about their future. She'd probably make herself right at home and learn to milk cows from Muriel, and then what? It was all he had to give her, and there was no way in the world he was going to drag Katie into the hard life he had grown up with. As far as he was concerned, it had killed his mother. She had died of cancer, without proper medical care, or the money to pay for it. His father didn't even have insurance. He always thought his mother had died of poverty and fatigue, and too much hardship in her lifetime. And even with Katie's money to back her up, he loved her too much to condemn her to this existence, or even let her see it too closely. At twenty-two, his sister already looked exhausted. She had married right out of high school while he was in Vietnam, and had three kids in three years with the boy who had been her high school sweetheart. By the time she was twenty-one, she looked beaten and dreary. There was so much more that he wanted for her too, but just looking at her, he knew she'd never have it. She'd never get out. She had never even gone to college. And she was trapped now. Peter knew, just as his sister did, that she and her husband would work at her father's dairy farm for their lifetimes, unless he lost the farm, or they died. There was no other way out. Except for Peter. And Muriel didn't even resent that. She was happy for him. The seas had parted for him, and all he had to do was set off on the path Frank Donovan had offered.

'Do it, Peter,' Muriel whispered to him when he came to the farm to talk to them. 'Go to New York. Papa wants you to,' she said generously. 'We all do.' It was as though they were all telling him to save himself, to go for it, swim free of the life that would drown him,

27

if he let it. They wanted him to go to New York and try for the big time.

There was a lump in his throat the size of a rock when he drove away from the farm that weekend. His father and Muriel stood watching him go, and they waved until his car disappeared completely. It was as though all three of them knew this was an important moment in his life. More than college. More than Vietnam. In his heart, and his soul, he was cutting his bond to the farm.

When Peter got back to Chicago, he spent the night alone. He didn't call Katie. But he called her father the next morning. And he accepted his offer, as he felt his hands shake while he held the phone.

Peter started at Wilson–Donovan two weeks later, to the day, and once he got to New York, he woke up every morning feeling as though he had won the Kentucky Derby.

Katie had been working at an art gallery in Chicago, as a receptionist, and she quit her job the same day he did, and moved back to New York to live with her father. Frank Donovan was delighted. His plan had worked. His little girl was home. And he had found a brilliant new marketing man in the bargain. For all concerned, the arrangement was a good one.

And for the next several months, Peter

concentrated more on business than romance. It annoyed Katie at first, but when she complained to her father about it, he wisely told her to be patient. And eventually, Peter relaxed and became less anxious about whatever unfinished projects he had at the office. But generally, he wanted to do everything perfectly, to justify Frank's faith in him, and show him how grateful he was to be there.

He didn't even go home to Wisconsin anymore, he never had time to. But in time, much to Katie's relief, he began to make more room in his schedule for some diversion. They went to parties, and plays, she introduced him to all her friends. And Peter was surprised to realize how much he liked them, and how at ease he felt in her life.

And little by little, over the next several months, none of the things that had once terrified him about Katie seemed quite so worrisome to Peter. His career was going well, and much to his astonishment, no one was upset by where he was, or how he got there. In fact, everyone seemed to like and accept him. And swept away by a wave of good feelings, he and Katie got engaged within the year, and it didn't come as a surprise to anyone, except maybe Peter. But he had known her long enough, and he had come to feel so comfortable in her world, he felt he belonged there. Frank Donovan said it was meant to be, and Katie smiled. She had never doubted for an instant that Peter was right for her. She had always known it, and been absolutely sure that she wanted to be his wife.

Peter's sister, Muriel, was thrilled for him when he called her with the news, and in the end, Peter's father was the only one who objected to their union, much to Peter's disappointment. As much as his father had thought the job at Wilson–Donovan was a great opportunity, he was equally opposed to the marriage. And he was absolutely convinced that eventually, Peter would regret it for the rest of his life.

'You'll always be the hired hand, if you marry her, son. It's not right, it's not fair, but that's the way it is. Every time they look at you, they'll remember who you were back at the beginning, not who you are now.' But Peter didn't believe that. He had grown into her world. It was his now. And his own world had begun to seem part of another life. It just didn't seem part of him anymore, it was completely foreign. It was as though he'd grown up in Wisconsin accidentally, or as though it had been someone else and he'd never really been there at all. Even Vietnam seemed more real to him now than his early days on the farm in Wisconsin. It seemed hard to believe sometimes that he'd actually spent more than twenty years there. In little more than a year, Peter had become a businessman, a man of the world, and a New Yorker. His family was still dear to him, and always would be. But the thought of life as a dairy farmer still gave him nightmares. But try as he could to convince his father that he was doing the right thing, he just couldn't do it. The senior Haskell was immovable in his objections, although finally he agreed to come to the wedding, but probably only because he was worn down by listening to Peter argue, and trying to convince his father that what he was doing was right.

In the end, Peter was devastated when his father didn't come to the wedding. He had had an accident on the tractor the week before, and was laid up with a bad back and a broken arm, and Muriel was about to give birth to her fourth child. She couldn't come, and her husband Jack didn't want to leave her to fly to New York. Peter felt bereft at first, and then, like everything else in his new life, eventually he got caught up in the swirl of activity around him.

They went to Europe for their honeymoon,

and for months after that, they never seemed to have time to go to Wisconsin. Katie always had plans for him, or Frank did. And despite all their promises and good intentions, somehow Peter and Katie never made it to Wisconsin, to visit his family on the farm. But Peter had promised his father they'd go for Christmas, and nothing was going to stop him this time. He didn't even tell Kate about the plan. He was going to surprise her. He was beginning to suspect it was the only way to get there.

But when his father had a heart attack and died just before Thanksgiving, Peter was overwhelmed by his own emotions. He felt guilt and grief and regret for all the things he had never done, and always meant to. As it turned out, Kate had never even met him.

Peter took her to the funeral. It was a grim affair, in the pouring rain, as she and Peter stood to one side, looking wooden. Peter was clearly devastated, and Muriel was a good distance from him, sobbing as she stood beside her husband and babies. It seemed an odd contrast of farm folk and city slickers. And Peter began to realize how separate he had become from them, how far he had traveled since he left, how little they had in common now. Katie had been uncomfortable with them, and she made a point of it to Peter. And Muriel was surprisingly cool to her, which was unlike her. When Peter said something about it to Muriel, she muttered awkwardly about the fact that Katie didn't belong there. Although she was Peter's wife, she hadn't even known their father. She was expensively dressed in a black coat and a fur hat, and she seemed irritated to be there, and Muriel said so, much to Peter's chagrin. She made a pointed comment to Peter and they had argued about it, and then they'd both cried. But the reading of the will only brought up more stress between them. Their father had left the farm to Muriel and Jack, and Kate had been visibly outraged the moment she heard what the lawyer said.

'How could he do that to you?' she had raged in the privacy of his old bedroom. It had a linoleum brick floor and the old tan paint on the walls was cracked and peeling. It was a far cry from the house Frank had bought them in Greenwich. 'He disinherited you!' Kate fumed, and Peter tried to explain it. He understood it far better than his wife.

'It's all they have, Kate. This miserable godforsaken place. This is their whole life here. I have a career, a good job, a life with you. I don't need this. I didn't even want it, and Dad knew that.' Peter didn't consider it a slight or an injustice. He wanted Muriel to have it. The farm meant everything to them.

'You could have sold it and split the money with them, and they could have moved some-place better,' she said sensibly, but it only showed Peter that she didn't understand.

'They don't want to do that, Kate, and that's probably what Dad was afraid of. He didn't want us to sell the farm. It took him his whole life to buy it.' She didn't tell him what a disaster she thought it was, but he could see it in the way she looked at him, and in the silence that grew between them. As far as Kate was concerned, the farm was even worse than Peter had told her when they were in college, and she was relieved that they'd never have to come back here again. At least she wasn't going to come back. And if she had anything to say about it, after his father had disinherited him, Peter wasn't going to either. As far as she was concerned, Wisconsin was now relegated to the distant past. She wanted Peter to move on.

Muriel was still upset when they left, and Peter had the uncomfortable feeling that he was saying good-bye to her, and not just his father. It was as though that was what Kate wanted, although she never came right out and

34

said it to him. It was as though she wanted all his ties to be to her, all his roots and his bonds, his allegiance and affection. It was almost as if Kate was jealous of Muriel, and the piece of his life and history that she represented, and his not getting a piece of the farm was a good excuse to end it once and for all.

'You were right to leave here years ago,' Kate said quietly as they drove away, she seemed to be unaware of the fact that Peter was crying. All she wanted was to go back to New York as fast as they could get there. 'Peter, you don't belong here,' she said firmly. He wanted to argue with her, to tell her she was wrong, to stick up for them, out of loyalty, except that he knew she was right, and he felt guilty about it. He didn't belong there. He never had.

And as they boarded the plane in Chicago, he felt relief sweep over him. He had escaped again. At some level, he had been terrified that his father would leave him the farm and expect him to run it. But his father had been wiser than that, and knew Peter better. Peter had nothing to do with the farm now. He didn't own it, it couldn't devour him, as he had feared it might. He was free at last. It was Jack and Muriel's problem now.

And as the plane lifted off the ground and headed for Kennedy, he knew he had left the farm behind, and everything it represented. He only hoped he hadn't also lost his sister at the same time.

He was quiet on the flight home, and over the next weeks, he mourned his father in silence. He said very little about it to Kate, mostly because he had the feeling she didn't want to hear it. He called Muriel once or twice, but she was always busy with the kids, or rushing out to help Jack with the dairy. She never had time to talk, and when she did, Peter didn't like the comments she made about Katie. Her open criticism of his wife created a definite chasm between them, and after a while, he stopped calling. He threw himself into his work, and found solace in what happened at the office. He was completely at home there. In fact, his whole life in New York seemed like the perfect existence to him. He fit in perfectly, at Wilson-Donovan, among their friends, in the social life Kate had carved out for them. It was almost as though he had been born into it, and had never had another life before that.

To his friends in New York, Peter was one of them. He was smooth and sophisticated, and people laughed when he said he'd grown up on a farm. Most of the time, no one believed him. He seemed more like Boston, or New

York. And he was good-natured about making the adjustments the Donovans expected of him. Frank had insisted they live in Greenwich, Connecticut, as he did. He wanted 'his baby' close to him, and besides, she was used to it, and she liked it. Wilson-Donovan was based in New York, and they kept a studio apartment there, but the Donovans had always lived in Greenwich, Connecticut, an hour's ride from New York. It was an easy commute, and Peter rode in on the train with Frank daily. Peter liked living in Greenwich, he loved their house, and he loved being married to Katie. Most of the time, they got on splendidly, and the only major disagreement they'd had was over the fact that she thought he should have inherited the farm and then sold it. But they had long since ceased to argue about it, in deference to each other's conflicting opinions.

The only other thing that bothered him was that Frank had bought their first house for them. Peter had tried to object to it, but he didn't want to upset Katie. And she had begged him to let her father do it. Peter had complained, but in the end, she won. She wanted a big house so they could start a family quickly, and Peter certainly couldn't afford the kind of house she was used to, and her father thought she should live in. These were the problems Peter had been so afraid of. But the Donovans handled it all graciously. Her father called the handsome Tudor house a 'wedding gift.' And to Peter, it looked like a mansion. It was big enough to accommodate three or four kids, had a beautiful deck, a dining room, a living room, five bedrooms, a huge den for him, a family room, and a fabulous country kitchen. It was a far cry from the battered old farmhouse his father had left his sister in Wisconsin. And Peter had to admit sheepishly that he loved the house.

Her father also wanted to hire someone to clean and cook for them, but there Peter drew the line, and announced that he would do the cooking himself if he had to, but he was not going to allow Frank to provide them with hired help. Eventually, Katie learned to do the cooking, for a little while at least. But by Christmas, she was so violently ill from morning sickness, she couldn't do anything, and Peter had to do most of the cooking and clean the house. But he didn't mind a bit, he was thrilled about their baby. It seemed almost a mystical exchange to him, a special kind of consolation for the loss of his father, which still pained him more than he ever said.

It was the beginning of a happy, fruitful

eighteen years for them. They had three sons in their first four years, and ever since, Katie's life had been filled with charity committees, parents' associations, and car pools, and she loved it. The boys were involved in a thousand things, soccer, baseball, swimming teams, and recently Katie had decided to run for the Greenwich school board. She was totally involved in her community, and very concerned with world ecology, and a number of issues Peter knew he should have been interested in, but wasn't. He liked to say that Katie was involved in global issues for both of them. He was just trying to keep his head above water at work.

But she knew a lot about that too. Katie's mother had died when she was three, and she had grown up being her father's constant companion. As she grew up, Katie knew everything about his business, and that never changed even after she and Peter married. There were times when she knew things about the company even before Peter did. And if he shared a bit of news with her, he was always startled to realize it wasn't news to her. It caused some problems over the years, but Peter was willing to accept Frank's place in their life. Katie's bond to him was a great deal stronger than Peter had expected, but there was no harm in it. Frank was a fair man, and he always exercised good judgment about how far to go with his opinions. At least Peter thought he did, until Frank tried to tell them where to send their son to nursery school. That time, Peter put his foot down, and kept it there until high school, or at least he tried to. But there were times when Katie's father was completely immovable, and it upset Peter even more when Katie sided with him, although she usually tried to phrase it as diplomatically as possible when she echoed her father's opinions.

But despite her diplomacy, Kate's ties to her father remained strong over the years, and she agreed with him more frequently than Peter would have wanted. It was Peter's only complaint in an otherwise happy marriage. And he had so many blessings in his life that he didn't feel he had a right to complain over the occasional battle of wills with Frank. As far as Peter was concerned, when he examined his life, the blessings far outweighed the pains or the burdens.

The only real sadness in his life was when his sister died at twenty-nine, of cancer, just as his mother had, though Muriel was far younger. And like his mother, his sister had been unable to afford decent treatment. She and her husband had been so proud, they never even called and told him. She was at death's door when Jack finally called, and Peter was heartbroken when he flew to Wisconsin and saw her. She died only a few days after that. And in less than a year, Jack sold the farm, remarried, and moved to Montana. For years afterwards, Peter didn't know where he'd gone, or what had happened to his sister's children. And when he finally heard from Jack again, years after Muriel had died, Kate said too much water had gone over the dam, and he should let it go and forget them. Peter had sent Jack the money he'd asked for when he called, but he'd never gotten to Montana to see Muriel's children. And he knew that when, and if, he did, they would no longer know him. They had a new mother and a new family, and Peter knew that Jack had only called him because he needed money. He had no real sentiment for his late wife's brother, nor Peter for him, although Peter would have liked to see his nephews and nieces. But he was too busy to fly to Montana to see them, and in a way, they were part of another life. In some ways, it was easier to do as Kate said, and just let it go now, although he felt guilty about it whenever it crossed his mind.

Peter had his own life to lead, his own

family to think of, his own children to protect, and do battle for. And there had indeed been a battle royal, four years before when their oldest son, Mike, applied to high school. Apparently, every Donovan in memory had gone to Andover, and Frank felt that Mike should too, and Katie agreed with him. But Peter did not. He didn't want to send Mike away to school, he wanted him to stay at home until he went to college. But this time, Frank won hands down. It was Mike who cast the deciding vote, and his mother and grandfather had convinced him that unless he went to Andover, he'd never get into a decent college, let alone business school, and he'd miss every possible opportunity for a good job later on, and valuable connections in the meantime. It seemed ridiculous to Peter, who pointed out that he'd gone to the University of Michigan, night school in Chicago for his senior year, had never been to business school, and had never heard of Andover when he was growing up in Wisconsin. 'And I did all right,' he said with a smile. He was running one of the country's most important corporations. But he hadn't been prepared for what Mike would say when he answered back.

'Yeah, but you married it, Dad. That's different.' It was the worst blow the boy could

42

have dealt him, and something in Peter's eyes must have told Mike just how hard he'd hit him, because the boy was quick to explain that he didn't mean that the way it sounded and that two decades earlier things had been 'different.' But they both knew they weren't. And in the end, Mike had gone to Andover, and now, like his grandfather, he was going to Princeton in the fall. Paul was at Andover now too, and only Patrick, the youngest, was talking about staying home for high school, or maybe going to Exeter, just to do something other than what his brothers had done. He had another year to think about it, and he was talking about boarding school in California. It was something Peter would have liked to change, but knew he couldn't. Going away for their high school years was a Donovan tradition that couldn't even be discussed. Even Kate, despite her closeness to her father, had gone to Miss Porter's. Peter would have preferred having his kids at home, but to him it was a small compromise, he said, he lost their company for a few months a year, but they were getting a great education. There was no question about that, and Frank always said they were making important friendships that would endure all their lives. It was hard to quibble with that, so Peter didn't. But it was a lonely feeling when his sons left for boarding school every year. Kate and the boys were the only family he had. And he still missed Muriel and his parents, though he never admitted that to Kate.

Peter's life had moved ahead impressively over the years. He was an important man. His career had gone brilliantly. And appropriately, they had moved to a larger house in Greenwich, when he could afford to buy it himself. This time there was no question of accepting a house from Frank. The house Peter bought was a handsome home on six acres in Greenwich, and although the city appealed to him at times, Peter knew how important it was to Katie to stay where they were. She had lived in Greenwich all her life. Her friends were there, the right elementary schools for their kids, the committees she cared about, and her father. She loved living close to him. She still kept a close eye on his house for him, and on weekends, she and Peter often went over to discuss family matters, or business, or just for a friendly game of tennis. Katie went over to see him a lot.

They went to Martha's Vineyard in the summer to be near him too. He had a fabulous estate there that he'd owned for years, and the Haskells had a more modest one, but Peter had to agree with Kate, it was a great place for the children, and he truly loved it. The Vineyard was a special place to him, and as soon as he could afford to buy a place of their own, Peter had forced her to give up the cottage her father loaned them on his property, and bought her a lovely house just down the road. And the boys loved it when Peter built them their own bunkhouse, which allowed them to invite their friends, which they did constantly. For years now, Peter and Kate had been surrounded by children, particularly at the Vineyard. There always seemed to be half a dozen extra kids staying at their house.

Theirs was an easy comfortable life, and in spite of the compromises Peter knew he had occasionally made on the domestic end of things, as to where and how they lived, and the boys going to boarding school, he also knew that he had never sacrificed his principles or integrity, and as far as the business was concerned, Frank gave him a free hand. Peter had come up with brilliant ideas that had rapidly affected the firm positively, and he had brought them growth and development far beyond anything Frank had ever dreamed. Peter's suggestions had been invaluable, his decisions bold but sure. Frank had known exactly what he was doing when he brought

him in, and even more so when he made him
president of Wilson-Donovan at thirty-seven.
His running of the company had been
masterful right from the start. It had been seven
years since then, four of them spent on the
development of Vicotec, which had been
costly in the extreme, but once again
absolutely brilliant. It had been Peter's baby
from the first, and it had been his decision to
pursue that line of development at the scientific end, and he had convinced Frank to go
along with him. It was an enormous invest-
ment but in the long run, they both agreed,
well worth it. And for Peter, there was an
added bonus. It was the culmination of his life-
long dream, to help humanity, while still
forging ahead in the greedy, self-serving,
mundane world of business. But if nothing
else, in memory of his mother and Muriel,
Peter wanted Vicotec to be brought into existence as quickly as they could do it. If a product
like it had been available to them, their lives
might have been saved, or at the very least
prolonged. And now he wanted to save others
like them. People on farms and in rural areas,
or even in cities, but isolated by poverty or
circumstances that would kill them without a
drug like this one.

He found himself thinking about it again in

the cab, and about the meetings he had had in Europe all week. Just knowing how far Vicotec had come was incredibly rewarding. And as the car sped rapidly toward Paris, he was sorry that, as usual, Katie hadn't come along.

To Peter, it was the perfect city. It always took his breath away. There was something about Paris that made his heart race. He had come here on business for the first time fifteen years before, and at the time, he had felt as though he had been put on earth for that single moment in time when he first saw it. He had arrived in Paris alone on a national holiday, and he still remembered driving down the Champs-Elysées with the Arc de Triomphe straight ahead, and the French flag flying nobly in the breeze from inside the arch. He had stopped the car, gotten out, and as he stood there and looked at it, he had been embarrassed to realize that he was crying.

Katie used to tease him and say that he must have been French in a past life because he loved Paris so much. It was a place that meant a great deal to him, and he was never quite sure why. There was something incredibly beautiful and powerful about it. He had never had a bad time there. And he knew that this time would be no different. Despite the rather taciturn style of Paul-Louis Suchard, he knew that his meeting with him the next day could be nothing less than a celebration.

The taxi whizzed through the midday traffic as Peter continued to watch familiar landmarks slip by, like the Invalides and the Opéra, and a moment later, they drove into the Place Vendôme, and Peter felt almost as though he had come home as he saw it. The statue of Napoleon stood atop the column in the middle of the square, and if one squinted one could easily imagine carriages with coats of arms on the sides bouncing along, filled with white-wigged and satin-breeched French nobles. The picturesque absurdity of it made Peter smile as the cab stopped in front of the Ritz, and the doorman hurried forward to open the car door. He recognized Peter, as he appeared to recognize all of the arriving guests, and signaled quickly to a bellboy to take Peter's single piece of luggage, while Peter paid the driver of the cab.

The facade of the Ritz was surprisingly unassuming, with only a small canopy to distinguish it, and it looked no more impressive than the host of impressive shops all around it. Chaumet and Boucheron were nearby with their sparkling wares, Chanel was at the corner of the square, and JAR's, the highly exclusive jeweler, whose initials stood for its founder Joel A. Rosenthal, was tucked away just behind it. But certainly among the most important elements of the Place Vendôme was the Ritz Hotel, and Peter always said that there was nowhere else in the world like it. It was the ultimate decadence and luxury, offering its guests unlimited comfort in total style. He always felt a little guilty staying there on a business trip, but he had come to love it too much over the years to stay anywhere else. It was a rare element of fantasy in a life that was otherwise completely sensible and ordained by reason. Peter loved the subtlety, the elegance, the exquisite decor of the rooms, the sumptuous beauty of the brocades on the walls, the beautiful antique fireplaces. And from the moment he stepped into the revolving door, he felt the instant undercurrent of excitement.

The Ritz never disappointed him, and never failed him. Like a beautiful woman one only visits occasionally, she was waiting for him each time with her arms open, and her hair done, her makeup perfect, and looking even more enchanting than she had been the time before when he last saw her.

Peter loved the Ritz almost as much as he loved Paris. It was part of the magic and the charm, and as he came into the lobby from the revolving door, he was immediately greeted by a liveried concierge, and hastened up the two steps to the reception desk to register. Even being at the desk, waiting to sign in, was fun. He loved watching the people there. On his left was a handsome, older South American man, with a striking young woman in a red dress standing beside him. They were speaking quietly to each other in Spanish. Her hair and nails were impeccably done and Peter noticed that she was wearing an enormous diamond on her left hand. She glanced at him and smiled as he watched her. He was an extremely attractive man, and nothing in his demeanor now suggested to the woman standing next to him that he had once been a farm boy. He looked like exactly what he was, a wealthy, powerful man, who moved in the circles of the elite, and those who ran the empires of the world. Everything about Peter suggested power and importance, and yet there was something appealing about him too, something gentle and young and he was undeniably very good-looking. And if one took the time to look, there was something more about him too, something intriguing in his eyes, more than most people knew, or cared to see there. There was a softness about Peter, a kindness, a kind of compassion that is rare in men of power. But the woman in the red dress didn't see that. She saw the Hermès tie, the strong, clean hands, she saw the briefcase, the English shoes, the well-cut suit, and she had to force her eyes back to her companion.

On Peter's other side were three very well dressed older Japanese men in dark suits, all of them smoking cigarettes and conferring discreetly. There was a younger man waiting for them, and a concierge at the desk speaking to them in Japanese, and as Peter turned away from them, still waiting his turn, he noticed a flurry at the door, as four powerful-looking dark-skinned men came through the revolving door, and seemed to take control of it, as two more similar men followed right behind them, and then like a gumball machine spitting out its wares, the revolving door blurted out three very attractive women in bright-colored Dior suits. It was the same suit, in different colors, but the women themselves looked very different. Like the Spanish woman Peter had noticed standing next to him, these women were also immaculate, with their hair impeccably done. They all wore diamonds at their necks and ears, and as a group, they made quite an impression. In an instant, the six bodyguards accompanying them seemed to surround them, just as a much older, very distinguished Arab man emerged from the revolving door just behind them.

'King Khaled . . .' Peter heard someone whisper nearby, 'or it could be his brother . . . all three of his wives . . . staying here for a month . . . They have the entire fourth-floor hallway overlooking the gardens . . .' He was the ruler of a small Arab nation, and as they made their way through the lobby, Peter counted eight bodyguards, and an assortment of people who seemed to be trailing behind them. They were immediately accompanied by one of the concierges, and made their way slowly through the lobby with all eyes upon them. So much so that almost no one noticed Catherine Deneuve hurry into the restaurant for lunch, and they all but forgot the fact that Clint Eastwood was staying there, while making a movie just outside Paris. Faces and names such as theirs were commonplace at the Ritz, and Peter wondered if he would ever be blasé enough to simply not care, and just ignore them. But just being here, and watching it all, always seemed like such fun that he couldn't bring himself to look away or pretend to be bored, as some of the habitués did, and he couldn't help staring at the Arab king and his bevy of lovely consorts. The women were talking and laughing quietly, and the bodyguards kept a close watch on them, letting no one come anywhere near them. They surrounded them like a wall of stern statues, while the king walked along quietly, talking to another man, and then suddenly Peter heard a voice just behind him, and was startled.

'Good afternoon, Mr Haskell. Welcome back. We are very happy to see you again.'

'So am I, happy to be back.' Peter turned and smiled at the young concierge who had been assigned to sign him in. They were giving him a room on the third floor. But in his opinion, there could be no bad rooms at the Ritz. He would have been happy anywhere they put him. 'You seem to be as busy as usual.' He was referring to the king and the small army of bodyguards, but the hotel was always filled with people just like him.

'As usual . . . *comme d'habitude* . . .' The young concierge smiled, and put away the form that Peter had filled out. 'I will show you to your room now.' He had checked his passport, and gave the room number to one of the bellboys, signaling to Peter to follow him down the steps and across the lobby.

They passed the bar and the restaurant, filled with well-dressed diners, and people meeting for drinks or lunch, to discuss business, or more intriguing plans. And as they went by, Peter glimpsed Catherine Deneuve then, still beautiful, and laughing as she talked to a friend at a corner table. It was everything he loved about this hotel, the faces, the people, the very look of them was exciting. And as they walked the long, long hall to the back elevator, they passed the block-long expanse of vitrines filled with expensive wares from all the boutiques and jewelers of Paris. Halfway there, he saw a gold bracelet he thought Katie would like, and made a mental note to come back here to buy it. He always brought her something from his trips. It was her consolation prize for not going, or it had been years before, when she was either pregnant, or nursing, or tied down with their sons when they were very young. Nowadays she really didn't want to travel with him, and he knew that. She enjoyed her committee meetings and her friends. With both older boys away at boarding school, and only one at home, she really could have come, but she always had an excuse, and Peter didn't press her anymore. She just didn't want to. But he still brought her presents, and the boys too, if they were home. It was a last vestige of their childhoods.

They reached the elevator at last, and the

Arab king was nowhere to be seen by then, they had gone upstairs a few minutes earlier to their dozen or so rooms. They were regulars there, his wives normally spent May and June in Paris, and sometimes stayed until the collections in July. And they came back again in the winter for the same reason.

'It's warm this year,' Peter said easily, chatting to the concierge as they waited for the elevator. It was glorious outside, balmy and hot, it made you want to lie under a tree somewhere, and look up at the sky, watching the clouds roll by. It really wasn't a day to do business. But Peter was going to call Paul-Louis Suchard anyway, and see if he would make time to see him before their scheduled meeting the next morning.

'It's been hot all week,' the concierge said conversationally. It put everyone in a good mood, and there was air-conditioning in the rooms, so there were never any complaints about temperature. And they both smiled as an American woman with three Yorkshire terriers walked past them. The dogs were so fluffed and so covered with bows that it made the two men exchange a glance as they watched her.

And then, almost as though the area they stood in had become electrically charged,

Peter suddenly felt a surge of activity behind him. He had been looking at the woman with the dogs, and even she looked up in surprise. Peter wondered if it was the Arabs with their bodyguards again, or some movie star, but one could sense an instant heightening of excitement. He turned to see what was happening, and a phalanx of men in dark suits with earpieces seemed to be coming toward them. There were four of them, and it was impossible to see who was behind them. It was easy to see that they were bodyguards, from the earpieces they wore and the walkie-talkies they carried. And if it had been any colder, they would surely have been wearing raincoats.

They moved toward where Peter and the concierge stood, almost in unison, and then moved aside just enough to reveal a handful of men just behind them. They were men in lightweight suits, they looked American, and one of them was taller than the others and noticeably blonder. He looked almost like a movie star, and something about him seemed to magnetize everyone. They were all hanging on his every word, and the three men with him looked extremely earnest and deeply engrossed, and then suddenly laughed at what he was saying.

Peter was intrigued by him, and glanced at

him long and hard, suddenly sure that he had seen him somewhere, but couldn't remember, and then instantly it came to him. He was the controversial and very dynamic young senator from Virginia, Anderson Thatcher. He was forty-eight years old, had been lightly touched by scandal more than once, but in each case the fearsome fumes had been quickly dispelled, and more than once, and far more importantly, he had been touched by tragedy. His brother Tom, while running for the presidency, had been killed six years before, just before the election. He had been a sure winner, and there had been all kinds of theories about who had done it, and even two very bad movies. But all they'd ever turned up finally was one lone, mad gunman. But in the years since, Anderson Thatcher, 'Andy' as he was known to his friends apparently, had been seriously groomed and had come up through the ranks of his political allies and enemies, and was now thought to be a serious contender for the next presidential election. He had not announced his candidacy yet, but people in the know thought he would shortly. And over the past several years, Peter had followed him with interest. Despite some of the less savory things he'd heard about him personally, he thought he might be an interesting candidate on the

57

next ticket. And just looking at him now, surrounded by campaign officials and body-guards, there was an obvious charisma about him, and it fascinated Peter to watch him.

Tragedy had struck him for the second time when his two-year-old son had died of cancer. Peter knew less about that, but he remembered some heartbreaking photographs in *Time* when the child died. There had been one photograph in particular of his wife, looking devastated as she walked away from the cemetery, surprisingly solitary, as Thatcher took his own mother's arm and led her from the service. The agony that had been portrayed on the young mother's face had made him shudder. But all of it had warmed people's hearts to them, and it was intriguing to see him now, deeply engrossed in conversation with his cohorts.

And it was a moment later, while the elevator still refused to come, that the group of men moved slightly away, and only when they did so, did Peter catch a glimpse of yet another person behind them. It was the merest hint, the quickest impression, and then suddenly he saw her standing there, the woman he had seen in the photograph. Her eyes were cast down, and the impression she gave was of incredible delicacy, she seemed very small and very frail, and almost as though she would fly away at any moment. She was the merest wisp of a woman, with the biggest eyes he had ever seen, and something about her that made you want to stare at her in fascination. She was wearing a sky-blue Chanel linen suit, and there was something very gentle about her, and very self-contained as she walked behind the men in her party. Not one of them seemed to notice her, not even the bodyguards, as she stood quietly waiting for the elevator behind them. And as Peter looked down at her, she glanced suddenly up at him. He thought she had the saddest eyes he'd ever seen, and yet there was nothing pathetic about her. She was simply removed, and he noticed that her hands were delicate and graceful as she reached into her handbag and put away a pair of dark glasses. But not one of them spoke to her or even seemed to notice her as the elevator finally came. They all pressed in ahead of her, and she followed quietly behind them. There was a startling dignity about her, as though she were in her own world, and every inch a lady. Whether or not they knew she was alive seemed to be of no importance to her.

As Peter watched her, fascinated, he knew exactly who she was. He had seen numerous photographs of her over the years, in happier times, when she married him, and even before that with her father. She was Andy Thatcher's wife, Olivia Douglas Thatcher. Just as Thatcher did, she came from an important political family. Her father was the much respected governor of Massachusetts, and her brother a junior congressman from Boston. Peter thought he remembered that she was about thirty-four years old, and she was one of those people who fascinates the press, and whom they can't bring themselves to leave alone, although she gave them very little to go on. Peter had seen interviews with him, of course, but he didn't recall any with Olivia Thatcher. She seemed to stay entirely in the background, and he found himself mesmerized by her as he got in the elevator just behind her. She had her back to him, but she was so close that, with no effort at all, he could have put his arms around her. The very thought of it almost made him gasp, as he looked down at the dark sable-colored hair that was so lovely. And as though she felt Peter thinking about her, she turned and looked at him, and he met her eyes again, and for a moment he felt time stop. He was struck again by the sadness in her eyes, and it was as though, without saying a word, she was saying something to him. She had the most expressive eyes he'd ever seen, and then suddenly he wondered if he'd imagined it, if there was nothing more in her eyes than in anyone else's. She turned away almost as suddenly as she had looked at him, and she didn't look at him again as he left the elevator, feeling somewhat shaken.

The porter had already taken his bag up to his room, and the *gouvernante* had already checked the room for him, and found everything perfectly in order, and as he looked around when he stepped into it, Peter felt once again as though he had died and gone to Heaven. The brocades on the walls were a warm peach, the furniture all antique, the fireplace apricot marble, and the window and bedcoverings were in the same matching silks and satins. There was a marble bathroom, and every possible amenity and convenience. It was like a dream come true, and he sank into a comfortable satin chair, and looked out at the immaculately tended garden. It was perfection.

He tipped the concierge, and then walked slowly around the room, and went out and leaned against the balcony, admiring the flowers below, and thinking about Olivia Thatcher. There was something haunting about her face, her eyes, he had thought that about photographs of her too, but he had never seen anything as powerful as what he had seen in her eyes when she looked up at him. There was something so painful there, yet there was something strong too. It was as though she had been saying something to him, or to anyone who looked at her. In her own way, she was far more powerful and more compelling than her husband. And Peter couldn't help thinking that she didn't look like someone who would play the political game. In fact, to the best of his knowledge, she never had, and she still wasn't now, even with her husband such a close contender for the nomination.

He wondered what secrets lay hidden behind her facade, or was he imagining all of it? Perhaps she wasn't sad at all, but simply very quiet. No one had been speaking to her, after all. But why had she looked at him like that? What had she been thinking?

He was still distracted by thoughts of her after he washed his face and hands and called Suchard five minutes later. He couldn't wait a moment longer to see him. But it was Sunday. And Suchard sounded unenthused about an impromptu meeting. But nonetheless, he agreed to meet Peter an hour later. Peter walked around his room impatiently, decided to call Kate, and as usual, she wasn't in. It was only nine o'clock in the morning for her, and he imagined that she was out doing errands somewhere or visiting friends. Kate was rarely at home after nine o'clock, and never home before five-thirty. She was always busy. Nowadays, with even more activities, and her school board involvement, and only one child at home, she often came home even later.

When Peter finally left his room, he was wildly excited about seeing Suchard. This was the moment he'd been waiting for. The final green light before they could move ahead on Vicotec. It was only a formality, he knew, but still an important one in their pursuit of getting on the FDA 'Fast Track.' And Suchard was the most knowledgeable and respected head of their various research teams and departments. His benediction on Vicotec would mean more than anyone else's.

The elevator came more quickly this time, and Peter stepped into it swiftly. He was still wearing the same dark suit, but had changed to a fresh blue shirt with starched white cuffs and collar and he looked crisp and clean as he glanced at a slender figure in the corner. It was a woman in black linen slacks with a black T-shirt, she was wearing dark glasses. Her hair was pulled back, and she was wearing flats, and as she turned and looked at him, even with the dark glasses, he knew it was Olivia Thatcher.

After reading about her for years, he had suddenly seen her twice in one hour, and this time she looked completely different. She looked even slimmer and younger than she had in the Chanel suit, and she took her glasses off for a moment, and then glanced at him. He was sure she had recognized him too, but neither of them said anything, and he tried not to stare at her. But there was something about her that absolutely overwhelmed him. He couldn't figure out what it was about her that intrigued him. Her eyes, for sure, but it was far more than that. It was something about the way she moved and looked, the legend of all that he had heard about her. She seemed very proud, and very sure, and very quiet, and amazingly self-contained. And just looking at her like that made him want to reach out to her and ask her a thousand stupid questions. Just like all the reporters. Why do you look so sure of yourself? So removed? . . . But you look so sad too. Are you sad, Mrs Thatcher? How did you feel when your little boy died? Are you depressed now? They were the kind of questions everybody always asked her and she never answered. And yet, looking at her, he wanted to know the answers too, he wanted to reach out to her, to pull her close to him, to know what she felt, and why her eyes reached into his like two hands reaching for his, he wanted to know if he was crazy to read so much into her. He wanted to know who she was, and yet he knew he never would. They were destined to be strangers, never to speak a single word to each other.

Just being near her made him feel breathless. He could smell her perfume next to him, see the light shine on her hair, sense the smoothness of her skin, and mercifully, as he couldn't make himself stop staring at her, they reached the main floor, and the door opened. There was a bodyguard waiting for her, and she said nothing, but simply stepped into the lobby and began walking, and he followed. She had such an odd life, Peter thought, as he watched her go, feeling himself drawn to her like a magnet, and he had to remind himself that he had business to do, and no time for this childish fantasy. But it was obvious to him that there was something magical about her, it was easy to see why she was something of a legend. More than anything, she was a mystery. She was the kind of person you never knew, but wished you did. He wondered, as he walked outside in the bright sun and the doorman hailed him a cab, if anyone knew her. And as the cab drove him away, he saw her turn the corner and leave the Place Vendôme. She hurried away down the rue de la Paix, with her head down, her sunglasses on, the bodyguard following her, and in spite of himself Peter wondered where she was going. And then, forcing his eyes and his mind from her, as the cab sped off, he looked straight ahead at the streets of Paris rushing past him.

## Chapter Two

The meeting with Suchard was brief and to the point, as Peter expected it would be, but he was completely unprepared for what Paul-Louis Suchard said about their product. Not for a single instant had he anticipated Suchard's verdict. According to him, and all but one of the tests they'd done, Vicotec was potentially dangerous, lethal possibly, if misused, or even innocently mishandled, and as a result of the flaws it had shown, if it was usable at all, it was still years away from production and eventual release. Nor was it ready yet for the human trials Peter so desperately wanted.

Peter sat and stared at him as he listened. He could not believe what he had just heard, could not even remotely imagine that interpretation of their product. And he had become sufficiently knowledgeable about the chemical properties involved to ask him some very pointed and technically sophisticated questions. Suchard only had the answers to some of them, but on the whole he felt that Vicotec was dangerous, and that, conservatively, the product should be abandoned. Or if they wanted to take the risk of developing it further for the next several years, the problems might be worked out, but there was certainly no guarantee that they would ever be able to harness it and make it both useful and safe. And if they didn't, it would almost certainly become a killer. Peter felt as though someone had hit him with a brick.

'Are you sure there's no mistake in your processing, Paul-Louis?' Peter asked desperately, wanting to find their systems flawed, anything but his beloved 'baby.'

'Almost certainly there is no mistake,' Paul-Louis said in heavily accented English, but it was all too easy to understand what he had just said, much to Peter's horror. As usual, Paul-Louis looked morose, but he always did. And it was usually he who discovered the faults in their products. He was almost always the bearer of bad tidings. It was his vocation. 'There is one test we have not completed yet, it could mitigate some of our results, but it will not change them completely.' He went on to explain that it could provide for a little more optimism in terms of the time they might need for additional tests, but they were still talking years, not months, and certainly not weeks, as they had been hoping, before the FDA hearings.

'When will these tests be complete?' Peter asked, feeling ill. He couldn't believe what he'd been hearing. It felt like the worst day of his life, worse than anything he'd experienced in Vietnam, and certainly since then. It represented four years going down the tubes, if not completely, then at least partly.

'We need a few more days, but I believe that test is only a formality. I think we already know what Vicotec can and cannot do. We are well aware of most of its weaknesses and its problems.'

'Do you think it's salvageable?' Peter asked, looking terrified.

'I personally believe so . . . but some of my team do not. They feel it will always be too dangerous, too delicate, too great a risk in the hands of an unskilled person. But it will most certainly not do what you wanted. Not yet. And perhaps never.' They had wanted a form of chemotherapy that would be easier to administer, even for lay people, in remote, rural areas, where good medical care was not available to them. But none of it was going to be possible, from what Paul-Louis was saying. Even he felt sorry for Peter, when he saw his face. Peter looked as though he'd just lost his family, and all his friends, and he was only beginning to consider the ramifications. They would be endless. It was a huge disappointment, and a real shock to him as he listened to what Paul-Louis had to say. 'I'm very sorry,' Paul-Louis Suchard added quietly. 'I think that in time you will win this battle. But you must be patient,' he said gently, and Peter felt tears well up in his eyes, realizing how close they had come, and how far they still were from their objective. These were not the answers he had expected. He had expected their meeting to be merely a formality, and instead it was a nightmare.

'When will you have the test results for us, Paul-Louis?' He dreaded going back to New York to tell Frank, especially with incomplete information.

'Another two or three days, perhaps four. I cannot be quite sure yet. Certainly by the end of the week you will have your answers.'

'And if the results are good, you don't think it would alter your position now?' He was begging, pressing for all the good news he could. He knew how conservative Suchard was, maybe this time he was being too careful. It was hard to understand how his results could be so diametrically opposed to what all the others had said. Yet he had never been wrong before, and it was taking a terrible chance not to believe him. Obviously, they couldn't ignore what he was saying.

'It could change some of my position, not all of it. Perhaps if these next results are optimum, perhaps you will only be looking at another year of further research.'

'What about six months? If we work on it in all our laboratories, and concentrate all our research capabilities on this project?' With the gain they stood to make, it could be worth it. And profit was something Frank Donovan liked listening to, testing was not.

'Perhaps. That is a tremendous commitment, if you are willing to make it.'

'It's up to Mr Donovan, of course. I'd have to discuss it with him.' There was a lot he'd have to discuss with him now, and he didn't want to do it on the phone. He knew it was taking a chance, but he really wanted to wait for the last test results, and then talk to Frank after they knew exactly what Suchard had discovered. 'I'd like to wait until you finish the

71

last test, Paul-Louis. If you don't mind keeping all of this confidential until then.'

'Not at all.' They agreed to meet again as soon as the final test was completed, and Paul-Louis said he'd call him at the hotel.

Their meeting concluded on a gloomy note, and Peter felt exhausted as he took a cab back to the Ritz, and then got out and walked the last few blocks to the Place Vendôme. He was feeling desperately unhappy. They had worked so hard and he had believed in it so much, how could it go so sour? How could Vicotec prove to be a killer now? Why hadn't they discovered that before? Why did it have to happen this way? His one big chance to help humanity, and instead he had backed a killer. The irony of it tasted very bitter, and as he walked back into the hotel, even the hubbub of the cocktail hour and guests coming and going in a flurry of well-dressed activity didn't cheer him. The usual Arabs, Japanese, French movie stars, models from all over the world went unnoticed as he strode across the lobby and walked up the stairs to his room, thinking about what to do now. He knew he had to call his father-in-law, yet he wanted to wait until he had the rest of the information. He would have liked to talk to Kate about it, but he knew that whatever he said to her would have reached his father-in-law's ears before morning. It was one of the true weaknesses in their relationship. Kate was unable and unwilling to keep anything to herself, whatever was said between husband and wife was always shared with her father. It was a remainder of their old relationship when she'd been growing up alone with him, and try as he had over the years, Peter had been unable to change it. He had resigned himself eventually, and he was careful not to tell her anything unless he wanted to share it with Frank too, and this time he most emphatically didn't. Not yet anyway. He wanted to wait until he heard from Paul-Louis again, and then he would face whatever he had to.

Peter sat in his room that night, staring out the window, and feeling the warm air, unable to believe what had happened. It was incredible. And at ten o'clock, he was standing at his balcony, trying not to dwell on the possibility of failure. But all he could think of now were the dreams, and how close they had come, the hopes dashed and lives changed by what Paul-Louis had said to him, and might discover shortly. There was still hope, but there was certainly very little chance of an early release now. And appearing at the FDA hearings in September would be pointless. They wouldn't allow them to begin human trials, if there was still so much to work out. There was suddenly so much to think about. It was hard to wrap his mind around all of it, and finally at eleven o'clock, Peter decided to call Katie. It would have been nice to be able to tell her what was troubling him, but at least hearing her voice might cheer him up.

He dialed the number easily, but there was no answer. It was five o'clock in the evening, and even Patrick wasn't home. He wondered if Katie might have gone to friends for dinner. And as he set the receiver down, he was suddenly overwhelmed by a feeling of depression. Four years of hard work had all but gone down the drain in a single day, and along with it, almost everything he'd ever dreamed of. And there was no one to talk to about it. It was grim.

He stood at the balcony again for a little while, and thought about going out for a walk, but even strolling through Paris suddenly held little appeal, and instead, he decided to get some exercise to rid himself of his private demons. He glanced at the little card on the desk, and then walked swiftly down the stairs to the spa two floors below him. It was still open fortunately, and he had brought a dark blue bathing suit with him, just in case he had the opportunity to use it. He usually liked using the Ritz pool, but this time he hadn't been sure how much time he'd have to do it. As it turned out now, while he waited for Suchard to complete his tests, he had time to do a lot of things. He just wasn't in the mood to do them.

The attendant on duty seemed a little surprised when he walked in. It was almost midnight by then, and there was no one there. The spa appeared to be deserted and everything was silent. The single attendant had been reading a book quietly, and assigned Peter a changing room and gave him a key, and a moment later, he walked through the wading pool of disinfectant toward the main pool area. It was a large, handsome pool, and he was suddenly glad he had come here. It was just what he needed. He thought a swim might clear his head after everything that had happened.

He dove neatly into the pool from the deep end, and his long, lean body sliced through the water. He swam a considerable distance underwater, and then surfaced finally, and swam long clean strokes down the length of the pool, and then as he reached the far end, he saw her. She was swimming quietly, mostly underwater, and then she surfaced occasionally and went down again. She was so small and lithe that she almost disappeared in the large pool. She was wearing a simple black bathing suit, and when she surfaced, her dark brown hair looked black against her head, and her huge dark eyes seemed startled when she saw him. She recognized him instantly, but made no sign of recognition to him. She just dove under the water again and went on swimming as he watched her. It was so odd watching her, she was always so near, and yet so totally removed, in the elevator, both times, and now here. She was always tantalizingly close, and yet so far away that she might as well have been on another planet.

They swam silently at opposite ends of the pool for a while, and then passed each other several times, as they both did laps, working earnestly to flee their private torments, and then as though by design they both stopped at the far end of the pool. They were out of breath, and not knowing what else to do, unable to take his eyes from her, Peter smiled at her, and then she smiled in answer. And then just as suddenly, she swam away again before he could speak to her or ask her any questions. He hadn't been planning to anyway, but he suspected that she was used to that, people who hounded her, or wanted to know things they had no right to ask her. He was surprised to see that she wasn't accompanied by a bodyguard, and he wondered if anyone even knew she was down here. It was almost as though they didn't pay any attention to her. When he had seen her with the senator, they hadn't looked at her, or spoken to her, and she seemed perfectly content to be in her own world, just as she was now, as she continued swimming.

She came up at the far end from Peter this time, and not really intending to, he began to swim slowly toward her. He had no idea what he would have done if she had spoken to him with any real interest. But he couldn't imagine her doing that anyway. She was someone one looked at, or was fascinated by, an icon of sorts, a mystery. She was not a real person. And as though to prove what he thought, just as he approached, she stepped gracefully out of the pool, and with one swift gesture, wrapped herself in a towel, and when he looked up again, she was gone. He had been right after all. She wasn't a woman, only a legend.

He went back to his own room shortly after that, and thought about calling Kate again. It was nearly seven o'clock in Connecticut by then, and she was probably at home, having dinner with Patrick, unless they were out with friends.

But the odd thing was that he really didn't want to talk to her. He didn't want to put up a front for her, or tell her things were fine, nor could he tell her what had happened with Suchard. He couldn't trust her not to tell her father, but not being able to say anything to her made him feel oddly isolated as he lay on his bed at the Ritz in Paris. It was a special kind of purgatory, in a place meant only to be Heaven. And he lay there, in the warm night air, feeling better than he had before, physically at least. The swim had helped. And seeing Olivia Thatcher again had fascinated him. She was so beautiful, yet so unreal, and everything about her made him somehow feel that she was desperately lonely. He wasn't sure what made him think that, if it was just what he had read about her, or what was real, or what she had conveyed to him with those brown velvet eyes that looked so full of secrets. It was impossible to tell from looking at her, all he knew was that seeing her made him want to reach out and touch her, like a rare butterfly, just to see if he could do it, and if she would survive it. But like most rare butterflies, he suspected that if he touched her, her wings would turn to powder.

He dreamt of rare butterflies after that, and a woman who kept peeking at him from behind trees, in a lush, tropical forest. He kept thinking that he was lost, and as he would panic and begin to scream, he would always see her, and she would lead him silently to safety. He wasn't entirely sure who the woman was, but he thought it was Olivia Thatcher.

And when he woke in the morning, he was still thinking of her. It was the oddest feeling, more of a delusion than a dream. Seeing her close to him all night, in his dream, had actually given him the feeling that he knew her.

The telephone rang then. It was Frank. It was four o'clock in the morning for him, in Paris it was ten, and he wanted to know how the meeting with Suchard went. 'How did you know I'd see him yesterday?' Peter asked, trying to wake up and gather his wits about him. His father-in-law got up at four in the morning every day. And by six-thirty or seven, he was in the office. Even now, within months of retirement, or so he said, he hadn't altered his routine by so much as a minute.

'I know you left Geneva at noon. I figured you wouldn't waste any time. What's the good news?' Frank sounded buoyant, and Peter remembered only too clearly the shock of everything Paul-Louis Suchard had told him.

'They haven't finished their tests, actually,' Peter said, sounding intentionally vague, and wishing that Frank hadn't called him. 'I'm going to wait here for the next few days until they're finished.'

Frank laughed as he listened to him, and for once the sound of it grated on Peter's nerves. What in God's name was he going to tell him? 'You can't leave your baby alone for a minute, can you, son?' But he understood. They had all invested so much in Vicotec, money as well as time, and in Peter's case, his life's dreams had gone into backing their new product. At least Suchard hadn't said it was dead, Peter thought to himself, as he sat up in bed. All he had said was that it had problems. Serious ones to be sure, but there was still hope for his dream child. 'Well, enjoy yourself in Paris for a few days. We'll hold the fort for you here. There's nothing dramatic happening at the office. And tonight, I'm taking Katie to dinner at "21". As long as she doesn't mind your cooling your heels there, then I think I can get by without you.'

'Thanks, Frank. I'd like to be here to discuss the results with Suchard when he's through.' It didn't seem fair not to give Frank at least a hint of warning. 'There have been a few kinks apparently.'

'Nothing serious, I'm sure,' Frank went on without giving it a second thought. The results in Germany and Switzerland had been just too good to cause them any real worry. Peter had thought so too, until Paul-Louis warned him that Vicotec was a potential killer. He just hoped now that they would all be proven wrong, and that the problems they uncovered by week's end were all minor. 'What are you going to do with yourself while you hang around waiting?' Frank sounded amused more than anything. He liked his son-in-law, they had always been good friends. Peter was reasonable and a smart man, and he had proven to be an excellent husband for Katie. He let her do what she wanted to do, and didn't try to interfere with her having things the way she liked them. He let her live where she wanted to, send the boys to the right schools, 'right' being Andover and Princeton. He came to Martha's Vineyard for a month every year, and he respected the relationship Frank and Katie had shared since her childhood. In addition, he was a brilliant president for Wilson-Donovan. He was a good father to the boys too. In fact, there was very little Frank didn't like about him, except that occasionally Peter could be stubborn about certain issues, like boarding school or family matters that Frank still sometimes felt weren't really his business.

His marketing ideas had made history, and thanks to him, Wilson-Donovan was the most successful pharmaceutical company in the industry. Frank himself had been responsible for growing the firm from a solid family business to a giant entity, but it was Peter who had helped it grow into an international empire. The *New York Times* wrote about him constantly, and the *Wall Street Journal* called him the wonder boy of the pharmaceutical world. In fact, only recently they had wanted an interview with him about Vicotec, but Peter had insisted that they weren't ready. And Congress had recently asked him to appear before an important subcommittee to discuss the ethical and economic issues involved in pharmaceutical pricing. But he hadn't yet told them when he could appear before them.

'I brought some work with me,' Peter said, glancing at the sunlit balcony, and with absolutely no desire to do it, in answer to his father-in-law's earlier question. 'I thought I'd do some work on my computer and send it back to the office. I'll keep busy with that and a walking tour,' he said, thinking that he had the whole day before him.

'Don't forget to stock up on champagne,'

Frank said jovially. 'You and Suchard are going to have some celebrating to do. And we'll celebrate some more as soon as you get back to the office. Should I call the *Times* today?' he asked casually, as Peter nervously shook his head, and stood up, looking very long and lean and naked.

'I'd wait. I think it's important to wait for the last tests, if nothing else to ensure our credibility,' he said soberly, wondering if anyone could see him through the open window. His dark hair was tousled, and he wrapped the sheet around his waist. The terry cloth robe from the hotel was just out of reach on a peach brocade chair halfway across his bedroom.

'Don't be such a nervous Nellie,' Frank exhorted him. 'The tests are going to be fine. Call me as soon as you hear,' he said, suddenly anxious to get going himself, and get to the office.

'I will. Thanks for calling, Frank. Give my love to Kate, in case I don't reach her before you see her. She was out all day yesterday, and it's too early to call her now,' he said, by way of explanation.

'She's a busy girl,' her father said proudly. She was still a girl to him, and in some ways she hadn't changed since college. She still looked almost the way she had twenty-four years before when Peter had met her. She was lithe and blond, 'cute-looking,' her friends still said, and very athletic. She wore her hair short and had blue eyes like his, and there was something pixieish about her, except when she didn't get what she wanted. She was a good mother, and a good wife to Peter, and an exceptional daughter to Frank. They both knew that. 'I'll give her your love,' Frank reassured him, and then hung up, as Peter sat in his room, wearing a sheet, and staring out the window. What was he going to say to him if it all blew up in their faces? How were they going to justify the millions they had spent, the billions they wouldn't make, at least not for a while, and not until they spent still more to correct the problems? Peter couldn't help wondering if Frank would be willing to do that. Would he be willing to pursue Vicotec as far as they had to, to make it perfect, or would he insist that they abandon the project? As chairman of the board, the decision was still his, but Peter was going to do everything he could to fight for it. He was always willing to go the long hauls for the big wins. Frank liked the quick, showy wins. Just getting him through the past four years of development had been hard enough, another year or two might be just too much, particularly in view of what it would have to cost them.

He ordered coffee and croissants from room service, and then picked up the phone. He knew he was supposed to wait for Suchard's call, but he just couldn't help it. He called Paul-Louis and was told that Dr Suchard was in the laboratory and could not be interrupted. They were having a very important meeting. And all Peter could do was apologize, and go back to the agony of waiting. It seemed an eternity of days, waiting to hear from him. It had been less than twenty-four hours since their meeting the day before, and already Peter was ready to jump out of his skin with unbearable tension.

He put his robe on before the breakfast came, and he thought of going swimming again, but it seemed so decadent during working hours. He took out his computer instead, and sat working with it, while munching a croissant and sipping his coffee, but it was impossible to concentrate, and by noon, he showered and dressed and gave up any hope of working.

It took him a long moment to decide what to do. He wanted to do something frivolous, and truly Parisian. A walk along the Seine, or in the Septième, down the rue du Bac, or just sitting in the Latin Quarter, drinking and watching the passersby. He wanted to do anything but work and think of Vicotec. He just wanted to get out of his room and become part of the city.

He put on a dark business suit, and one of his perfectly tailored white shirts. He wasn't meeting anyone, but he hadn't brought anything else, and as he walked out into the brilliant June sun on the Place Vendôme, he hailed a cab and asked the driver to take him to the Bois de Boulogne. He had forgotten how much he loved being there, and he sat for hours, in the warm sun, on a bench, eating ice cream, and watching the children. It was a long way from the laboratories wrestling with Vicotec, farther still from Greenwich, Connecticut, and as he sat there lost in his own thoughts in the Paris sun, it even seemed a long way from the mysterious young wife of Senator Thatcher.

# Chapter Three

When Peter left the Bois de Boulogne that afternoon, he took a cab to the Louvre, and strolled briefly through it. It was beautifully organized, and the statues in the courtyard were so powerful that he stood and stared at them for a long time, mesmerized, feeling a silent communion with them. He didn't even mind the glass pyramid that had been put right in front of the Louvre, which had caused so much controversy among both foreigners and Parisians. He walked for a while, and then finally took a cab home. He had been out for hours, and he felt human again, and suddenly more hopeful. Even if the tests didn't go well, they would somehow salvage what they already knew, and then press forward. He wasn't going to let an important project like this die because of a few problems. The FDA hearings were not the end of the world, he'd been through them before over the years, and if it took five years instead of four, or even six eventually, then so be it.

He was feeling relaxed and philosophical when he walked back into the Ritz again. It was late afternoon, and there were no messages for him. He stopped and bought a newspaper, and made a point of going to the girl in charge of the vitrines, and bought the gold bracelet for Katie. It was a solid, handsome chain, with a single large gold heart dangling from it. She loved hearts, and he knew she'd wear it. Her father bought her really expensive things, like diamond necklaces and rings, and knowing he couldn't compete with him, Peter usually kept his gifts to the kind of thing he knew she'd wear, or that would have special meaning.

And when he went upstairs, he glanced around the empty room, and felt suddenly anxious. The temptation to call Suchard was great again, but this time he resisted. He called Katie instead, but when he dialed, all he got was the answering machine again. It was noon in Connecticut, and he figured she was out to lunch, and God only knew where the boys were.

Mike and Paul should have been home from school by then, Patrick had never left, and in another week or so, Katie would be moving everyone to the Vineyard. Peter would stay in town and work, and join them on weekends, as he always did, and then he'd spend his four-week vacation with them in August. Frank was taking July and August off that year, and Katie was planning a big Fourth of July barbecue to open the season.

'Sorry I missed you,' he said to the machine, feeling foolish. He hated talking to electronics. 'The time difference makes it difficult. I'll call you later . . . bye . . . oh . . . it's Peter.' He grinned, and hung up, wishing he hadn't sounded so stupid. The answering machine always made him feel awkward. 'Captain of industry unable to speak to answering machine,' he said, making fun of himself, as he sprawled across the settee in the peach satin room and looked around him, trying to decide what to do for dinner. He had the option to go to a bistro nearby, or to stay at the hotel and eat in the dining room, or stay in his room, order room service, watch CNN, and work on his computer. In the end, he opted for the last choice. It was the simplest.

He took off his jacket and his tie, and rolled his immaculate shirtsleeves up. He was one of those people who still looked impeccable at the end of the day, not just at the beginning. His sons teased him about it, and claimed he had been born wearing a tie, which made him laugh, remembering his youth in Wisconsin. He would have liked some of that for them, and a little less Greenwich, Connecticut, and Martha's Vineyard. But Wisconsin was far, far behind him. With both his parents and his sister long gone, he had no reason to go there. He still thought of Muriel's children in Montana at times, but somehow, by now it seemed too late to try to make contact. They were almost grown up, and they wouldn't even know him. Katie was right. It was too late now.

There was nothing interesting on the news that night, and he got engrossed in his work as the night wore on. He was surprised by how good the dinner was, but much to the waiter's chagrin, he didn't pay much attention. They set it up beautifully, but he set the laptop on the table next to him, and went right on working.

'*Vous devriez sortir, monsieur,*' the waiter said. 'You should go out.' It was a beautiful night, and the city looked exquisite beneath a full moon, but Peter forced himself not to pay attention.

He promised himself another late night swim, as a reward, when he was through, and he was just thinking about it at eleven o'clock when he heard a persistent beeping sound, and wondered if it was the radio, or the television, or perhaps something had gone wrong in the computer next to his bedside. There was a nagging bell and a high-pitched whine, and finally, confused about what it was, he opened the door into the hall, and discovered instantly that with the door open, it grew louder. Other guests were looking into the hall as well, and some of them looked worried and frightened.

'*Feu?*' 'Fire?' he asked a bellboy hurrying by, and he looked back at Peter with uncertainty, and barely stopped to answer.

'*C'est peut-être une incendie, monsieur,*' which told Peter that it could be. No one seemed to be sure, but it was definitely an alarm of some kind, and more and more people began emptying into the hallways. And then suddenly it seemed as though the entire staff of the hotel sprang into action. Bellmen, captains, waiters, maids, the *gouvernante* for their floor, housekeepers of all kinds walked sedately but quickly through the floors, knocking on doors, ringing bells, and urging everyone to come outside as quickly as possible, and *non, non, madame*, please do not change your gown, that will be fine. The *gouvernante* was handing out robes, and bellboys were carrying small bags, and helping women with their dogs. No explanation had been offered yet, but they were all told that everyone had to evacuate at once, without delaying for an instant.

Peter hesitated, wondering if he should take his laptop with him, but then just as quickly decided to leave it. He had no company secrets on it, just a lot of notes and information and correspondence that he needed to take care of. In a way, it was almost a relief to leave it. He didn't even bother to put his jacket back on, he just put his wallet and his passport into his pants pocket, and took his room key, and then hurried downstairs between Japanese ladies in hastily donned Gucci and Dior, a huge American family 'escaping' from the second floor, several Arab women in extraordinary jewels, a handful of handsome Germans pushing ahead of everyone down the stairs, and a flock of miniature Yorkshire terriers and French poodles.

There was something wonderfully comical about all of it, and Peter couldn't help smiling to himself as he made his way quietly downstairs, trying not to think of the comparison with the *Titanic*. The Ritz was hardly sinking. And all along their path they were met by personnel of the hotel, helping, reassuring, giving a hand where necessary, greeting everyone, and apologizing for the inconvenience. But still no one had mentioned exactly why all of it had occurred, if it was due to a fire, a false alarm, or some other grave threat to the guests of the hotel. But once they made their way past the well-filled vitrines, through the lobby, and out into the street, Peter saw that the CRS troops were there, fully dressed and armed and shielded. They were roughly the equivalent of an American SWAT team, and seeing King Khaled and his group quickly spirited away in government cars suggested to Peter that it was perhaps a bomb scare. There were two well-known French actresses there as well, with 'friends,' an amazing assortment of older men with young girls, and Clint Eastwood was there in jeans and a T-shirt, having just come in from shooting. By the time the entire hotel had vacated all its rooms, it was nearly midnight. But it was impressive to see how quickly it had been done, how sanely, and how safely. The hotel staff had done a masterful job of shepherding its guests into the Place Vendôme and now, at a safe distance, they were setting up rolling tables with little pastries and coffee, and for those who felt in need of it, there was stronger drink too. It would have been almost fun, if it hadn't been so late and wasn't so inconvenient, and there wasn't the faint aura of danger around them.

'There goes my late night swim,' Peter said to Clint Eastwood as they stood side by side, looking up at the hotel, checking for smoke, but there was none. The CRS had gone inside ten minutes before to look for bombs. Apparently, the management had gotten a call that there was a live one.

'There goes my sleep,' the actor said mournfully. 'I have a four A.M. call tomorrow. This could take a long time, if they're looking for a bomb.' He was thinking of sleeping on the set, but the other guests did not have that option. They just stood on the street, still somewhat amazed, as they clutched their pets, their friends, and their little leather cases filled with jewelry.

And as Peter watched another wave of CRS troops go in, and following the order himself to move farther back from the hotel, he turned and suddenly saw her. He spotted Andy Thatcher, surrounded, as usual, by hangers-on and bodyguards, and looking completely unconcerned by the commotion. He was continuing an animated conversation with the people around him, all, save one, were men, and the lone woman in the group looked like a political bulldog. She was smoking furiously, and Thatcher looked engrossed in what she was saying. But Peter noticed that Olivia was standing just beyond the group, and no one was speaking to her. They paid no attention to her at all, as he watched her with his customary fascination. She stood off to one side, ignored even by the bodyguards, as she sipped a cup of the hotel's coffee. She was wearing a white T-shirt and jeans, and he thought that she looked like a kid in a pair of penny loafers, and the eyes that had so mesmerized him seemed to be taking in the whole scene, as her husband and his group moved slowly forward. Thatcher and one of his men talked to several of the CRS troops, but they only shook their heads. They had not yet found what they had come for. Someone brought out folding chairs, and waiters offered them to the guests, as wine was brought out too, and people stayed in surprisingly good temper about the inconvenience. It was slowly becoming a late night street party in the Place Vendôme. And in spite of himself, Peter continued to watch Olivia Thatcher with interest.

She seemed to have drifted even farther from her group after a while, and even the bodyguards seemed to have lost track of her and paid no attention whatsoever to her. And the senator had had his back to her ever since they'd come out of the hotel, he never spoke to her once, as he and his entourage settled into chairs, and Olivia moved even farther to the rear of the several hundred guests in the Place Vendôme to get another cup of coffee. She looked quite peaceful standing there, and didn't seem in the least bothered that her husband's entire party ignored her. And as he looked at her, standing there, Peter was more and more fascinated, and couldn't help staring.

She offered an elderly American woman a chair, and patted a little dog, and eventually set her empty cup back on a table. A waiter offered Olivia another cup, but she smiled and shook her head graciously as she declined it. There was something wonderfully gentle and luminous about her, as though she had just drifted to earth and were really an angel. It was hard for Peter to accept the fact now that she was just a woman. She looked too peaceful, too gentle, too perfect, too mysterious, and when people came too close to her, too frightened. She was obviously ill at ease under close scrutiny, and she seemed happiest when no one was paying attention to her, which no one was that night. She was so unpretentiously dressed, and so unassuming standing there, that even the Americans in the crowd didn't recognize her, although they had seen her hundreds of times in every newspaper and magazine in the country. She had been every paparazzi's dream for years, as they leapt out at her, and caught her unprepared, particularly in the years when she had been with her sick and dying child. But even now, she intrigued them, as something of a legend, and a kind of martyr.

And as Peter watched her continually, he couldn't help noticing that she was drifting farther and farther back, behind the other guests, and he actually had to strain now to see her. He wondered if there was a reason for it, or if she had just moved back there without thinking. She was far from her husband and his entourage by then, and they couldn't have seen her at all, unless they moved back themselves and tried to find her. More guests had returned to the hotel, from late night restaurants or nightclubs like Chez Castel, or simply from dinners with friends, or the theater. And gawkers had come to see what was happening. The whispers in the crowd blamed it all on King Khaled. There was an important British minister in the hotel too, and there had been a rumor that it could have been the IRA, but someone had supposedly planted a bomb, or said they had, and by order of the police, no one was going back into the hotel until the CRS found it.

It was well after midnight, and Eastwood had long since left to sleep in his trailer on the set. He wasn't going to waste the next few hours standing in the Place Vendôme, waiting around until morning. And as Peter glanced around he noticed Olivia Thatcher slowly move away entirely from the guests of the hotel, and drift nonchalantly to the other side of the square. She had turned her back on the people standing there, and then suddenly she seemed to be walking smoothly and swiftly toward the corner. And he couldn't help wondering where she was going. He looked to see if she had a bodyguard in tow, he was sure that if anyone knew what she was doing, they would have sent one. But she was clearly on her own, as she began to hurry, and she never once glanced over her shoulder. He couldn't take his eyes off her, and without thinking, he moved away from the crowd himself and began to follow her to the corner of the Place Vendôme. There was so much activity outside the hotel, and spilling everywhere, that it appeared that no one had seen either of them leaving. What Peter didn't realize was that for a few steps at least, a man was following him, but at the sound of a flurry in the square, he lost interest and hurried back to the heart of the action, where two well-known fashion models had put a CD player on and had started dancing with each other, in front of a nervous-looking CRS. CNN had arrived by then, and they were in the process of interviewing Senator Thatcher about his views on terrorists abroad and at home, and he told them in no uncertain terms how he felt about it. In view of what had happened to his brother nearly six years previously, he was particularly unsympathetic to this kind of nonsense. He gave a rousing little speech, and the people around him who heard applauded him when it was over, and then the CNN crew went on to interview some of the others. Interestingly, they never asked to speak to his wife, they felt that the senator had obviously spoken for both Thatchers, and then the crew hurried over to the dancing models and inter-viewed them right after Andy. They said they thought the evening was great fun, and it should happen at the Ritz more often. They were staying in the hotel for a three-day shoot for *Harper's Bazaar*, and they both said they loved Paris. Then they sang a little song, and did a mock soft shoe in the Place Vendôme. It was a lively group, and despite the possible danger presented by the missing bomb, it was a festive night.

But Peter was far from all of it by then, as he followed the senator's wife around the corner and out of the Place Vendôme. She seemed to know where she was going, and she didn't hesitate for a moment. She just kept walking. She walked at a good clip, and Peter took long strides to keep up with her, but he let her keep ahead, and he had no idea what he would say to her, if she stopped and turned around, and asked him what he was doing. He had no idea what he was doing, or why. He just knew that he had to be there. He had been compelled to follow her from the Place Vendôme, and he told himself he wanted to be sure she was safe at that hour of the night, but he had no idea at all why he seemed to feel he should be the one to do that.

He was amazed when she walked all the way to the Place de la Concorde, and then stood there, smiling to herself, as she looked at the fountains, with the Eiffel Tower lit up in the distance. There was an old bum sitting there, and a young man strolling by, and two couples kissing, but no one paid any attention to her, and she looked so happy as she stood there. It made him want to go over and put an arm around her, and look at the fountains with her. But instead, he just stood at a polite distance from her, smiling at her. And then much to his astonishment, she glanced over at him, and there were questions in her eyes. It was as though she knew suddenly that he was there, and why, but she still felt he owed her an explanation. Clearly, he had followed her, and she looked neither angry nor panicked, and much to his embarrassment, she turned and walked slowly toward him. She knew who he was, she had recognized him as the man from the pool the night before, but he blushed in the darkness as she came toward him.

'Are you a photographer?' She looked up at him and asked very quietly. She looked very vulnerable and suddenly very sad. It had happened to her before, a thousand times, a million, ad nauseam and infinitum. Photographers followed her everywhere, and felt victorious each time they robbed her of a private moment. She was accustomed to it now, she didn't like it but she accepted it as part of her life.

But he shook his head, having glimpsed how she felt, and he was sorry to have intruded. 'No, I'm not . . . I'm sorry . . . I . . . I just wanted to be sure you . . . It's very late.' And then suddenly, looking down at her, he felt less embarrassed and more protective. She was so incredible and so delicate. He had never met anyone like her. 'You shouldn't walk around alone so late at night, it's dangerous.' She glanced at the young man and the old clochard, and she shrugged, looking up at him with interest.

'Why were you following me?' She asked it very directly, and the brown velvet eyes were so soft as she looked at him that he wished he could reach out and touch her face.

'I . . . I don't know,' he said honestly. 'Curiosity . . . chivalry . . . foolishness . . . stupidity . . .' He wanted to tell her that he was overwhelmed by her beauty, but he couldn't. 'I wanted to be sure you were all right.' And then he decided to be direct with her. The circumstances were unusual, and she looked like the kind of person you could be straight with. 'You just walked away, didn't you? They don't know you're gone, do they?' Or perhaps they did by now, and were scurrying everywhere, but she didn't really care and she looked it. She looked like a mischievous child as she looked up at him. He had seen what she did, and she knew it.

'They'll probably never know the difference,' she said honestly, looking unremorseful, but surprisingly full of mischief. Even from what he had seen, she was truly the forgotten woman. No one in her group ever paid any attention to her, or spoke to her, not even her husband. 'I had to get away. Sometimes it's very oppressive to be . . . in my shoes.' She looked up at him, not sure if he had recognized her, and if not, she didn't want to spoil it.

'All shoes are oppressive sometimes,' he said philosophically. His were too at times, but he knew that hers were far more so. And then he looked down at her sympathetically again. Since he had come this far after her, there was no harm in going a little further. 'Can I buy you a cup of coffee?' It was an old line, and they both smiled, and she hesitated for a long moment while she tried to decide if he meant it, or was just being funny, and he saw her hesitation, and smiled warmly. 'It was a sincere offer. I'm relatively well behaved, and can at least be trusted for a cup of coffee. I'd suggest my hotel, but they seem to be having a problem.'

She laughed at that, and seemed to relax as she watched him. She knew him from the hotel, in the elevator and at the pool. He was wearing an expensive shirt and it looked clean, and he was wearing suit trousers and good shoes. And something in his eyes told her that he was both respectable and kind, and she nodded. 'I'd like a cup of coffee, but not at your hotel,'' she said primly, 'it's a little too busy for me tonight. How about Montmartre?' she said cautiously, and he grinned. He liked the suggestion.

'That's a great idea. May I offer a cab?' She nodded, and they walked to the nearest taxi stand, and he helped her in, and she gave the address of a bistro she knew that stayed open very late, and had tables out on the sidewalk. It was still a warm night, and neither of them had any desire to go back to the hotel, although they both seemed a little shy with each other. It was she who broke the ice first, as she looked at him with a teasing expression.

'Do you do that a lot? Follow women, I mean.' Suddenly, the whole thing amused her, and he had the grace to blush in the taxi as he shook his head.

'I've actually never done that before. It's absolutely the first time, and I'm still not sure why I did it,' except that she looked so vulnerable and so frail, that for some insane reason he wanted to protect her, but he didn't say that.

'I'm actually very glad you did,' she said, looking genuinely amused and surprisingly comfortable with him, as they reached the restaurant, and a moment later, they were sitting at an open-air table with two steaming cups of coffee. 'What a great idea.' She smiled at him. 'Now tell me all about you,' she said, putting her chin on her hands, and looking surprisingly like Audrey Hepburn.

'There's not much to tell,' he said, still looking faintly embarrassed, but excited to be there.

'I'm sure there is. Where are you from? New York?' she guessed, fairly accurately. At least he worked there.

'More or less. I work in New York. I live in Greenwich.'

'And you're married, and have two children.' She filled in the gaps for him, smiling at him wistfully as she did so. His life was so happy and so ordinary probably, so unlike hers with all its tragedies and disappointments.

'Three sons,' he corrected her. 'And yes, I'm married.' And then as he thought of his abundance of sons, he felt guilty toward her and the little boy she had lost to cancer. He had been her only child and he knew, as did the entire world, that she had had no children since then.

'I live in Washington,' she said quietly, 'most of the time.' She did not offer to tell him whether or not she had children, and knowing what he did of her, he didn't ask.

'Do you like Washington?' he asked gently, and she shrugged as she sipped her coffee.

'Not really. I hated it when I was young. I suppose if I thought about it, I'd hate it more now. It's not the city I dislike, it's the people and what they do to their lives there. Theirs, and everyone else's. I hate politics and everything it stands for.' And as she said it, he could see how fervently she meant it. But with a brother, a father, and a husband deeply entrenched in politics, she had little hope of escaping its clutches now. And then she looked at him, she hadn't introduced herself yet, and she would have liked to believe that he had no idea who she was, and she was just a woman in loafers, jeans, and a T-shirt. But she could see in his eyes that he knew her secret. It may not have been why he was there, having coffee with her at two A.M., but he wasn't unaware of it either. 'I suppose it would be unrealistic to think you don't know my name . . . or do you?' she asked with wide eyes, and feeling sorry for her again, he nodded. The anonymity would have been nice for her, but it wasn't her destiny, not in this lifetime.

'I do, and yes, it would be unrealistic to think people don't know who you are. But that shouldn't change anything. You have a right to hate politics, or anything, or go for a walk on the Place de la Concorde, or say anything you want to a friend. Everybody needs that.' He sensed easily how badly she did.

'Thank you,' she said softly. 'You said before that everybody's shoes pinch sometimes. Do yours?'

'Now and then,' he said honestly. 'We all get into tight spots sometimes. I'm the head of a company, and sometimes I wish that no one knew that and I could do anything I wanted.' Like right now. For one tiny moment with her, he would have liked to be free again and forget he was married. But he knew he could never do that to Katie. He had never cheated on her in his life, and he didn't intend to start now, not even with Olivia Thatcher. But that was also the last thing on her mind. 'I think we all get tired of our lives sometimes, and the responsibilities placed upon us. Probably not as tired as you do,' he said sympathetically, 'but I think, in our own ways, we all wish we could walk out of the Place Vendôme sometimes, and disappear for a while. Like Agatha Christie.'

'I've always been intrigued by that story,' Olivia said with a shy smile, 'and I've always wanted to do that.' She was impressed that he knew about that. She had always been fascinated by why Agatha Christie had simply disappeared one day. They had found her car crashed against a tree. And the famous author had vanished. She did not reappear until several days later. And when she did, she offered no explanation whatsoever for her absence. At the time, it had caused an enormous ruckus, and there had been headlines all over England about her disappearance. In fact, around the world.

'Well, you have done it now, for a few hours anyway. You've walked right out of your life, just as she did.' He smiled at her, and she looked at him with eyes full of mischief as she smiled.

Olivia laughed at the idea, and for a moment she loved it. 'But she was gone for days. This is just for a few hours.' She looked faintly disappointed as she said it.

'They're probably all going completely crazy by now, looking for you everywhere. They probably think you were kidnapped by King Khaled.' She laughed even harder at that, and she looked like a kid when she did, and a few minutes later, Peter ordered them both a sandwich. And when the sandwiches came, they both devoured them. They were starving.

'I don't think they're even looking for me,

do you know that? I'm not sure that if I truly disappeared anyone would even notice, unless they had a rally to attend that day, or a campaign speech in a women's club. I'm very useful at times like that. Otherwise, I'm not very important. I'm sort of like one of those artificial trees they bring out to decorate the stage. You don't need to feed or water them, you just roll them out to look good when you need a little window dressing to set the main showpiece off.'

'That's an awful thing to say,' Peter chided her, though from what he had seen, he wasn't sure he disagreed with her. 'Is that how you really feel about your life?'

'More or less,' she said, knowing that she was daring a great deal. If he turned out to be a reporter, or worse yet, someone from the tabloids, she'd be mincemeat by morning. But in a way, she almost didn't care. She needed to trust someone sometimes, and there was something incredibly warm and appealing about Peter. She had never talked to anyone as she did to him now, and she didn't want to stop, or go back to her life, or ever return to the Ritz Hotel. She wanted to stay here in Montmartre with him forever.

'Why did you marry him?' he dared to ask after she put down her sandwich again, and she looked into the night thoughtfully for a moment and then back into Peter's eyes.

'He was different then. But things changed very quickly. A lot of bad things happened to us. Everything seemed right in the beginning. We loved each other, we cared, he swore to me he would never go into politics. I saw what my father's career did to us, to my mother particularly, and Andy was just going to be a lawyer. We were going to have children, horses, and dogs, and live on a farm in Virginia. And we did, for about six months, and then it was all over. His brother was the politician in the family, not Andy. Tom would have been president eventually, and I would have been happy never to see the White House except when they lit the tree at Christmas. But Tom was killed six months after we were married, and the campaign types came after Andy. I don't know what happened to him, if he felt obligated after his brother was killed, obliged to step into his shoes and do "something important for his country," I've heard that line until it choked me. And eventually, I think he fell in love with it. It's heady stuff, this thing called political ambition. I've come to understand that it demands more from you than any child, and seems to offer more excitement and passion than any woman. It devours everyone who gets near it. You can't love politics and survive. You just can't. I know that. Eventually, it eats everything you have inside, all the love and goodness and the decency, it eats whoever you once were, and leaves a politician in its place. It's not much of an exchange. Anyway, that's what happened. Andy went into politics, and then to make it up to me, and because he said we would, we had a baby. But he didn't really want it. Alex was born during one of his campaign trips, and Andy wasn't even there then. Or when he died.' Her face kind of froze over as she said it. 'Things like that change everything . . . Tom . . . Alex . . . politics. Most people don't survive that. We didn't. I don't know why I thought we should have. It really was too much to ask, and I think when Tom died, he took most of Andy with him. The same thing happened to me with Alex. Life deals out hard hands sometimes. Sometimes you just can't win, no matter how hard you try, or how much money you have on the table. I put a lot on this game, I've been at it for a long time. We've been married for six years, and none of it has been easy.'

'Why do you stay?' It was an amazing conversation to have with a stranger, and they were both surprised at the boldness of his questions and the candor of her answers.

'How do you go? What do you say? Sorry your brother died and your life got all screwed up . . . sorry our only baby . . .' She started to say the words but couldn't, and he took her hand and held it, and she didn't pull it away. The night before they had been strangers in a swimming pool, and suddenly, at a café in Montmartre, a day later, they were almost friends.

'Could you have another child?' Peter asked cautiously, you never knew what had happened to people, what they could and couldn't do, but he wanted to ask her, and hear her answer.

But she shook her head sadly. 'I could, but I wouldn't. Not now. Not again; I don't ever want to care that much again for another human being. But I also don't want another child in this world I live in now. Not with him. Not in politics. It almost ruined my life and my brother's when we were young . . . and more importantly than that, it ruined my mother's. She's been a good sport for nearly forty years, and she has hated every moment of it. She's never said that, and she'd never admit it to anyone, but politics has ruined her life. She lives in constant terror of how people will interpret every move she makes, she's afraid to do or be or think or say anything. That's how Andy would like me to be, and I can't do that.' And then as she said the words to him, she looked genuinely panicked, and he knew instantly what she was thinking.

'I won't hurt you, Olivia. I will never, ever repeat any of this. To anyone. It's between us, and Agatha Christie.' He smiled and she looked at him cautiously, deciding whether or not to believe him. But the odd thing was she trusted him. Just looking at him, she could sense that he wouldn't betray her. 'Tonight never happened,' he said carefully. 'We'll go back to the hotel separately, and no one will ever know where we've been, or that we were together. I've never met you.'

'That's comforting,' she said, looking truly relieved and very grateful, and she believed him.

'You used to write, didn't you?' he asked, remembering something he had read about her years before, and wondering if she still did write.

'I did. So did my mother. She was actually very talented, she wrote a novel about Washington that set it on its ear, early in my father's career. It was published, but he never let her publish anything again, and she really should have. I'm not as talented, and I've never published, but I've wanted to write a book for a long time, about people and compromises, and what happens when you compromise too much or too often.'

'Why don't you write it?' He was sincere, but she only laughed and shook her head.

'What do you think would happen if I did? The press would go wild. Andy would say I had jeopardized his career. The book would never see the light of day. It would be burned in a warehouse somewhere, by his henchmen.' She was the proverbial bird in the gilded cage, unable to do anything she wanted, for fear it might hurt her husband. And yet she had walked away from him, and had disappeared to sit in a café in Montmartre and empty her heart to a stranger. It was an odd life she led, and he could tell how close she was to breaking out of it as he watched her. Her hatred of politics and the pain it had brought to her was obvious and abundant. 'And what about you?' She turned her deep brown eyes to Peter then, wondering about him. All she really knew was that he was married, had three sons, was in business, and lived in Greenwich. But she also knew he was a good listener, and when he held her hand, and looked at her, she felt something stir deep inside her, it was a part of her she thought had died, and suddenly she could feel it breathing. 'Why are you here in Paris, Peter?'

He hesitated for a long time, still holding her hand and looking into her eyes. He hadn't told anyone, but she had trusted him, and he needed to tell her now. He knew he had to tell someone.

'I'm here for the pharmaceutical company I run. We've been working on a very compli-cated product for four years, which isn't actually such a long time in this field, but it has seemed like a long time to us, and we've spent an enormous amount of money. It's a product that could revolutionize chemotherapy, and it's very important to me. It seemed like my one contribution to the world, something important that makes up for all the frivolous, selfish things I've done. It means everything to me, and it has passed all our tests with flying colors, in every country we work in. The last tests are being conducted here, and I came to wrap things up. We're asking for permission to do early human trials, from the FDA, based on our testing. Our laboratories here are going through the final steps, and until this point, the product has been flawless. But the tests here show something very different. They are not completed yet, but when I arrived here yesterday, the head of our laboratories told me that there could be serious problems with the drug. To put it bluntly, instead of a godsend to help save the human race, it could be a killer. I won't know the whole story till the end of the week, but it could be the end of a dream, or the beginning of long years of testing. And if that's the case, I have to go home, and tell the chairman of my company, who is co-incidentally my father-in-law, that our product is either on the shelf or out the window. It's not going to be a popular announcement.'

She seemed impressed as she looked at him and nodded. 'I should think not. Have you told him what they said yesterday?' She was sure he had, and it was almost a rhetorical question, but she was stunned when he shook his head and looked faintly guilty.

'I don't want to say anything till I have all the information,' he said, dodging the issue. Her eyes looked deep into his as she watched him.

'This must be quite a week for you, waiting to hear,' she said sympathetically, and only beginning to glimpse from the look in his eyes how important it was to him. 'What did your wife say?' She said it, assuming that other people enjoyed a relationship she didn't. She had no way of knowing his particular problem of not being able to say anything to Katie without her telling her father.

But he stunned her again, this time even more so. 'I didn't tell her,' he said softly, and Olivia looked at him in amazement.

'You didn't? Why not?' She could not imagine the reason.

'It's a long story.' He smiled sheepishly at Olivia and she wondered. There was something in his eyes that whispered to her of loneliness and disappointment. But it was so subtle, she wondered if he was even aware of it himself. 'She's extremely close to her father,' he said slowly, thinking about what he was saying. 'Her mother died when she was a child, and she grew up alone with him. There's absolutely nothing she doesn't tell him.' He looked up at Olivia again, and he could see that she understood him.

'Even things that you tell her in confidence?' Olivia looked outraged at the indiscretion.

'Even those,' he smiled. 'Kate has no secrets from her father.' It tugged at his heart as he said it. He wasn't sure why, but it bothered him more than it had in years as he explained it.

'That must be uncomfortable for you,' Olivia said, searching his eyes, trying to see if he was unhappy, or even knew it. He seemed to be suggesting that Kate's loyalty to her father, even to that degree, was not only acceptable to him, but normal. And yet his eyes said something else. She wondered if that was what he had meant when he said everyone's shoes pinched sometimes. To Olivia, to whom privacy and discretion and loyalty meant almost everything, Peter's shoes would have given her bunions.

'It's just the way things are,' he said simply. 'I accepted it a long time ago. I don't think they mean any harm by it. But it means that sometimes I just can't tell her things. They have a tremendous attachment to each other.' Olivia decided, for his sake, to stay off the subject. She had no intention of peeling away protective layering, or of hurting him by pointing out how unsuitable his wife's behavior was. After all, Olivia hardly knew him, and she had no right.

'It must have been lonely for you today, worrying about the outcome of those tests, and having no one to talk to.' She looked at him sympathetically. She had gone straight to the heart of it with the words she used. They exchanged a warm smile of understanding. They both had heavy burdens on their shoulders.

'I tried to keep busy, since I couldn't tell

anyone,' he said quietly. 'I went to the Bois de Boulogne, and watched the kids play. And then I went for a walk along the Seine, and to the Louvre, and eventually I went back to the hotel, and worked, and then the alarm went off.' He grinned. 'And it's been a pretty good day ever since then.' And it was going to be a new day soon. It was almost five o'clock in the morning, and they both knew they had to go back to the hotel before too much longer. They went on talking for another half hour after that, and finally at five-thirty they reluctantly left the café, and went to find a taxi. They walked slowly along the streets of Montmartre, in her T-shirt and his shirtsleeves, hand in hand, like two young kids on a first date, and they looked incredibly comfortable with each other.

'It's odd how life is sometimes, isn't it?' she asked, looking up at him happily, thinking of Agatha Christie, and wondering if she had done something like this, or something even more daring, during her disappearance. Once she returned, the famous author had never explained. 'You think you're all alone, and then someone comes out of the mists, completely unexpectedly, and you're not alone any longer,' Olivia said quietly. She had never, ever dreamt though that she would meet anyone like him. But he met a deep need for her. She was starving for friendship.

'It's a good thing to remember when things get rough, isn't it? You never know what's right around the corner,' Peter said, smiling at her.

'In my case, I fear what's right around the corner might be a presidential election. Or worse yet, another madman's bullet.' It was a hideous thought which brought back the ugly memories of her brother-in-law's assassination. It was clear she had loved Andy Thatcher deeply once upon a time, and it still saddened her that life had been so hard on them and thrown them so many terrible curveballs. In some ways, Peter felt sorry for both of them, but for the most part, it was Olivia he felt for. He had never seen anyone ignore another human being the way Andy Thatcher had ignored his wife, each time Peter saw them. There was a total indifference to her, as though she didn't exist at all, or he didn't even see her. And his lack of interest in her clearly extended to his advisors. Maybe she was right, maybe to them, she was simply a decoration. 'What about you?' she asked Peter with renewed concern about him. 'Will it be very bad for you if your product turns out to be a disaster when the tests come in? What will they do to you in New York?'

'Hang me up by my feet and flay me,' he said with a rueful grin, and then he grew serious again. 'It won't be easy. My father-in-law was going to retire this year, I think partly as a vote of confidence in me, but I don't think he'll do that if we lose this product. I think it will be very rough, but I'll just have to stand by it.' But it wasn't just that for him. Putting Vicotec on the market was a way of saving people who had died like his mother and sister years before. And that meant the world to Peter. More even than profit or Frank Donovan's reaction. And now they might lose the whole product. It almost killed him to think that.

'I wish I had your courage,' she said sadly, and the look in her eyes was the one he had seen the first time he met her, the look of sorrow that knew no limit.

'You can't run away from things, Olivia.' But she knew that already. Her two-year-old son had died in her arms. What more courage was there in life than that? He didn't need to lecture her about courage.

'What if your survival depends on running away?' she asked with a serious look at him, and he put an arm around her shoulders.

'You have to be very sure before you do that,' he said, looking at her seriously, wishing he could help her. She was a woman who needed a friend desperately, and he would have loved to be that person, for more than just a few hours. But he also knew that once he left her at the hotel, he'd never be able to call her and talk to her, let alone see her.

'I think I'm getting very sure,' she said softly. 'But I'm not there yet.' It was a painfully honest statement. As desperately unhappy as she was, she still needed to make the decision.

'And where would you run to?' he asked as they finally found a cab, and asked for the rue Castiglione. He didn't want to drive her right to the hotel, and they didn't know yet if everyone had been able to go back inside, or if they were still gathered in the square, waiting.

But for Olivia, Peter's last question was easy. She had been there before, and had known even then that it would always be her safe haven. 'There's a place I used to go a long time ago, when I came here to study for a year in college. It's a little fishing village in the south of France. I found it when I first came, and I used to go there for weekends. It's not chic, or fashionable, it's very simple, but it was the one place I could always go to think when I needed to find myself again. I went there for a week after Alex died, but I was afraid the press would find me eventually, so I left before they did. I would hate to lose it. I'd love to go back there again one day, and stay for a while, maybe even finally write the book I keep thinking I have in my head, to see if I can do it. It's a magical place, Peter. I wish I could show it to you.'

'Maybe you will one day,' he said almost glibly, pulling her closer to him, but it was a gesture of comfort and support. He made no attempt to make any advances to her, or to try and kiss her. He would have liked nothing in this world more, but out of respect for Olivia, and his wife, he absolutely wouldn't do it. In some ways, Olivia was a fantasy for him, and just having talked to her all night was a gift he would cherish forever. It was like something in a movie. 'What's this place called anyway?' he asked, and she smiled at him and gave him the name like a gift. It was almost like a pass-word between them.

'La Favière. It's in the south of France, near a place called Cap Benat. You should go there if you ever need to. It's the best thing I can give anyone,' she whispered as she lay her head against his shoulder, and for the rest of the ride back, he just held her there, sensing without words that it was what she needed. He wanted to tell her that he would always be her friend, that he would be there for her if she needed him, that she should never hesitate to call him, but he wasn't quite sure how to say all of it to her, and instead he just held her. For a mad moment, he even wanted to tell her that he loved her. He wondered how long it had been since anyone had said that to her, how long since anyone had even talked to her as though they cared about her, and had any interest at all in what she was feeling. 'You're a lucky man,' she said softly to him as the cab stopped on the rue Castiglione down the street from the Place Vendôme, just as they had told the driver.

'What makes you say I'm lucky?' Peter asked curiously. The only thing that seemed lucky to him just then was having been with her all night, emptying their souls in each other's hands and sharing their secrets.

'Because you're content with your life, you believe in what you've done, and you still believe in the decency of the human race. I wish I still did, but I haven't in a long time.' But she hadn't been as lucky. Life had been kind to him for the most part, and extremely hard on Olivia Thatcher. She didn't tell him she suspected his marriage was a lot less fulfilling than he told himself, because she thought he didn't even know that. In some ways, he was lucky because he was still so blind, but he was sincere and caring and he had worked hard, and he was willing to close his eyes to his wife's indifference to him, and her involvement in her own life, and his father-in-law's outrageous invasion of what should have been their life. He was fortunate in Olivia's eyes, because he saw none of the emptiness around him. He sensed it perhaps, but he didn't really see it. And he was basically such a kind, decent, loving person. She had felt so much warmth from him that night, that even now, just before dawn, she didn't want to leave him.

'I hate to go back,' she whispered sleepily into his white shirt, nestled against his shoulder in the back of the cab. After all their talking, they were both spent, and she was beginning to fade now.

'I hate to leave you,' he said honestly, trying to force himself to remember Kate again, but it was this woman he wanted to be with, and not Kate. He had never talked to anyone as he had talked to Olivia that night, and she was so giving and understanding. She was so lonely and so hurt and so starved. How could he make himself leave her? It was hard to remember why he should now.

'I know I'm supposed to go back, but I can't remember why.' She smiled sleepily, thinking of what a heyday the paparazzi would have if they could have seen them for the last six hours. It was hard to believe they had been away for that long. They had talked for hours in Montmartre, and now it was agony going back where they belonged, but they knew they had to. Peter suddenly realized he had never talked to Kate the way he had talked to Olivia that night. Worse yet, he was falling in love with her, and he had never even kissed her.

'We both have to go back,' he said mournfully. 'They must be half crazy with worry about you by now. And I have to wait to hear about Vicotec.' If not, he would have loved to run away with her.

'And then what?' She was referring to Vicotec. 'Our various worlds fall apart, separately, and we keep on going. Why do we have to be the brave ones?' She looked and sounded like a petulant child, and he smiled as he looked at her expression.

'I guess because that's what we got picked for. Somewhere, sometime, someone said, "Hey you, get on this line, you're one of the brave ones." But actually, Olivia, you're a lot stronger than I am.' He had sensed that that night, and respected her a great deal for it.

'No, I'm not,' she said simply. 'I never volunteered for all this. This wasn't multiple choice, and I picked it. It just happened. That's not brave, it's just destiny.' She looked up at him silently then, wishing that he was hers, and knowing he never would be. 'Thank you for following me tonight . . . and for the cup of coffee.' She smiled, and he touched her lips with his fingers.

'Anytime, Olivia . . . remember that. Anytime you want a cup of coffee I'll be there . . . New York . . . Washington . . . Paris . . .' It was his way of offering her his friendship, and she knew it. Unfortunately for both of them, it was all he was able to offer.

'Good luck with Vicotec,' she said as they got out of the cab, and she looked up at him. 'If it's right for you to help all those people, Peter, it'll happen. I believe that.'

'So do I,' he said sadly, missing her already. 'Take care of yourself, Olivia.' He wanted to say so many things, to wish her well, to hold on to her, to run away with her to her fishing village near Cap Benat. Why was life so unfair sometimes? Why wasn't it more generous?

Why couldn't they just disappear like Agatha Christie?

They stood at the corner for what seemed like a long time, and then after he squeezed her hand for a last time, she finally walked around the corner, and swiftly across the square, a small, lithe figure in a white T-shirt and a pair of blue jeans. And as he watched her go, he wondered if he would ever see her again, even in the hotel. When he followed her, she stood at the door of the Ritz, and waved for a last time, and as he looked at her, he hated himself for not having kissed her.

## Chapter Four

Much to his own astonishment, Peter slept till noon that day. He was exhausted after coming home at six o'clock in the morning. And when he awoke, all he could think of was Olivia. He felt quiet and sad without her, and when he looked out the window, it was raining. He sat thinking about Olivia for a long time, over croissants and coffee, and he kept wondering what had happened when she had gone back to her room early that morning. He wondered if her husband had been furious with her, or terrified, sick with worry, or just concerned. He couldn't imagine Katie doing a thing like that. But two days earlier, he couldn't have imagined himself doing it either.

He wished he could have gone on talking

to Olivia all night. She was so honest and open with him. And as he finished his coffee, he thought of some of the things she'd said, about her own life, and his. Looking at his marriage through her eyes suddenly gave him a different perspective, and he felt uncomfortable about Katie's relationship with her father. They were so close that he actually felt shut out, and it irked him that he couldn't tell Katie about Suchard, and the reason for the delay in Paris. Even if he didn't want to tell Frank, he would have liked to tell his wife, and he knew with total certainty that he couldn't.

It was strange to think that it had been easier last night, talking about it to a perfect stranger. Olivia had been so sympathetic and so kind to him, and she had easily understood how agonizing it was for him, just waiting. He wished he could have talked to her again, and as he showered and dressed, he found that all he could think about was her . . . her eyes . . . her face . . . that wistful look as she walked away, and the ache he'd felt as he watched her. It was all so unreal. It was almost a relief when the phone rang an hour later, and it was Katie. Suddenly, he needed to reach out to her, to bring her close to him, to reassure himself that she really loved him.

'Hi there,' she said, it was seven in the morning for her, and she sounded bright and alert, and already in a hurry. 'How's Paris?'

For an instant, he hesitated, not sure what he could tell her. 'Fine. I miss you,' he said, and suddenly waiting to hear from Suchard felt like a crushing weight to him, and the night before only an illusion. Or was it Olivia who was real now, and Katie the dream? Still tired from the night before, it all seemed very confusing.

'When are you coming home?' she asked, sipping a cup of coffee and finishing her breakfast in Greenwich. She was catching an eight o'clock train to New York and she was rushing.

'I'll be home in a few days, I hope,' he said thoughtfully. 'By the end of the week for sure. Suchard had some delays in his tests, and I decided to wait here. I thought it might make him finish a little more quickly.'

'Is anything important causing the delays, or just technicalities?' she asked, and it was almost as though he could see Frank waiting with her for the answer. He was sure Frank had already told her everything Peter had said the day before. And as always, he knew he had to be careful what he told her. It would all go straight back to her father.

'Just some minor things. You know how meticulous Suchard is,' Peter said nonchalantly.

'He's a nitpicker, if you ask me. He'll find a problem even if you never had one. Daddy says it went great in Geneva.' She sounded proud of him, but a little cool. Over the years, their relationship had taken some odd turns. She was less affectionate than she used to be with him, and less demonstrative unless she was in a playful mood and alone with him. And she seemed not to be particularly warm to him that morning.

'It sure did go great in Geneva.' He smiled, trying to visualize her, but suddenly all he could see was Olivia's face, sitting in his Greenwich kitchen. It was an odd sort of hallucination, and it worried him. Katie was his life, not Olivia Thatcher. He opened his eyes wider and stared at the rain falling beyond his window, trying to concentrate on what he was seeing. 'How was dinner with your father last night?' He tried to change the subject. He didn't want to discuss Vicotec with her. They'd have plenty to talk about that weekend.

'Great. We made lots of plans for the Vineyard. Dad's going to try and stay for the whole two months this year.' She sounded pleased, and Peter forced himself not to think about what Olivia had said to him about compromising everything. This had been his life for nearly twenty years, and he still had to live it.

'I know he's staying up there for the whole two months, you're all deserting me in the city.' He smiled at the thought, and then thought about his sons. 'How are the boys?' It was obvious from his tone how much he loved them.

'Busy. I never see them. Pat finished school, Paul and Mike got home the day you left, and this place looks like a zoo again. I spend all my time picking up socks and jeans, and trying to match pairs of size thirteen sneakers.' They both knew they had been blessed, they were all good kids. And Peter loved being with them, he always had. Hearing about them from Kate suddenly made him miss them.

'What are you doing today?' he asked, sounding wistful. He had another day of waiting to hear from Suchard, with nothing much to do except sit in his room and work on his computer.

'I have a board meeting in town. I thought I'd have lunch with Dad, and I want to pick up some things for the Vineyard. The boys ate our sheets last year, and we can use some new towels and other odds and ends too.' She sounded busy and distracted, and the fact that she was seeing her father again had not gone unnoticed.

'I thought you had dinner with Frank last night,' Peter said, frowning. His perspective was suddenly just a fraction different.

'I did. But I told him I was going into town today, and he invited me to a quick lunch in his boardroom.' What could she possibly have to say to him? It made Peter wonder as he listened. 'What about you?' She turned the tables on him, and he stared at the rain falling on the rooftops of Paris. He loved Paris even in the rain. He loved everything about it.

'I thought I'd do some work in my room today. I have a lot of little stuff I brought over on my computer.'

'That doesn't sound like much fun. Why don't you at least have dinner with Suchard?' He wanted a lot more from him than dinner, and he didn't want to distract him from what he was supposed to be doing.

'I think he's pretty busy,' Peter said vaguely.

'Me too. I'd better run or I'll miss my train. Any message for Dad?' Peter shook his head, thinking that if he had one, he'd call himself, or fax him. He didn't send messages to Frank via Katie.

'Just have fun. I'll see you in a few days,'

Peter said, and nothing in his voice would have told her he'd just spent the night baring his soul to another woman.

'Don't work too hard,' she said evenly, and then she hung up, and he sat there for a long time, thinking about her. The conversation was unsatisfactory, but typical of her. She was interested in what he did, and deeply involved with anything that had to do with the business. But at other times, she had no time for him at all, and they never talked anymore about their inner thoughts, or shared their feelings. Sometimes he wondered if it frightened her to be close to anyone but her father. Losing her mother as a young child had given her a fear of loss and abandonment, and she was afraid of getting too attached to anyone but Frank. To Katie, her father had proven himself long since, and he had always been there. Peter had been there for her too. But her father was her priority. And he expected a lot of Katie. He was very demanding of her time, her interest, and her attention. But he gave a lot too, and he expected to be acknowledged for the generosity of his gifts with an equal amount of time and affection. But Katie needed more in her life too, she needed her husband and her sons. And yet, Peter suspected that she had never loved anyone as much as she loved

Frank, not even him, or their sons, although she would never admit it. And when she thought anyone was threatening Frank, she fought like a lioness to protect him. It was the reaction she should have had for her own family, and not her father. That was the unnatural quality in the relationship that had always bothered Peter. She was attached to her father beyond all reason.

Peter worked on his computer all that afternoon, and finally at four o'clock, he decided to call Suchard, and then felt foolish once he did it. This time Paul-Louis took the call from the laboratory but he was curt with him, and told Peter he had no further news. He had already promised to call the moment the final tests were finished. 'I know, I'm sorry . . . I just thought . . .' Peter felt stupid for being so impatient, but Vicotec meant so much to him, more than to anyone else, and it was on his mind constantly. That, and Olivia Thatcher. It became impossible to work finally, and at five o'clock, he decided to go to the pool and see if he could burn off some of his tension by swimming.

He looked for Olivia in the elevator, and at the spa. He looked for her everywhere, but he didn't see her. He wondered where she was today, what she thought about the night before. If it was a rare interlude for her, or a kind of turning point. He found that he was haunted by everything they had said, the way she'd looked, the deeper meaning of everything she'd told him. He kept seeing those huge brown eyes, the innocence of her face, the earnestness of her expression, and the slim figure in the white T-shirt as she walked away. Even swimming didn't exorcise her from his mind, and he didn't feel much better when he went back upstairs and turned the television on. He needed something, anything, to distract him from the voices in his head, the vision of a woman he barely knew, and the worry of Vicotec going down the drain with Suchard's testing.

The world was in its usual state when he watched CNN. There was trouble in the Middle East, a small earthquake in Japan, and a bomb scare at the Empire State Building in New York that had driven thousands of terrified people into the street, which only served to remind him of the night before, as he watched Olivia walk out of the Place Vendôme and followed her. And as he thought of it, he suddenly wondered if he was losing his mind. The announcer on CNN had just said her name, and there was a blurred photograph of her back in the white T-shirt, as she hurried away, and an even fuzzier photograph of a man a good distance behind her. But all you could see was the back of his head, and no other distinguishing feature.

'The wife of Senator Anderson Thatcher disappeared last night, during a bomb threat at the Hotel Ritz in Paris. She was seen walking from the Place Vendôme at a hurried pace, and this man was photographed following her. But no further information about him is known, whether he was following her maliciously, or according to plan, or simply by coincidence. He was not one of her bodyguards, and no one seems to know anything about him.' Peter realized instantly that the photograph was of him as he first followed her from the square, but fortunately no one had recognized him, and it was impossible to identify him from the picture. 'Mrs Thatcher has not been seen since approximately midnight last night, and there are no further reports about her. A night watchman says he thought he saw her come in early this morning, but other reports claim that she never returned to the hotel after this photograph was taken. It is impossible to say at this time if there has been foul play, or if perhaps, with so much political strain, she has simply gone somewhere, perhaps to take respite with friends in or near Paris for a few hours, although as time goes on that appears less and less likely. The only thing we do know for certain is that Olivia Douglas Thatcher has vanished. This is CNN, Paris.' Peter stared at the screen in disbelief. A montage of photographs had just been shown of her, and as he continued to watch the TV, her husband came on, and a local reporter conducted an interview with him for the English-speaking channel Peter was watching. The reporter implied that she had been depressed for the past two years, ever since the death of their young son, Alex. And Andy Thatcher denied it. He also added that he felt sure that his wife was alive and well somewhere, and that if she had been taken by anyone, they would be hearing from the responsible group shortly. He seemed very sincere and amazingly calm. His eyes were dry, and he showed no signs of panic. The reporter said then that the police had been at the hotel with him and his staff all afternoon, manning the phones and waiting for word of her. But something about the way Andy Thatcher looked made Peter think he was wiling away the hours by working on his campaign, and not as frantic about his wife's whereabouts as anyone else would be. But Peter was suddenly terrified as he wondered what had happened to her after she had left him.

He had left her at the hotel shortly after 6 A.M., and he had seen her go into the hotel. What could possibly have happened to her? He felt more than a little responsible, and wondered if it was foul play, and if she had been grabbed on the way to her room. But as he turned it around in his mind, he kept stopping in the same place. The thought of kidnapping worried him so much, and yet it felt so wrong to him. And the words *Agatha Christie* kept rolling around in his head again and again. He couldn't bear the thought that something terrible might have happened to her, but the more he thought about it, the more he suspected that it hadn't. She had walked away the night before. She could easily have done it again. Maybe she really couldn't face going back to her life, although he knew that she felt she had to. But even last night she had told him that she didn't think she could do it for much longer.

Peter began pacing around his room as he thought about her, and a few minutes later, he knew what he had to do. It was awkward, certainly, but if her safety depended on it, it was worth it. He had to tell the senator that he had been out with her, where they'd gone, and that he had brought her back to the hotel that morning. He wanted to mention La Favière to him too, because the more Peter thought about it, the more certain he was that she had gone there. It was the one place where he knew instinctively she would take refuge. And as little as he knew her, it still seemed obvious to him. And although Andy Thatcher surely knew how much La Favière meant to her, perhaps he had overlooked it. Peter wanted to tell him about it now, and suggest that they send the police there at once to search for her. And if she wasn't there, then he felt sure she was truly in trouble.

Peter didn't waste time waiting for the elevator. He headed straight for the stairs, and ran up two flights to the floor where he knew they were staying. She had mentioned her room number the night before, and he saw instantly that there were police and secret service standing in the halls, conversing. They seemed subdued, but not in any particular gloom. Even right outside her suite, no one seemed particularly worried. And they watched him as he approached. He looked respectable, and had put his jacket on as he left his room. He was carrying his tie in his hand, and he wondered suddenly if Anderson Thatcher would see him. He didn't want to discuss this with anyone, and it was going to be embarrassing telling him that he had had coffee with his wife in Montmartre for six hours, but it seemed important to Peter to be honest with him.

When he reached the door, Peter asked to see the senator, and the bodyguard in charge asked if he was acquainted with him, and Peter had to admit that he wasn't. Peter told him who he was, and felt foolish for not having called first, but he had been in such a hurry the minute he realized she was gone, and wanted to share as quickly as possible where he thought she might be hiding.

As the bodyguard stepped into the suite, Peter could hear laughter and noise within, he could glimpse smoke, and he was aware of what sounded like a lot of conversation. It almost sounded like a party. He wondered if it had to do with search efforts to find Olivia, or if, as he had suspected earlier, they were actually discussing the campaign, or other political issues.

The bodyguard came back outside in an instant, and apologized politely for Senator Thatcher. Apparently, he was in a meeting, perhaps if Mr Haskell would be good enough to call, they could discuss their business over the phone. He was sure Mr Haskell would understand, in light of everything that had just happened. And as it so happened, Mr Haskell would have. What he didn't understand was why they were laughing in that room, why people weren't scurrying around, why they weren't panicking over losing her. Did she do this all the time? Or did they just not care? Or did they suspect, as he did, that she had just had enough for now, and had taken a hike for a day or two to gather her wits about her?

He was tempted to say that his message had to do with the senator's wife's whereabouts, but he knew he could have been wrong too, and he was realizing more clearly now, as he thought about it, how awkward it was going to be to explain their tryst of the night before in the Place de la Concorde. And why exactly had he followed her? Badly put, the whole thing could have created a huge scandal, for her as well as him. And he realized now that he had been wrong to come. He should have called, and he went back to his own room to do that. But as soon as he did, he saw her photograph on CNN again. This reporter was exploring the idea of suicide rather than kidnapping. They were showing old photographs of her dead child, and then shots of her at the funeral, crying. And the haunted eyes which stared back at him begged him not to betray her. They interviewed an expert on depression after that, and talked about the kind of crazy things people did when they lost hope, and they suspected Olivia Thatcher had when her son died. And Peter wanted to throw something at them. What did they know of her pain, her life, her grief? What right did they have to pick her life apart? They went all the way back to photographs of her at her wedding, and at her brother-in-law's funeral six months after she'd married Andy.

Peter had the phone in his hand when they began talking about the tragedies of the Thatcher family, starting with Tom Thatcher being assassinated six years before, the son who died, and now Olivia Thatcher's tragic disappearance. They were already calling it tragic when the operator came on and asked how she could help Peter. And he was about to give her the number of the Thatchers' room, and then just as suddenly, he knew he couldn't do it. Not yet. He had to see for himself first. And if she wasn't there, then he would know something had happened to her, and he would call Andy as soon as he could. In truth, he didn't owe her anything, but after the night before, he felt he owed her his silence. He just hoped that he wasn't risking her life by stalling until he got there.

And as he put the phone down again, the announcer on CNN was saying that thus far her parents, Governor Douglas and his wife, had not been available for comment on the mysterious disappearance of their daughter in Paris. The voice droned on, and Peter went to grab a sweater from the closet. He only wished he had brought a pair of jeans with him, but there had been no way of knowing he would have anywhere to use them. It was hardly the kind of thing he wore to meetings.

He called the desk after that, and after being told there were no more flights to Nice at this time of night, and the last train was leaving in five minutes, he asked for a car, and a map that would get him from Paris to the south of France, and when they offered him a driver, he explained that he wanted to drive himself, although it would certainly have been faster and easier with a driver. But it would also be much less private. They told him they'd have everything ready for him in an hour, and he should come to the front door and pick up the car, and the maps would be in it. It was just after seven then, and at eight o'clock, when he went downstairs, a new Renault was waiting for him, with a stack of maps on the front seat. And the doorman very obligingly explained to him how to get out of Paris. He had no bags with him, no luggage at all. All he'd brought was an apple, a bottle of Evian water, and his toothbrush in his pocket. And as he got behind the wheel of the car, it had a little bit of the flavor of a wild-goose chase. He had already worked out at the desk that, if he needed to, he could abandon the car in Nice or Marseilles, and fly back to Paris. But that was only if he didn't find her. If he did, he wondered if she'd ride back with him. At least they could talk on the way back. She obviously had a lot on her mind, and maybe he could help her sort it out on the road to Paris.

The Autoroute du Soleil was still fairly well traveled at that time of night, and it was only after he reached Orly that the traffic began to thin out and he picked up some speed for the next two hours, until he reached Pouilly. And by then, Peter felt strangely peaceful. He wasn't sure why, but he felt as though he was doing the right thing for her. And for the first time in days, he felt free of all his encumbrances and all his worries. There was something about getting in a car and driving hard through the night that made him feel he had left all his troubles behind. It had been wonderful talking to her the night before, like finding a friend in an unexpected place. And as he drove, all he could see was her face, her eyes haunting him, just as they had the first time he saw her. He thought of her the night he had seen her in the pool too, swimming away from him, like a small, lithe black fish . . . and then running across the Place Vendôme the night before, to freedom . . . the hopeless look in her eyes when she'd gone back . . . the sense of peace about her when she spoke of the little fishing village. It was crazy to follow her across France, and he was aware of it. He scarcely knew her. And yet, just as he had to follow her from the square the night before, he knew he had to do this now. For reasons still unknown to him, or anyone at that point, he had to find her.

## Chapter Five

The road to La Favière was boring and long, but thanks to the speeds he was able to achieve, it went faster than he expected, and it took him exactly ten hours. He drove slowly into town at six o'clock, just as the sun came up. The apple was long since gone, and the Evian bottle was almost empty on the seat beside him. He had stopped for coffee once or twice, and had left the radio on to keep him awake. He drove with all the windows down, but now that he had reached his destination, he was truly exhausted. He had been awake all night, for the second time in two days, and even his excitement at being there and the adrenaline that had spurred him on were beginning to fade, and he realized he had to sleep an hour before he began his search for her. It was too early to look for her anyway. Except for the fishermen beginning to arrive at the dock, everyone in La Favière was still sleeping. Peter pulled off to the side of the road, and climbed into the backseat. It was cramped, but it was exactly what he needed.

It was nine o'clock when he woke, and he heard children playing near the car. Their voices were raised as they ran by, and Peter could hear seagulls overhead. There were a variety of sounds and noises as he sat up, feeling as though he had died. It had been a long night, and a long drive. But if he found her, it would be worth it. As he sat up and stretched, he caught a glimpse of himself in the rearview mirror and laughed. He looked a mess, definitely enough to frighten small children.

He combed his hair, and brushed his teeth with the last of the Evian, and looked as respectable as he could as he got out of the car to begin his search. He had no idea where to begin, and he slowly followed the children he'd heard, to the bakery, where he bought a pain au chocolat, and walked back outside to look out over the water. The fishing boats were already out, small tugs and little sailboats were still in port, and there were clumps of old people huddled in groups, discussing the state of things, as the younger men continued their fishing. The sun was high in the sky by then, and as Peter looked around, he decided she'd been right. It was the perfect place to escape to, peaceful, beautiful, and there was something about it that was very rare and warm, like an embrace from an old friend. And near the port was a long sandy beach. He finished his pain au chocolat, and began to walk slowly along the sand, wishing he had a cup of coffee. He felt mesmerized by the sun and the sea, and wondered how he would find her. He walked almost all the way down the beach, and sat on a rock, thinking of her, and wondering if she'd be angry if he found her, if she was even here, when he looked up and saw a slip of a girl come around the point from another beach just beyond it. She was barefoot, in T-shirt and shorts, she was small and slim and her dark hair was blowing in the breeze as she looked up at him and smiled, and he could only stare. It was as it was meant to be. So effortless, so simple. She was there, smiling at him from across the beach, as though she'd been waiting for him. And with a smile meant only for him, Olivia Thatcher walked slowly toward him.

'I don't suppose this is a coincidence,' she said softly as she sat down on the rock beside him. He was still more than a little over-whelmed, and he hadn't moved since he'd first seen her. He was too bowled over by having found her.

'You told me you were going back,' he said, his eyes digging deep into hers, not angry, no longer surprised, simply there, and completely at ease with her.

'I was. I meant to. But when I got there, I found I couldn't.' She looked sad as she said it. 'How did you know where I was?' she asked gently.

'I saw it on CNN.' He smiled, and she looked horrified.

'That I'm here?'

He laughed at the question. 'No, my friend. They said only that you were gone. I spent the whole day imagining you back in your life as a senator's wife, however reluctantly, and at six o'clock I turned on the news, and there you were. Kidnapped, apparently, and they have a photograph of me following you out of the Place Vendôme, as your possible kidnapper, but fortunately you can't see much.' He was smiling. It was all so absurd, and a little bit crazy. He didn't say anything about some of the reports about her depression.

'Good Lord, I had no idea.' She looked pensive as she absorbed what he had just told her. 'I was going to leave Andy a note, saying I'd be back in a few days. But in the end, I didn't do that either. I just left. And came here. I took the train,' she said by way of explanation, and he nodded, still trying to understand everything that had brought him here. He had followed her twice now, pulled by a force he couldn't explain but couldn't resist either. Her eyes looked deep into his, and neither of them moved. His eyes were a caress, but neither of them made any move to touch each other. 'I'm glad you came,' she said softly.

'So am I . . .' And then he looked suddenly like a boy again, as the breeze ruffled his dark hair and swept it across his eyes. They were the color of the summer sky as he watched her. 'I wasn't sure if you'd be angry if I found you.' He'd been worried about that all the way from Paris. She might have thought of his following her as an unforgivable intrusion.

'How could I? You've been so kind to me . . . you listened . . . you remembered.' She was bowled over that he had found her there, that he had cared enough to even try. It was a long trip from Paris. And suddenly she sprang to her feet, looking more than ever like a little girl, and held out a hand to him. 'Come, let me take you to breakfast. You must be starving after driving all night.' She tucked a hand into his arm as they walked slowly toward the port. She was barefoot, on narrow, graceful feet, and the sand was hot, but she didn't seem to mind it. 'Are you very tired?'

He laughed, remembering how exhausted he had been when he arrived. 'I'm all right. I slept for about three hours when I got here. I don't exactly get much sleep when you're around.' But life wasn't dull around her either. That was certain.

'I'm really sorry,' she said, and a moment later, she walked him into a tiny restaurant, and they both ordered omelettes, croissants, and coffee. And when it came, it was a fragrant, sumptuous meal and Peter devoured it. She picked at hers. She was watching him, and drinking the strong black coffee.

'I still can't believe you came here,' she said softly. She looked pleased but somewhat wistful. Andy would never have done anything like this. Not even way back in the beginning.

'I tried to tell your husband about this place,' he said honestly, and she looked suddenly very worried.

'What did you say? Did you tell him where you thought I'd gone?' She didn't want Andy to come here. She didn't mind seeing Peter now, in fact she was glad he had come, but she was still not ready to see Andy. He was most of the reason why she had come here.

'I didn't tell him anything in the end,' Peter put her mind at rest very quickly. 'I wanted to, but I was put off when I went to your suite to see him. The police were there, secret service, bodyguards, and it sounded as though he was having a meeting.'

'I'm sure it didn't have anything to do with me. He has an uncanny sense about when it's right to be worried, and when it isn't. That's why I didn't leave him the note. I suppose it was wrong, but he knows me well enough to know that I'm all right. I don't think he really believes that I was kidnapped.'

'I got that impression too when I went to the suite,' Peter said slowly. There hadn't been that intense aura of panic one would have expected if he really thought she was in danger. He didn't really think Anderson Thatcher was worried, which was why he had felt free to come himself, and call him later. 'Are you going to call him now, Olivia?' Peter asked, concerned. He thought she should at least do that.

'I will eventually. I don't know what I want to say yet. I'm not sure I can go back, although I suppose I'll have to, briefly at least. I owe him some kind of explanation.' But what was there to explain, that she didn't want to live with him anymore, that she had loved him once but it was gone, that he had betrayed every hope, every shred of decency, everything she'd ever cared about, or wanted from him? In her mind, there was nothing left to go back to. She had discovered that the night before when she put her key in the door of the suite, and found she just couldn't turn it. She couldn't go back in. She would have done anything she had to, to escape him. And in turn she meant nothing to him anymore. She knew that. She hadn't in years. Most of the time, he was completely oblivious to her existence.

'Olivia, are you leaving him?' Peter asked gently, as they finished breakfast. It was none of his business, but he had driven ten hours to make sure that she was all right and no harm had come to her. That gave him some right to at least a minimum of information, and she knew that.

'I think so.'

'Are you sure? In your world, that will probably create a tremendous uproar.'

'Not as much as finding you here with me,' she laughed, and he chuckled. He couldn't disagree with her on that one. And then she grew serious again. 'The uproar doesn't frighten me. It's all a lot of noise, like children's toys on Halloween. That's not the problem. I just can't live with the lies anymore, the pretence, the falseness of a life in politics. I've had enough of it to last for ten lifetimes. And I know I couldn't survive another election.'

'Do you think he'll run for the big one next year?'

'Possibly. More than likely,' she said, thinking it over. 'But if he does, I can't do it with him. I owe him something, but not that. It's too much to ask. We started out with all the right ideas, and I know Alex meant a lot to him too, although he was never there when he should have been. But most of the time, I understood that. I think he changed when his brother died. I think a piece of Andy died with him. He sold out everything he's ever been or cared about for politics. I just can't do that. And I don't see why I should have to. I don't want to end up like my mother. She drinks too much, she gets migraines, she has nightmares, she lives in constant terror of the press, her hands shake all the time. And she's always terrified of creating a situation that will embarrass my father. No one can live with that kind of pressure. She's a mess and she has been for years. But she looks great. She's had her eyes done and her face lifted, and she covers up how scared she is. And Daddy drags her out for every single meeting, lecture, campaign speech, and rally. If she were honest, she'd admit that she hates him for it, but she'd never do that. He ruined her life. She should have left him years ago, and maybe if she had, she'd still be a whole person. I think the only reason she stayed with him is so he didn't lose an election.' Peter listened to her with a serious expression, deeply affected by what she was saying. 'If I'd known Andy would go into politics, I'd never have married him. I guess I should have suspected,' Olivia said with a look of sorrow.

'You couldn't know his brother would be killed, or that he'd be dragged into it,' Peter said fairly.

'Maybe that's just an excuse, maybe it would have all fallen apart anyway. Who knows.' She shrugged, and looked away, out the window. The fishing boats looked like toys dotting the horizon. 'It's so beautiful here . . . I wish I could stay here forever.' She sounded as though she meant it.

'Do you?' he asked gently. 'If you leave him, will you come back here?' He wanted to know where to imagine her, where to see her in his mind's eye, when he thought of her during long, cold winter nights in Greenwich.

'Maybe,' she answered, still unsure of so

many things. She knew she still had to go back to Paris and talk to Andy, though she was reluctant to do that. Having let the kidnapping myth grow for two days, she could just imagine the circus he would make of it when she got back to Paris.

'I talked to my wife yesterday,' Peter said quietly, while Olivia sat thinking in silence about her husband. 'It was strange talking to her, after everything we said the other night. I've always defended everything she did . . . and her relationship with her father, although I didn't really like it. But after talking to you, it suddenly irks me.' He was so honest with her, so able to say anything he felt. She was so open, so deep, and yet she was cautious not to hurt him, and he sensed it. 'She had dinner with him the other night. She had lunch with him yesterday. She's going to spend two months with him this summer, day and night. Sometimes I feel as though she's married to him, and not to me. I guess I've always felt that. The only thing I've consoled myself with is that we have a good life, our sons are great, and her father lets me do what I want in the business.' Oddly enough, it had seemed like so much for so long, and now suddenly it didn't.

'Does he let you do what you want?' She pressed him now, as she hadn't dared to in

Paris. But this time he had brought up the subject. And now they knew each other better. His coming to La Favière had brought him even closer to her.

'Frank pretty much does let me do what I want. Most of the time.' He went no further. They were on dangerous ground. She was ready to leave Andy for reasons of her own, but he had no desire to rock his domestic boat with Katie. Of that much he was certain.

'And if Vicotec goes bad in the tests they're doing now? What will he do then?'

'Continue to stand behind it, I hope. We'll just have to do more research, although it will certainly be expensive.' That was the under-statement of all time, but he couldn't imagine Frank backing down now. He thought Vicotec was brilliant. They'd just have to tell the FDA they weren't ready.

'We all make compromises,' Olivia said quietly. 'The only problem is when we think we've made too many. Maybe you have or maybe it doesn't matter, as long as you're happy. Are you?' she asked, with enormous eyes. She wasn't asking as a woman, but only as his friend now.

'I think so.' He looked puzzled suddenly. 'I always thought so, but to be honest, Olivia, listening to you, I wonder. I've given in on so many things. Where we live, where the boys go to school now, where we spend our summers. And then I think, so what, who cares? The trouble is maybe I do. And maybe I wouldn't even give a damn if Katie were there for me, but all of a sudden I listen to her and I realize she's not there. She's either out at a committee meeting somewhere, doing something for the kids or herself, or with her father. It's been that way for a while, at least since the boys left for boarding school, or maybe even before that. But I've been so busy, I never let myself notice. But all of a sudden, after eighteen years, there's no one for me to talk to. I'm here talking to you, in a fishing village in France, and I'm telling you things I could never tell her . . . because I can't trust her. That's a very damning statement,' he said sadly, 'and yet . . .' He looked up at her pointedly, and reached across the table for Olivia's hand. 'I don't want to leave her. I've never even thought of it. I can't imagine leaving her, or life other than the one I share with her, and our boys . . . but all of a sudden I realize something I've never known, or dared to face before. I'm all alone now.' Olivia nodded silently. It was something she was more than familiar with, and something she had suspected about Peter since the first time they'd talked in

Paris. But she felt sure that he'd been unaware of it. Things had just rolled along until suddenly he found himself in a place he had never expected. And then he looked at Olivia with the ultimate honesty, yet another thing he had discovered about himself in the last two days. 'No matter how I felt, or how she let me down, I'm not sure I'd ever have the guts to leave her. There'd be so much to unravel.' Even thinking about starting his life all over again seriously depressed him.

'It wouldn't be easy,' Olivia said quietly, thinking of herself and still holding his hand. She didn't think less of him because of what he was saying to her. On the contrary, she thought more of him, because he was able to say it. 'It terrifies me too. But at least you have a life with her, as flawed as it may be. She's there, she talks to you, she cares in her own way, even if she is limited, or too attached to her father. But she must have loyalty to you too, and to your children. You have a life together, Peter, even if it is less than perfect. Andy and I have nothing. We haven't in years. He's been gone, almost since the beginning.' Peter suspected that it was more than true and he didn't try to defend him.

'Then maybe you should leave.' He worried about her now though, she seemed so vulnerable and so frail. He didn't like to think of her alone, even here, in her quaint little village. He kept thinking how painful it was going to be not seeing her again. After only two days, she had become important to him, and he couldn't imagine what it would be like not talking to her. The legend he had glimpsed in the elevator had become a woman.

'Could you go back to your parents for a while, until things calm down again, and then come back here?' He was trying to help her work things out, and she smiled at him. They truly were friends, partners in crime now.

'Maybe. I'm not sure my mother would be strong enough to handle it, particularly if my father tries to fight me, and sides with Andy.'

'How pleasant.' Peter looked instantly disapproving. 'Do you think he would do that?'

'He might. Politicians usually stick together. My brother agrees with anything Andy does, just on principle. And my father always supports him. It's nice for them, rotten for the rest of us. And my father thinks Andy should run for president. I don't suppose my defection would be viewed with approval. It's bound to hurt his chances, or knock him out of the race completely. A divorced president is unthinkable. Personally, I think I'd be doing him a favor. I think that's one job that would be a nightmare. A life from hell. I have no doubt in my mind about that one. It would kill me.' He nodded, amazed to be discussing this with her at all. As complicated as his own life was, particularly with Vicotec blowing in the wind, it was certainly a lot simpler than hers was. At least his life was private. But her every move was scrutinized. And no one in his family had the remotest intention of running for public office, except Katie for the school board. Olivia, on the other hand, was related to a governor, a senator, a congressman, and possibly a president in the not too distant future, provided she didn't leave him. It was amazing.

'Do you think you might stay, if he decides to run, I mean?'

'I don't see how I could. It would be the ultimate sellout. But I suppose anything is possible. If I lose my mind, or he has me bound and gagged and put in a closet. He could tell people I was sleeping.' Peter smiled at that, and they walked slowly out of the restaurant arm in arm after he paid for their breakfast. He was surprised by how cheap the food was.

'If he did that, then I'd have to come and rescue you again,' he said with a grin, as they sat down on the dock and dangled their feet over the water. He was still wearing a white shirt and the trousers to his suit, and she was still barefoot. They made an intriguing contrast. 'Is that what you did this time?' she asked, leaning against him easily with a broad grin. 'Rescue me?' She looked pleased by the description. No one had rescued her in years, and it was a welcome gesture.

'I thought I was . . . you know, from kidnappers, or terrorists, whoever that guy in the white shirt was who followed you out of the Place Vendôme. He looked like a really shady character to me. I definitely thought a rescue was in order.' He was smiling at her, and the sun was hot as it shone down on them, swinging their feet as they sat on the dock like children.

'I like that,' she said, and suggested they go back to the beach. 'We could walk to my hotel and go swimming from there.' But he laughed at that. He was certainly not dressed to swim in his trousers. 'We could buy you some shorts or swimming trunks. It's a shame to waste this weather.'

He looked at her wistfully. It was a shame to waste any of it, but there were limits to what they had a right to. 'I should be getting back to Paris. It took me almost ten hours to get here.'

'Don't be ridiculous. You can't come all this way just for breakfast. Besides, you have nothing to do there except wait to hear from Suchard, and he may not even call you. You can call the hotel for messages and call him from here if you have to.'

'That certainly takes care of it,' he said, laughing at her rapid disposal of his obligations.

'You could rent a room in my hotel, and we could both drive back tomorrow,' she said matter-of-factly, putting off their departure for another day, but Peter wasn't at all sure he should let her do that, though the invitation was more than tempting.

'Don't you think you should at least call him?' Peter suggested quietly, as they walked down the beach hand in hand in the blazing sun. And as he looked at her, radiant next to him, he realized that never in his life had he known such freedom.

'Not necessarily,' Olivia said, looking anything but contrite. 'Look at the publicity he'll get out of this, the sympathy, the attention. It would be a terrible shame to spoil it for him.'

'You've been in politics too long.' Peter laughed at her in spite of himself, and sat down on the sand next to her, as she pulled him down beside her. He had taken his shoes and socks off by then and was carrying them. He felt like a beach bum. 'You're beginning to think like they do.'

'Never. Even at my worst, I'm not rotten enough. I couldn't be. I don't want anything badly enough. The only thing I ever wanted in my life I lost. I have nothing left to lose now.' It was the saddest statement he'd ever heard, and he knew she was talking about her baby.

'You might have more children one day, Olivia,' he said gently, as she lay down next to him on the sand with her eyes closed, as though she could keep the pain away if she refused to see it. But he could see tears in the corners of her eyes and he wiped them away gently. 'It must have been awful . . . I'm so sorry. . .' He wanted to cry with her, to hold her in his arms, to take away all the grief she'd had for the past six years. But he felt helpless to do anything as he watched her.

'It was awful,' she whispered with her eyes still closed. 'Thank you, Peter . . . for being my friend . . . and for being here.' She opened her eyes and looked at him then. Their eyes met and held for a long time. He had come a long way for her, and suddenly in this little French town, hidden from everyone who knew them, they both knew they were there for each other, for as long as it was possible, as long as they dared. He leaned on one elbow looking down at her and knew with absolute certainty he had never felt this way for anyone, and he had never known anyone like her. He couldn't think of anything or anyone else now.

'I want to be there for you,' he said gently, looking down at her, tracing her face and her lips with his fingers. '. . . and I have no right to be. I've never done anything like this.' He was tormented by her, and yet she was the balm that soothed all his other ills. Being with her was the best thing that had ever happened to him, and also the most confusing.

'I know that,' she said softly. From her gut, from her soul, from her heart, she knew everything about him. 'I don't expect anything from you,' she explained, 'you've already been there for me more than anyone in the last ten years. I can't ask more than that . . . and I don't want to make you unhappy,' she said, looking up at him sadly. In some ways, she knew so much more about life than he did, about grief, about loss, about pain, but even more about betrayal. 'Shhh . . .' he said, putting a finger to her lips, and then without another sound, he lay close to her, and took her in his arms and kissed her. There was no one there to see anything, to care what they did, or take photographs, or stop them. All they had were their consciences and the obstacles they'd brought along with them, which lay like debris from the sea, washed up on the beach all around them. Their children, their mates, their memories, their lives. And yet none of it seemed to matter as he kissed her with all the passion that had been pent up over the years and had been long forgotten. They lay in each other's arms for a long time, and her kisses were as hungry as his, her soul even more needy. It was a long time before they remembered where they were, and forced themselves to pull apart and lay there smiling at each other.

'I love you, Olivia,' he said breathlessly. He was the first to speak as he pulled her closer, as they lay side by side on the beach, looking up at the sunshine. 'That must sound crazy to you after two days, except that I feel I've known you all my life. I have no right to even say it to you . . . but I love you.' He looked down at her with something in his eyes that had never been there, and she was smiling.

'I love you too. God only knows what it'll bring to us, probably not much, but I've never been so happy in my life. Maybe we should both run away. To hell with Vicotec, and Andy.' They both laughed at the cavalier way she said it, and it was extraordinary to realize that at that precise moment not a single soul knew where either of them were. She was thought to have been kidnapped or worse, and he had simply disappeared with a rented car, a bottle of Evian, and an apple. It was heady stuff knowing that no one in the world could find them.

And then Peter thought of something. Maybe at that very moment Interpol was on its way there. 'Why is it that your husband didn't figure out you might have come here?' It had been so obvious to him, surely it would have been to Andy.

'I've never told him about this. I've always kept it as my secret.'

'You did?' Peter looked stunned when she said it. She had told him the first night they'd talked. And she hadn't told Andy? He was flattered. Her trust in him seemed extraordinary, but it was mutual. There was nothing in the world he wouldn't have told her, or hadn't. 'I guess we're safe here then. For a few hours at least.' He was still determined to go back late that afternoon, but after they bought a bathing suit for him, and swam in the ocean side by side, his resolve began to weaken. It was a lot more exciting than swimming in the Ritz pool had been. He hadn't even known her then, and she had tantalized him as she swam by him.

But here, she swam very close to him, and he could hardly bear it.

She said swimming in the ocean frightened her, she had never liked sailing for that reason. She worried about the currents and the tides, and what kind of fish were swimming around her. But she felt protected with him, and they swam out to a small boat tied to a buoy. They climbed into it and rested for a little while, and it took all the strength he had, not to make love to her right in the little dinghy. But they'd already made an agreement. Peter was adamant that if something happened between them, it would spoil everything. They would both be consumed by guilt, and they both knew that whatever this was that had blossomed between them overnight could have no future other than friendship. They couldn't afford to risk destroying it by doing something foolish. And although Olivia's marriage was far more precarious than his, and less intact, she agreed with him. Having an affair with him would only complicate matters when she went back to Paris to talk to Andy. But it was certainly difficult keeping their relationship as close to platonic as they could, and limiting it to kisses. They both talked about it again when they got back to the beach, and tried not to get too carried away, but it was far from easy. Their bodies were wet and smooth as they lay very near, as they talked of all the things that were important to them. They talked about their childhoods, hers in Washington, and his in Wisconsin. He talked about how out of place he had always felt at home, and how much more he had wanted, and how lucky he had been when he found Katie.

She asked about his family, and he told her about his parents and his sister. He told her of his mother and sister dying of cancer, and why Vicotec meant so much to him.

'If they'd had a product like that available to them, it might have made a difference,' he said sadly.

'Maybe,' she said philosophically. 'But sometimes you can't win, no matter how many miracle drugs you have at your disposal.' They'd tried everything, and they still hadn't been able to save Alex. And then she turned to him, thinking of his sister.

'Did she have kids?' He nodded, and tears filled his eyes as he looked into the distance. 'Do they come to visit?'

He felt ashamed when he answered. He looked Olivia in the eye, and knew how wrong he had been. Suddenly, being with her made him want to change that. It made him want to change a lot of things, some of which were easier than others.

'My brother-in-law moved away, and remarried within the year. I didn't hear from him for a long time. I don't know why, maybe he wanted to put it all behind him. He didn't call and tell me where they were till he and his new wife needed money. I think they had a couple more kids by then. And I let Katie tell me that it had been too long, that they probably didn't give a damn, and the kids didn't know me. I let it go, and I haven't heard from them in a long time. They were living on a ranch in Montana the last time I heard from them. Sometimes I wonder if Katie likes the fact that I have no family, except for her and the boys and Frank. She and my sister never really hit it off, and she was furious that Muriel inherited the farm and I didn't. But my father was right to give it to them. I didn't want it or need it, and my father knew that.' He looked at Olivia again then, knowing what he had known for years, and refused to acknowledge, in deference to Katie. 'I was wrong to let those kids slip out of my life. I should have gone out to Montana to see them.' He owed that to his sister. But it would have been painful, and it had been so much easier to listen to Katie.

'You still could,' Olivia said kindly.

'I'd like to do that. If I can still find them.'

'I'll bet you can, if you try.'

He nodded, knowing what he needed to do now. And then he was startled by her next question.

'What if you'd never married her?' Olivia asked him with curiosity. She loved playing games with him, and asking him questions that were difficult to answer.

'Then I'd never have the career I have now,' he said simply. But Olivia was quick to shake her head in disagreement.

'You're absolutely wrong. And that's your whole problem,' she said without hesitating for an instant. 'You think that everything you have is because of her. Your job, your success, your career, even your house in Greenwich. That's crazy. You would have had a brilliant career anyway. She didn't do that, *you* did. You would have had a fabulous career wherever you were, maybe even back in Wisconsin. You have that kind of mind, and I suspect that kind of ability to seize opportunity, and run with it. Look what you've done with Vicotec. You said yourself that was entirely your baby.'

'But I haven't done it yet,' he said modestly.

'You will though. No matter what Suchard says. One year, two, ten, who cares. You'll do it,' she said, with absolute conviction. 'And if this doesn't work, something else will. And it has nothing to do with who you're married to.' She wasn't wrong, he just didn't know that. 'I'm not denying the Donovans gave you an opportunity, but other people would have too. And look what you've given them. Peter, you think they've done it all for you, and you're still embarrassed about it. You've done it all yourself and you don't even know it.' It was certainly a perspective he'd never had before, and listening to her gave him confidence. She was a remarkable woman. She gave him something no one ever had before, and certainly not Katie. But he gave her something too, a kind of warmth and caring and tenderness she had longed for. They were a rare combination, and she was grateful for it.

It was the end of the afternoon when they went back to her hotel, and ordered salade niçoise, and bread and cheese to eat on the terrace. And at six o'clock he looked at his watch, and realized he had to head back to Paris. But after a day of swimming and sun, and restraining the passion he felt for her, he was almost too tired to move, let alone drive ten hours.

'I don't think you should,' she said, looking very pretty and young and tan and somewhat worried. He would have liked to stay with her forever. 'You haven't had a decent night's sleep for two days, and you won't get back until four in the morning, even if you leave in the next ten minutes.'

'I have to admit,' he said, looking pleasantly fatigued, 'it's not terribly appealing. But I should get back.' He had called the Ritz and there were no messages for him at least, but he still had to go back to Paris, and eventually Suchard would call him. He was just relieved that neither Katie nor Frank had called him that morning.

'Why not stay the night, and drive to Paris tomorrow?' she said sensibly, and he looked at her and debated.

'Will you come back with me if I go tomorrow?'

'Maybe,' she said, looking suddenly very fey as she looked out at the ocean.

'That's what I love about you, a real passion for commitment.' But she had a passion for other things, and the little he had tasted of her had already nearly driven him to distraction. 'All right, all right,' he said finally. He really was too tired to undertake the drive that night, and preferred to do it after a good night's sleep, the following morning.

But when they went to rent the other single

remaining room at her hotel, they found that it had already been rented. There were only four rooms in all, and she had the best one. It was a small double room with a view of the ocean, and they stood looking at each other for a long moment.

'You can sleep on the floor,' she said finally with a mischievous grin, attempting to honor their commitment to each other not to do anything they'd regret later. But at times it was difficult to remember.

'It's depressing to admit,' he grinned, 'but that's the best offer I've had in a long time. I'll take it.'

'Fair enough. And I promise to behave. Scout's honor.' She held up two fingers and he pretended to look disappointed.

'That's even more depressing.' They were both laughing as they went off arm in arm to find him a clean T-shirt, a razor, and a pair of blue jeans. And they found all of it in the local store. The T-shirt advertised FANTA, the jeans fit him perfectly, and he insisted on shaving in her tiny bathroom before dinner, and he looked better than ever when he emerged. She was wearing a white cotton lace skirt, a halter top, and a pair of espadrilles she had bought on the trip down, and with her shining dark hair and her tan, she looked really lovely. It was hard to realize now that this was the woman he had read about, and been fascinated by for so long. She didn't seem like the same person anymore. She was his friend, and the woman he was falling in love with. And there was something very sweet about the way they felt about each other physically and emotionally, and in spite of the opportunity, refused to indulge it. It was wonderfully romantic and old-fashioned.

They held hands and kissed, and went for a long walk at midnight on the beach, and when they heard music in the distance, they danced on the sand, holding each other close, and then he kissed her.

'What are we going to do when we go back?' he said finally, as they sat down side by side, still listening to the music in the distance. 'What am I going to do without you?' It was a question he had asked himself over and over.

'What you always did,' she said quietly. She had no intention of breaking up his marriage, or even encouraging him to think about it. She had no right to do that, no matter what happened between her and Andy. And besides, despite the attraction they shared, in some ways, she barely knew him.

'What is it I always did?' he asked, sounding suddenly unhappy. 'I can't remember anymore. Everything back there seems so unreal to me now. I don't even know if I was happy.' But the worst of it was that he was beginning to suspect he wasn't. And that was a new concept to Peter.

'Maybe it doesn't matter. Maybe you don't need to ask yourself those questions,' she said wisely. 'We have all this right now . . . we'll have the memory of today. That will hold me for a long time,' she said sadly, and then looked up at him. They both knew the truth about his life, that he had sold out without even knowing it, but she would never have said that. He had made excuses to himself, and let Kate and Frank run everything, from his home to his business. It had happened gradually. And the only thing that amazed him, as he looked at it now, from Olivia's eyes, was that he couldn't understand why he had never seen it. But it had been so much easier not to.

'What am I going to do without you?' Peter said miserably as he held her close to him. He couldn't imagine not having her to talk to. He had survived forty-four years without her, and now suddenly he couldn't bear the thought of a single moment separated from her.

'Don't think about it,' she said, and this time she kissed him. And it took all their strength to pull away from each other again and walk slowly back to the hotel, with their arms around each other. And as they walked slowly up to her small room, Peter smiled at her and whispered.

'You may have to stay awake and throw cold water on me all night,' he said with a rueful grin. He would have done anything to wave a magic wand and change their circumstances, but they both knew that they had no right to what they wanted, and it was a real test of their integrity not to indulge themselves and just grab it.

'I'll do that,' Olivia promised with a grin. She still hadn't called Andy, and seemed to have no intention of doing so at the moment. Peter didn't mention it again. He felt it was up to her to make that decision, but her stubbornness about it intrigued him, and he wondered if she was punishing him, or just afraid to call him.

Olivia was as good as her word when they got to her room. She handed all the pillows to him and one of the blankets, and helped him make an awkward bed on the carpet next to her side of the bed. He slept in his jeans and T-shirt and bare feet, and she changed into her nightgown in the tiny bathroom. And finally, they lay in the dark, she lay on the bed, and he on the floor next to her, and they held hands and talked in the dark for hours, but he made no move to kiss her, and it was nearly four o'clock when she finally stopped talking and drifted off to sleep. He stood up very quietly, and tucked her in, looking down at her sleeping like a little girl, and he leaned down and kissed her ever so gently. And then he lay down on the floor again, on his makeshift bed, and thought about her until morning.

## Chapter Six

It was nearly ten-thirty when they both woke up the next day, and the sun was streaming in through the window. Olivia woke up first and she was looking down at him from the bed when he first stirred. And she smiled at him the moment he saw her.

'Good morning,' she whispered cheerily, and he groaned as he rolled over on his back. Despite the thin carpet and the blanket, the floor had been hard and he was more than a little tired after falling asleep at seven. 'Are you stiff?' She saw his face as he turned, and offered to rub his back for him. They were both very proud of themselves that they had gotten through the night without mis-behaving.

'I'd love that.' He accepted her offer of a back rub with a broad smile, and rolled over on his stomach with another groan, which amused her. She was still lying on her stomach on the bed, reaching down to him, and gently massaging his neck, and he lay happily on his makeshift bed with his eyes closed. 'Did you sleep well?' she asked, doing his shoulders after his neck and trying not to think about how smooth his skin was. He had skin like a baby.

'I lay here thinking about you all night,' he said honestly. 'It's definitely a tribute to my being a gentleman that I behaved myself, or maybe it's just a sign of stupidity and old age.' He rolled over and looked at her then, and he took her hands in his, and then without any warning, he sat up easily, and kissed her.

'I had a dream about you last night,' she said, as he sat on the floor next to her, their faces next to each other's, and his hands played with her hair, as he kissed her lips again and again. He knew he was going to have to leave her shortly.

'What happened in the dream?' he whispered as he kissed her neck, his promises to himself slowly being forgotten.

'I was swimming in the ocean, and I started to drown .... and then you saved me. I think it's pretty representative of what's happened ever since I met you. I was drowning when I met you,' she said, looking at him, and this time he put his arms around her and kissed her. He was on his knees by then, and she was still on the bed, and suddenly his hands began to explore her breasts beneath her nightgown. She moaned softly at his touch, and wanted to remind him of their mutual promises, but in a single instant she forgot them, and reached out to him and pulled him toward her.

Their kisses were increasingly passionate as she pulled him slowly toward her in the bed, and a moment later their bodies were entwined, and they were tangled in the sheets, she still in her nightgown, and he was still wearing blue jeans. They lay there together for a long time, kissing each other and forgetting themselves and discovering things about each other that they had promised not to explore. As Peter kissed her, he wanted to devour her, to just swallow her whole, until she was a part of him, and he could keep her near him forever.

'Peter . . .' She whispered his name, and he held her close to him, and then he was kissing her again, and she was reaching for him in total starvation.

'Olivia . . . don't . . . I don't want you to

be sorry later . . . .' He tried to be responsible, for her sake more than his own or Kate's, but he couldn't stop himself either by then. Without saying another word, she peeled his jeans away from him, his T-shirt was already gone, and he tossed her thin nightgown high into the air, and it settled somewhere on the floor nearby as he began making love to her. And it was nearly noon when they caught their breath again, and they lay in each other's arms, completely spent and sated. But neither of them had ever looked happier, and Olivia smiled up at him from where she lay in his arms, her exquisite limbs completely entwined with his now.

'Peter . . . I love you . . .'

'That's a good thing,' he said, pulling her so close to him that they almost seemed like one person, 'because I've never loved anyone so much in my life. I guess I'm not a gentleman after all,' he said, looking only faintly regretful, and so pleased with what they'd done, and she smiled sleepily at him.

'I'm glad you're not.' She sighed and snuggled still closer to him.

They said nothing for a long time, and just lay there in each other's arms, grateful for every moment that they shared. And finally, knowing they would have to leave each other again, they made love again, one last time. And when they got up at last, Olivia clung to him and cried. She never wanted to leave him, but they knew they had to. She had decided to go back to Paris with him. And they left their hotel at four o'clock looking like two children banished from the Garden of Eden.

They stopped and got something to eat, and shared a glass of wine and some sandwiches sitting on the beach, looking out at the ocean.

'I'll be able to visualize you here, if you come back,' he said sadly, looking at her, and wishing, as she did, that they could stay there together forever.

'Will you come to see me?' she asked, smiling wistfully at him, her hair hanging over her eyes, with grains of sand along the side of her face where she'd been lying.

But for a long time Peter didn't answer. He wasn't sure what to say to her. He knew he couldn't make any promises. He still had a life with Kate, and only an hour before, Olivia had said she understood that. She didn't want to take anything away from him. All she wanted was to cherish what they had shared for the past two days. It was more than some people had in a lifetime.

'I'll try,' he said finally, not wanting to break a promise to her even before he made it. They both knew how difficult it was going to be, and they had already said that they couldn't continue their affair. It would have to remain nothing more than a memory. Their lives were too complicated, and they were both far too involved with other people. And once Olivia went back to her own world, the paparazzi who normally followed her would never let something like this happen. What they had shared here was a miracle and could never be repeated.

'I'd like to come back here and rent a house,' Olivia said solemnly. 'I think I could actually write here.'

'You ought to try it,' he said as he kissed her.

They threw the last of their lunch away, and stood for a moment, hand in hand, looking out at the ocean.

'I'd like to think we'll be back here one day. Together, I mean,' Peter said, promising her something he hadn't dared to say before, that there was some dim, distant hope for a future. Or maybe just another day. Another memory to carry with them. Olivia expected nothing of him.

'Maybe we will,' she said quietly. 'If it's

meant to be, maybe that will happen.' But they had obstacles to overcome first, hurdles they had to jump, burning hoops they had to leap through. He had Vicotec to see through to the end, his father-in-law to contend with, Kate waiting for him in Connecticut, and she had to go back and deal with Andy.

They walked quietly to his car, and she had bought some food for the road. She put it in the backseat and hoped he couldn't see the tears in her eyes, but even without looking at her, he could feel them. He could feel them in his heart. He was crying for the same reasons that she was. He wanted more than either of them had a right to.

He pulled her close to him, as they stood looking out to sea for a last time, and told her how much he loved her. She told him the same thing, and then they kissed again, and then finally got into his rented car to begin the long drive back to Paris.

They hardly spoke to each other for a while, and then finally they both relaxed again, and started talking. They were each dealing with what had happened in their own way, trying to absorb it, make it theirs, and accept the inevitable limitations.

'It's going to be so hard,' Olivia said,

smiling through tears in spite of herself as they passed la Vierrerie, 'knowing that you're out there somewhere and I can't be with you.'

'I know,' he said, feeling a lump in his throat as well. 'I was thinking the same thing when we left the hotel. It's going to drive me crazy. Who am I going to talk to?' And now that they had made love, in some ways he felt she was his now.

'You could call once in a while,' she said hopefully. 'I could let you know where I am.'

But they both knew that wherever he was, he was still going to be married. 'That doesn't seem fair to you.' None of it was. It was the danger in what they'd done, but they both knew it. And not making love wouldn't really have changed anything. In some ways, it might even have made it harder. At least this way, they had had it all, and they could take it with them.

'Maybe we should meet somewhere in six months, just to see what's happening in our lives.' She looked embarrassed for an instant, thinking of one of her favorite movies with Cary Grant and Deborah Kerr. It was a classic and she had cried over it a thousand times when she was younger. 'Maybe we could meet at the Empire State Building,' she said only half jokingly, and he shook his head quickly.

'That's no good. You'd never show up. I'd get mad about it, and you'd wind up in a wheelchair. Try another movie.' He smiled and she laughed at him.

'What are we going to do?' she asked, looking mournfully out the window.

'Go back. Be strong. Go back to whatever it is we did before to make it all work. I think that's easier for me than for you. I was so stupid and blind, I didn't even realize how unhappy I was. I think you have a lot to sort out though. The trick for me is going to be making it look like nothing has happened, as though I haven't seen the truth during my week in Paris. How would I ever explain that?'

'Maybe you won't have to.' She wondered how badly the Vicotec mess was going to rock his boat if it didn't do well in the tests. That remained to be seen, and Peter was getting increasingly worried about it.

'Why don't you write to me, Olivia?' he said finally. 'At least let me know where you are. I'll go crazy if I don't know. Will you promise me that?'

'Of course.' She nodded.

They talked as they drove through the

night, and it was nearly four A.M. when they arrived in Paris. He stopped a few blocks from the hotel, and although they were both tired by then, he pulled over.

'Can I buy you a cup of coffee?' he asked, remembering his opening line in the Place de la Concorde, and she smiled sadly.

'You can buy me anything you like, Peter Haskell.'

'What I want to give you can't be bought, at any price,' he said, referring to all he felt for her and had from the first moment he saw her. 'I love you. I probably will for the rest of my life. There's never going to be anyone like you. There never has been, never will be. Remember that, wherever you are. I love you.' He kissed her then, long and hard, and they clung to each other like two people drowning.

'I love you too, Peter. I wish you could take me with you.'

'I wish that too.' He knew that neither of them would ever forget what they had shared for the past two days, and what had passed between them that morning.

He drove her back to the hotel then, and let her out at the far end of the Place Vendôme. She had no bags with her, only the cotton skirt she wore. She had rolled up her jeans and T-shirt and was carrying them. She left nothing with him, except her heart, and she looked at him for a last time, and he kissed her again, and then she ran across the square, with tears streaming down her cheeks when she left him.

He sat there for a long time, thinking of her, and watching the entrance to the hotel where he had last seen her. He knew she had to be in her room by then, and this time she had promised him she would go back and not disappear again. And if she did, he wanted her to come to him, or at least let him know where she was. He didn't want her wandering around France. Unlike her husband, Peter was far more concerned with her safety. He was worried about everything, about what they'd done, about what would happen to her now when she went back, and whether or not she would once again be used and exploited, or if this time she would leave him. He worried about facing Kate again, when he went back to Connecticut, and if she would sense that something had changed between them. Or had it? Olivia had made him realize his success was his own, but he still felt he owed so much to Kate, in spite of what Olivia had said to him. He couldn't just let her down now. He had to go on as if nothing had happened. What had happened with Olivia had no past, no present, no future. It was simply a moment, a dream, an instant, a diamond they had found in the sand and held between them. But they both had other obligations which took precedence. It was Kate who was his past, his present, and his future. The only problem was the ache in his heart. And as he walked back into the Ritz, he thought his heart would break as he thought about Olivia. He wondered if he would ever see her again, and where she was at that exact moment. A life without her was beyond imagining, but that was all he had now.

And when he opened the door to his room, he saw the small envelope waiting for him. Dr Paul-Louis Suchard had called, and requested that Mr Haskell call him at his earliest possible convenience.

He was back to real life, to the things that mattered to him, his wife, his sons, his business. And somewhere in the distance, receding into the mists, was the woman he had found but could never have, the woman he was so desperately in love with.

He stood at his balcony as the sun came up, thinking about her. It all seemed like a dream, and perhaps it was. Perhaps none of it was

real. The Place de la Concorde . . . the café in
Montmartre . . . the beach at La Favière . . .
all of it. He knew that no matter what he felt
for her, or how sweet it had been, he had to
let it go now.

# Chapter Seven

When the wake-up call came at eight, Peter was dead to the world, and as soon as he hung up the phone, he wondered why he felt so awful. He felt as though there were lead in his soul, and then just as suddenly, he remembered. She was gone from him. It was over. He had to call Suchard, and fly back to New York and face Frank, and Katie. And Olivia had gone back to her husband.

It was hard to believe how miserable he felt as he stood in the shower, thinking of her, and forcing his mind back repeatedly to the business he had to deal with that morning.

He called Suchard precisely at nine, and Paul-Louis refused to tell him what the results were. He insisted that Peter come directly to the laboratory. He said that all of the tests were complete now. He wanted an hour of Peter's time, and said he could easily catch a two o'clock plane. Peter was annoyed that he wouldn't at least give him a summary of their results on the phone, and agreed to come to his office at ten-thirty. He ordered coffee and croissants, but could eat none of it, and he left the hotel at ten, and arrived ten minutes early. Suchard was waiting for him, and his face was grim. But in the end, the results were not quite as bad as Peter had feared, or Paul-Louis had predicted. One of the essential substances of Vicotec was clearly dangerous, and it was possible they would have to find a substitute, but the entire product did not have to be abandoned. It had to be 'reworked,' as Suchard said, and it could prove to be a lengthy process. When pressed, he admitted that the changes could be effected in six months or a year, perhaps less if a miracle occurred, though it was doubtful. More reasonably, the process would take about two years, which was pretty much what Peter had suspected after their first conversation. Perhaps, if they put extra teams on it, they could get Vicotec on its feet in less than a year, which wasn't the end of the world, though it was certainly disappointing. But the substance, as it existed now, and as they had planned to market it, was virtually a killer. It didn't have to be, and Suchard had several suggestions as to how to effect the necessary changes. But Peter knew that Frank would not consider any of this good news. He hated delays, and the extensive research that still had to be done would be costly. There was no hope of asking for early human trials now from the FDA, or attending the hearing they had set up for September in order to get it on the 'Fast Track.' What Frank wanted, of course, was early release of the drug as quickly as possible, resulting in massive revenues, which was different from what Peter wanted out of it. But whatever their reasons or their goals, right now they had nothing to ask for.

Peter thanked Paul-Louis for his input and his thorough research, and he sat lost in thought as he rode back to the hotel, trying to think of the right words to tell Frank. Paul-Louis's exact words still rang in his own ears uncomfortably: 'Vicotec, as it stands now, is a killer.' It was certainly not what they had intended, or what he would have wanted for his mother and sister. But somehow Peter couldn't see Frank taking the news reasonably, or even Katie. She hated things that upset her father. But even she would have to understand this time. No one wanted a series of tragedies, or even one, they could not afford to let that happen.

Peter closed his bags back at the hotel, and as he waited the last ten minutes for the car, he flipped on the news. And there she was. It was almost exactly what he had expected. The big news of the hour was that Olivia Douglas Thatcher had been found. And the tale they told was too strange to be true, and of course it wasn't. She had gone out to meet a friend, apparently, had a minor car accident, and had been suffering from mild amnesia for three days. Apparently no one in the small hospital where she was had recognized her or seen the news, and miraculously the night before, she had come to her senses again and was now happily reunited with her husband.

'So much for honest reporting,' Peter said, shaking his head and looking disgusted. They ran all the same old, tired photographs of her, and then ran an interview with a neurologist speculating on lasting brain damage from a minor concussion. But they concluded with a statement wishing Mrs Thatcher a complete and speedy recovery. 'Amen,' he said, and flipped off the tube. He looked around the room for a last time, and picked up his brief-case. His bag was already gone, and there was nothing left to do but leave his hotel room.

But it gave him an odd feeling of nostalgia this time leaving the room. So much had happened during this trip, and he wanted suddenly to run upstairs, just to see her. He would knock on the door of their suite, say he was an old friend . . . and Andy Thatcher would probably think he was crazy. Peter wondered if he suspected anything about the last three days, or if he didn't even care. It was hard to gauge and the story they had told the press was a thin tale at best. Peter thought it was ridiculous and wondered who had come up with that story.

And when he went downstairs, the usual cast of characters was there, the Arabs, the Japanese. King Khaled had gone to London after the bomb scare. There seemed to be a whole flock of new arrivals checking in as Peter made his way past the desk, and there was a large group of men in suits with walkie-talkies and earpieces as he stepped through the revolving door, and then he saw her in the distance. She was just getting into a limousine, and Andy was already in it with two of his people. He was turned away from her, talking to them, and as though sensing Peter nearby, Olivia glanced over her shoulder. She stopped, mesmerized, and looked at him. Their eyes met and held for a long time, and Peter was worried that someone might have noticed. He nodded slightly at her, and then, as though she had to tear herself away from him again, she slipped into the limousine, and the door closed, and Peter stood staring after her on the sidewalk, unable to see in the darkened windows.

'Your car is waiting, monsieur,' the doorman said politely, anxious to avoid a traffic jam in front of the Ritz. Two models were trying to leave for a shoot and Peter's limousine was blocking them. And they were getting hysterical, shouting at him and waving.

'Sorry.' He tipped the doorman and got in, and without another word, or even a last look at her, he looked straight ahead as the driver headed swiftly toward the airport.

And in their car, Andy was taking Olivia to see two congressmen and the Ambassador at the embassy. It was a meeting he'd had planned all week, and he had insisted she go with him. He had been furious with her at first, over the stir she'd caused, but within an hour of her safe return, he concluded that her disappearance was a bonus to him. He and his managers had worked out a series of possibilities, all of them designed to arouse sympathy, particularly in light of his current plans. He wanted to make her another Jackie Kennedy. She had the right looks for it, and that same waiflike quality, coupled with her natural style and elegance, and her courage in the face of adversity. His advisors had decided she was perfect. They were going to have to pay more attention to her than they had in the past, and groom her a little bit, but there was no question in their minds that she could do it.

She'd have to stop pulling her little disappearing acts though. She had done things like that for a while after Alex died, taken off for a few hours, disappeared for a night somewhere, she was usually at her brother's or her parents'. This had gone on for longer than in the past, but he had never truly had a sense that she was in danger. He knew she'd turn up eventually, he just hoped she didn't do anything stupid in the meantime. And he told her just what he thought of it before they left for the embassy, and told her what was expected of her now. At first she had said she wasn't going with him. And she had objected vehemently to the story they were releasing to the press about her.

'I sound like a complete moron,' she said, horrified. 'A brain-damaged one at that,' she said, complaining bitterly about the story.

'You didn't leave us much choice. What would you like us to say? That you were dead drunk in a hotel on the Left Bank for three days? Or should we tell the truth? What was the truth, by the way, or do I want to know it?'

'It's not nearly as interesting as anything you'd make up. I needed some time to myself, that's all.'

'That's what I thought,' he said, looking more bored than annoyed. He did plenty of disappearing acts himself, but he was subtler than his wife about it. 'Next time, you might leave me a note, or tell someone.'

'I was going to,' she said, looking embarrassed this time, 'and then I wasn't even sure you'd notice.'

'You must think I'm completely unaware of what goes on,' he said with a look of annoyance.

'Aren't you? About me, at least.' And then she gathered her courage in both hands and said what she had planned to all along. 'I'd like to speak to you this afternoon. Maybe when we get back from the embassy.'

'I have a lunch,' he said, losing interest in her immediately. She was back. She hadn't embarrassed him. They had satisfied the press. He needed her at the embassy, and after that he had other things to think of.

'This afternoon will be fine,' she said coolly. She could see the look in his eyes that told her he didn't have time for her. It was a familiar look to her, and not one that endeared him to her.

'Is something wrong?' he asked with a look of surprise at her. It was rare that she demanded his time, but he didn't in any way suspect what was coming.

'Not at all. I always disappear for three days at a time. What could be wrong?' He didn't like the look in her eyes or the way she said it.

'You were damn lucky I was able to clean that up for you, Olivia. If I were you, I wouldn't be so snotty about it. You can't expect to go wandering off like that, and have everyone be amused when you get home. If the press wanted to, they could really rake you over the coals for it. So why don't you just back off,' he said. He was all too aware that stunts like that could badly damage his chances.

'Sorry,' she said, looking grim. 'I didn't mean to cause you so much trouble.' He had never said a single word about being worried about her, or afraid she might have come to some harm. In truth, he had never thought about it. Knowing her as well as he did, he had remained convinced that she was hiding. 'Why don't we talk after you get back from your appointments this afternoon. It can wait till then.' She tried to say it calmly. But she was angry at him too. He always let her down. He hadn't been there for her in years now. And it was even more difficult now not to compare him to Peter.

Peter was all she could think of, and when they left for the embassy a little while later, it almost broke her heart when she saw him. She had been afraid to make any sign to him. She knew that the press would be watching her closely for a while. They were probably suspicious of the concocted story too, and every little tidbit they could ferret out would please them.

She was lost in her own thoughts, the whole time they were at the embassy. And Andy didn't ask her to join him for lunch afterwards. He had a long-standing appointment with a French politician. But when he came back at four o'clock, he was in no way prepared for what she told him. She was waiting quietly in the living room of the suite, sitting in a chair, and staring out the window. Peter was on a plane to New York by then, and it was all she could think of. He was going back to 'them,' the other people in his life, the ones who didn't care about him. And she was back in the hands of the exploiters too, but not for much longer.

'What's the big deal?' Andy asked as he came in. Two of his assistants were with him, but when he saw her face, and how serious she was, he rapidly dismissed them. He had only seen her look that way once or twice, when his brother died, and when Alex did. The rest of the time she always seemed withdrawn from him, and removed from the world he lived in.

'I have something I want to say to you,' she said quietly, not sure where to begin. All she knew was that she had to tell him.

'I figured out that much,' he said, looking more handsome than any man she knew. His blue eyes were huge, and his still-blond hair made him seem boyish. He had broad shoulders and a narrow waist, and as he sat down in one of the brocade chairs he crossed his long legs. But Olivia wasn't dazzled by him anymore, she wasn't even charmed. She knew how selfish he was, and how obsessed, and how little he cared about her.

'I'm leaving,' she said simply. That was it. It was out. It was over.

'Leaving where?' he said, looking puzzled. He didn't even understand what she was saying, and she could only smile at that. It was beyond his understanding and imagination.

'I'm leaving you,' she translated for him, 'as soon as we get back to Washington. I can't do this anymore. That's why I went away for the last few days. I had to think about it. But I'm sure now.' She wanted to be sorry about what she was saying to him, but they both knew she wasn't. And he didn't look sorry either, just startled.

'Your timing's not great,' he said pensively, but he didn't ask her why she was going.

'It never is. There's never a good time for something like this. It's like getting sick, it's never convenient.' She was thinking of Alex, and he nodded. He knew how hard that had hit her. But it had been two years. In some ways, he thought she had never recovered. And neither had their marriage.

'Is there anything specific that brought this on? Is something bothering you?' He didn't bother to ask her if there was someone else. He knew her better than that, and sensed easily that there wasn't. And he was absolutely convinced that he knew everything about her.

'There's a lot bothering me, Andy. You know that.' The two of them exchanged a long look, and neither of them would have denied that they had become strangers. She didn't even know who he was now. 'I never wanted to be a political wife. I told you that when we got married.'

'I can't help that, Olivia. Things change. I

never expected Tom to be killed. I never expected a lot of things. Neither did you. Things happen. You do your best to face them.'

'I've done that. I've been there for you. I campaigned with you. I've done everything you expected, but we're not married anymore, Andy, and you know it. You haven't been there for me in years. I don't even know who you are now.'

'I'm sorry,' he said quietly, and he sounded sincere, but he didn't offer to change it either. 'This is a bad time for you to do this to me.' He looked at her with a pointed look that would have frightened her if she had known what he was thinking. He needed her desperately, and there was no way he was willing to let her go now. 'There's something I've been meaning to discuss with you. I didn't make the final decision until last week.' And whatever decision it had been, it was equally clear to her that she had been no part of it. 'I wanted you to be among the first to know, Olivia.' 'Among the first,' but not the first, it was the whole story of the recent years of their marriage. 'I'm going to run for the presidency next year. It means everything to me. And I'm going to need your help to win it.' She sat staring at him, and if he had hit her with a baseball bat, he couldn't have hit her harder. It wasn't that she hadn't been expecting it. She knew it was a possibility, but now it was real, and the way he said it to her brought it home like a bomb in her hands, and she had no idea what to do now. 'I've been thinking a lot about this, knowing how you feel about political campaigns. But I would imagine there's a little appeal to being first lady.' He said it with a small smile, encouraging her, but she did not smile at him in answer. She looked horrified. The last thing in the world she wanted to be was first lady.

'There's no appeal to it whatsoever,' she said, shaking.

'But there is to me,' he said bluntly. It was the one thing he wanted, more than he wanted her, or any marriage. 'And I can't do it without you. There's no such thing as a separated president, much less a divorced one. That's not news to you.' She was a political pro, after growing up with her father. But as he looked at her, he had an idea. If nothing else, he had to salvage what he could from this, though he made no effort at all to convince her he still loved her. She was too smart for that, he had already put too many stamps in the coupon book. It had gone too far, and they both knew it.

'Let me suggest something to you,' he said thoughtfully. 'It's not exactly a romantic idea, but maybe it would suit both our needs. I need you. Practically speaking, for the next five years at least. One for the campaign, and four more for my first term. After that, we can either renegotiate, or the country will have to adjust to our situation. Maybe it's time for people to understand that even their president is human. After all, look at Prince Charles and Princess Di. England survived it, surely we will.' In his own mind, he was already the president, and people were going to have to adjust to him, just as she did.

'I'm not quite sure we're in those leagues,' she said ironically, but he didn't seem to notice.

'Anyway,' he went on, ignoring her, thinking ahead and concentrating on making it sound appealing, 'we're talking about five years. You're very young, Olivia. You can afford that, and it will give you a cachet you never had before. People will not just feel sorry for you, or curious about you, they will come to *adore* you. My boys and I can make that happen.' She wanted to vomit as she listened to him, but she let him continue. 'I will put five hundred thousand dollars in an account for you at the end of each year, after taxes. At the end of five years, you'll have two and a half million dollars.' He held up a hand to anticipate any comment. 'I know you can't be bought, but if you're going to go off on your own afterwards, that's a nice little nest egg with which to do it. And if we have another child,' he smiled at her, sweetening the deal, 'I will give you another million. We've been talking about that recently, and I think that could be an important issue. You don't want people to think that there's something strange about us, or say that we're both gay, or you're obsessed by tragedy. They say enough of that already. I think it's time for us to move on, and have another baby.' Olivia couldn't believe what she was hearing. '*We've been talking about a baby*,' meant he and his campaign people. It was beyond disgusting.

'Why don't we just rent a baby?' she said coldly. 'No one would have to know. We could just take it on the campaign trail with us, and then give it back when we get home. It would be a lot easier. Babies are so incredibly messy, and so much trouble.' He didn't like the look in her eyes when she said it.

'Comments like that are unnecessary,' he said quietly, looking like exactly what he was, a rich boy who had gone to all the best prep schools, followed by Harvard undergraduate and law school. He had lots of family money behind him, and he had always believed that there was nothing he couldn't have if he either bought it or worked hard enough for it. He was willing to do both, but not for her. And there was no way in the world she was going to have another baby with him. He was never around for the first one, even once he had cancer. It was part of why Alex's death had been so hard on her and somewhat easier for Andy. He hadn't been nearly as close to their son as she was.

'Your proposal is revolting. It's the most disgusting thing I ever heard,' she said with a look of outrage. 'You want to buy five years of my life, at a sensible price, and you want me to have another child because it will help you get elected. I may throw up if I sit here and listen to you for much longer.' The look on her face told him exactly what she thought of his proposal.

'You always liked children. I don't understand why that's a problem.'

'I don't like you anymore, Andy, and this is why, or part of it. How can you be this crass and insensitive? What has happened to you?' Tears burned her eyes, but she refused to cry for him. He wasn't worth it. 'I love children. I still do. But I'm not going to have a baby for a campaign, with a man who doesn't love me. What were you suggesting, that we do it by artificial insemination?' He hadn't slept with her in months, and she didn't really care. He didn't have time, and he had other resources he exploited regularly, and she didn't have the interest.

'I think you're overreacting,' he said, but he was faintly embarrassed by what she was saying. There was some truth to it, and even he knew it. But he couldn't back down now. It was too important to him to win her over. He had told his campaign manager that she would balk at having a baby. She had been terribly attached to their first child, distraught when he died, and he suspected that she would never be willing to have another. She was much too afraid now to lose it. 'All right, I'd like you to think about it, though. Say a million for each year. That's five million dollars for five years, and another two if you have a baby.' He was serious and all she could do was laugh now.

'Do you think I should hold out for two a year and three if I have a baby? What does that make,' she pretended to consider it, 'let's see . . . that's six if I have twins . . . nine if I have triplets. I could take Pergonal shots . . . maybe even quadruplets . . .' She turned and looked at him with wounded eyes. Who was this man she had once believed in? How could she have been so wrong about him? Listening to him, she wondered if he'd ever been human, yet deep in her heart, she knew he had been, way, way at the beginning. It was because of the person he once had been, and not the one he was now, that she stayed and listened. 'If I do any of this for you, and I doubt that I will, it will be out of some distorted sense of loyalty to you, not out of greed, or because I'm trying to get rich off you. But I know how badly you want this.' It would be her final gift to him, and then she'd never have to feel guilty for leaving.

'It's all I want, Olivia,' he said, so intent, he was pale. And she knew that for once he was being honest.

'I'll think about it,' she said quietly. She didn't know what to do now. That morning she had been convinced that she'd be back in La Favière by the end of the week, and now she was about to become first lady. It was a nightmare. But she felt as though she owed him something. He was still her husband, and he had been the father of her child, and she could help him get the one thing he wanted in life. It was an incredible gift to give anyone. And without her, she knew he couldn't do it.

'I want to announce it in two days. We're going back to Washington tomorrow.'

'Nice of you to tell me.'

'If you stuck around, maybe you'd get our travel plans,' he said bluntly, watching her, wondering what decision she'd make. But he knew her well enough to know he couldn't force her. He wondered if talking to her father would do anything, but he was afraid that in the end it might work against him.

It was a long agonizing night for her in the hotel, and she wished she could go for another long walk alone. She needed time to think, but understandably, she knew that the security people were skittish about her. And she wished more than anything that she could talk to Peter. She wondered what he would think, if he would say that she owed Andy this final gift, this one last great gesture of loyalty, or if he would say that she was crazy. Five years seemed like an eternity, and she knew that it would be five long years that she hated, particularly if he won the election.

But by morning, she had made up her mind, and met Andy over breakfast. He looked nervous and pale, not at the prospect of losing her, but with total terror that she wouldn't help him win the election.

'I suppose I should say something philosophical,' she said over coffee and croissants. He had asked everyone else to leave, which was rare for him. She hadn't been alone with him for years, except in bed at night, and this was the second time in two days. He looked at her strangely, convinced she was about to refuse him. 'But I guess we're beyond philosophy, aren't we? I just keep wondering how we got here. I keep remembering back to the beginning. I think you were in love with me then, and I can never quite figure out what happened. I remember the events, like newsreels that I replay in my head, but I can never quite figure out the exact moment when it all went sour. Can you?' she asked him sadly.

'I'm not really sure it matters,' he said, sounding subdued. He already knew what she was going to tell him. He had never thought she would be this vengeful. He had had his share of dalliances, he had done a lot of things, but he had never thought it really mattered to her. He realized now he'd been very foolish. 'I think things just happen over time. And my brother died. You don't know what that was like for me. You were there, but it was different for me. Suddenly everything that had been expected of him was expected of me. I had to stop being who I was and become him. I guess you and I got lost in the shuffle.'

'Maybe you should have told me then.' Maybe they should never have had Alex. Maybe she should have left him right in the beginning. But she wouldn't have given up the two years of Alex's life for anything. But even that didn't make her want another child now. She realized, as she looked at him, that she had to put Andy out of his misery. Waiting for her to finish what she had to say, he was dying. And she decided to do it quickly. 'I've decided to agree to stay with you for the next five years, at a million a year. I have no idea what I'm going to do with it, give it to charity, buy a castle in Switzerland, start a research fund in Alex's name, whatever it is, I'll figure it out later. You offered me a million a year, and I'll take it. But I have my conditions too. I want a guarantee from you that I'm out at the end of five years, whether or not you get reelected. And if you lose this time, all bets are off, and I'm gone the day after the election. And there's to be no pretense anymore. I'll pose for all the pictures you want, and go on the campaign trail, but you and I are no longer married. No one else has to know, but I want it clearly understood between us. I want my own bedroom wherever we go, and there will be no more children.' It was blunt, it was quick, it was direct, and it was over. Except that she had just plea-bargained herself into a five-year sentence, and he was so shocked he didn't even look pleased yet.

'How am I supposed to explain the separate bedroom?' He looked worried and pleased all at once. He had gotten almost everything he wanted, except a baby, and that had been his campaign manager's idea in the first place.

'Tell them I'm an insomniac,' she answered his question for him, 'or I have nightmares.' It was a good idea, and he figured they'd come up with some fantasy to cover it . . . he had so much work to do . . . the stress of the presidency . . . something like that.

'What about adoption?' He was negotiating down to the last points of the deal, but she remained firm on that one. 'Forget it. I'm not in the business of buying babies for politics. I won't do that to anyone, and certainly not an innocent child. They deserve a better life than this, and better parents.' One day she thought she might like to have another child, or even adopt one, but not with him, and not part of a business contract as loveless as this one. 'And I want all of this in a contract. You're a lawyer, you can draw it up yourself, just between us, and no one ever has to see it.'

'You need witnesses,' he said, still looking bemused. She had absolutely overwhelmed him with her answer. After all she'd said the night before, he'd been certain she wouldn't do it.

'Find someone you trust then,' she said quietly, but that was a tall order in his world. Everyone surrounding him would have sold him out in an instant.

'I don't know what to say to you,' he said, still looking astonished.

'There's not much left to say, Andy, is there?' In one fell swoop, he was running for the presidency, and their marriage was over. It made her sad, thinking about it, but there was no tenderness, not even friendship left between them. It was going to be a long five years for her, and for her own sake, she hoped he wouldn't win it.

'What made you do it?' he asked softly, more grateful than he had ever been to anyone in his life.

'I don't know. I felt I owed it to you. It didn't seem right to have the ability to give you something you wanted so much, or withhold it. You're not keeping me from anything I really want, except freedom. I want to write eventually, but that can wait.' She looked at him with interest, and for the first time in years, he realized that he never knew her.

'Thank you, Olivia,' he said quietly as he stood up.

'Good luck,' she said softly, and he nodded and left the room, without looking back at her. And she realized once he left that he'd never even kissed her.

## Chapter Eight

When Peter's plane touched down at Kennedy, there was a limousine waiting for him. He had arranged it all from the plane, and Frank was waiting for him at the office. In some ways, the news wasn't as bad as Peter had feared it would be, but it still wasn't good. And he knew that it would all be new to Frank, and would take a lot of explaining. Everything had been looking so good only five days before, when Peter left Geneva.

The Friday night traffic into town was miserable. It was rush hour, and it was June. Cars were jammed everywhere, and it was after six o'clock when Peter finally got to Wilson-Donovan, and he looked both strained and exhausted. He had spent hours going over Suchard's reports and notes on the plane, and for once he wasn't even thinking of Olivia. All he could think of was Frank, and Vicotec, and their future. The worst news of all was that they would have to cancel the FDA hearings asking for early release, but that was a practical matter. But Peter knew Frank would be bitterly disappointed. His father-in-law was waiting for him upstairs, on the forty-fifth floor of Wilson-Donovan, in the large corner suite that he had occupied for nearly thirty years since Wilson-Donovan had moved to the building. And his secretary was still outside. She offered Peter a drink when he arrived, but all he wanted was a glass of water.

'So, you made it!' Frank looked distinguished and jovial, in a dark pin-striped suit with a full mane of white hair, and Peter noticed out of the corner of his eye that there was a bottle of French champagne cooling in a silver bucket. 'What's all this secrecy? It's very cloak-and-dagger!' The two men shook hands, and Peter asked if he was well. But Frank Donovan looked healthier than he did. He was seventy, but he was vital and in good health, and very much in charge of everything, as he was now. He almost ordered Peter to tell him what had happened in Paris.

'I met with Suchard today,' Peter said as he sat down, wishing now that he had said something to warn him on the phone before that. The unopened champagne was staring at him like an accusation. 'He took forever on the tests, but I think it was worth it.' He felt his knees tremble like a kid's, and he almost wished he didn't have to be there.

'What does that mean? A clean bill of health, I assume.' He squinted at his son-in-law, and Peter shook his head and faced him squarely.

'I'm afraid not, sir. One of the secondary components went crazy on him in the first round of the tests, and he absolutely wouldn't give us clearance on it till he ran them all again and figured out if we had a serious problem here, or their testing systems were mistaken.'

'And which was it?' Both men looked grave now.

'Our product, I'm afraid. There's one single element we have to change. When we do, we'll be home free. But right now, in Suchard's words, as things stand, Vicotec is a killer.' Peter looked as though he were ready to face anything, but Frank merely shook his head in disbelief, and sat back in his chair, contemplating what Peter had just told him.

'That's ridiculous. We know better than that. Look at Berlin. Look at Geneva. They ran those tests for months, and we came up clean every time in their testing.'

'But we didn't in Paris. We can't ignore that. At least it only appears to be one single element, and he thinks it can be changed "fairly easily."' He was quoting Suchard now.

'How easily?' Frank scowled at him, wanting only one answer.

'He thinks, if we're lucky, the research could take six months to a year. If not, maybe two years. But if we put on double teams again, I think we might get it ready by next calendar year. I don't think we can do it any sooner.' He had calculated it all meticulously on his computer on the flight over.

'That's nonsense. We're asking for early human trials from the FDA in three months. That's how long we've got, and that's what it'll take us. It's your job to see to it. Get that French fool over here to help, if we have to.'

'We can't do it in three months.' Peter looked horrified by what Frank was saying. 'That's impossible. We have to withdraw the request for early trials from the FDA, and we'll have to postpone our appearance at the hearings.'

'I won't do that,' Frank bellowed at him. 'We'll look ridiculous. You've got plenty of time to work the kinks out before we go before them.'

'And if we don't, and they give us the release we want, we'll kill someone. You heard what Suchard said, it's dangerous. Frank, I want to see this product on the market more than anyone. But I'm not going to sacrifice people to do it.'

'I'm telling you,' his father-in-law spoke to him through clenched teeth. 'You have three months to work it out before the hearing.'

'I'm not going to FDA hearings with a product that's dangerous, Frank. Do you understand what I'm saying?' Peter had raised his voice to him, which was a first for him. But he was tired, it had been a long flight, and he hadn't had a real night's sleep in days. And Frank was acting like a lunatic, insisting that they were going to the hearings to request they start human trials and put Vicotec on the 'Fast Track,' when Suchard had just told them it was a killer. 'Did you hear me?' He reiterated to Frank, and the older man shook his head in silent fury.

'No, I did not. You know what I want from you on this. Now do it. I'm not throwing more money down the tubes to develop this further. It's either going to fly now or it won't fly at all. Is that clear?'

'Very,' Peter said quietly, back in control again. 'Then I guess it won't be flying. Whether or not to commit further research funds is your decision,' he said respectfully, but Frank only glared at him in anger.

'I'm giving you three months.'

'I need more than that, Frank. And you know it.'

'I don't care what you do. Just be sure you're ready for those September hearings.'

Peter wanted to tell him he was out of his mind, but he didn't dare. He had never known him to make dangerous decisions. He was being completely unreasonable and doing something that could bring the company down around them. It was ridiculous, and Peter could only assume he'd come to his senses in the morning. Like Peter, he was just disappointed.

'I'm sorry about the bad news,' Peter said quietly, wondering if Frank expected him to give him a ride to Greenwich in the limo. If so, the ride was going to be long and uncomfortable, but Peter was willing to do it.

'I think Suchard is out of his mind,' Frank said angrily, striding across his office and pulling open the door, as a sign for Peter to leave him.

'I was upset about it too,' he said honestly,

but at least he had been more reasonable than Frank, who seemed not to understand the ramifications of what he was saying. You could not ask for early clinical trials, aiming toward early release on a product that was still clearly dangerous and had not been perfected, or you were just plain begging for trouble. And Peter just couldn't see why Frank refused to understand that.

'Is that why you stayed in Paris all week?' Frank asked, obviously still furious at him. It wasn't Peter's fault, but he was the bearer of bad tidings.

'It is. I thought he'd move more quickly if I was there, waiting.'

'Maybe we shouldn't have bothered to have him test it.' Peter couldn't believe what he was hearing.

'I'm sure you'll feel differently when you give it some thought, and read the reports.' Peter handed him a stack of papers from his briefcase.

'Give it to research.' Frank pushed it away impatiently. 'I'm not going to read that garbage. They're just looking to delay us needlessly. I know the kind of work Suchard does for us. He's a nervous old woman.'

'He's a prize-winning scientist,' Peter said firmly, determined to hold his ground, but the meeting with Frank had been a nightmare from beginning to end, and he was anxious to leave, and get home to Greenwich. 'I think we should discuss this further on Monday, when you've had some time to digest it.'

'There's nothing to digest. I'm not even going to discuss it. I'm sure Suchard's report is nothing more than hysteria, and I refuse to pay attention to it. If you want to, that's your business.' And then he narrowed his eyes and wagged a finger at him. 'And I don't want this discussed with anyone. Tell both our research teams here to keep their mouths shut. All we need is this kind of gossip flying around and the FDA will withdraw our application for us.' Peter felt as though he were in a surrealistic movie. It really was time for Frank to step down, if he was going to make these kinds of decisions. They had no choice. They could not go to the FDA with Vicotec before it was ready. And he had no idea why Frank wouldn't listen. But Frank looked increasingly annoyed when he moved on to the next matter of business.

'We received notification from Congress, while you were gone,' he snapped at Peter. 'They want us to appear in front of a sub-committee in the fall, to discuss the high prices of pharmaceutical products in today's market.

More whining crap from the government, about why we're not handing out drugs free on street corners. We do plenty of that in clinics and third world countries. This is an industry for God's sake, not a foundation. And don't think we're going to price Vicotec like a giveaway. I won't have it!' The hair on Peter's neck stood up as his father-in-law said it. The whole purpose of the drug was to make it accessible to the masses, to make it available to people in remote or rural areas, or home situations that made it difficult, or even impossible, to get to medical practitioners for treatment, like his mother and sister. If Wilson-Donovan was going to price it like a luxury drug, they were going to defeat the purpose, and Peter had to fight back a wave of panic.

'I think price is going to be an important issue here,' Peter said calmly.

'So does Congress,' Frank barked at Peter. 'They're not calling on us just for this, it's the broader issues, but we still have to make a stand for high prices, or they're going to cram our words right down our throat when Vicotec hits the market.'

'I think we should keep a low profile,' Peter said, his heart sinking as he said it. He didn't like anything he was hearing. It was all about profit. They were developing a miracle drug, and Frank Donovan was going to take full advantage of it.

'I've already accepted. You're going. I thought you could do it in September, when you go to the FDA hearings. You'll be in Washington anyway.'

'Maybe not,' Peter said sternly, determined to put the battles off till later. He was exhausted. 'Would you like a ride out to Greenwich?' he asked politely, hoping to change the subject. He was still stunned by how stubborn Frank had been. It was way beyond reason.

'I'm having dinner in the city,' Frank said curtly. 'I'll see you this weekend.' Peter was sure that he and Katie had arranged something, and she would tell him when he got home. But all he could think about when he left was the insanity of Frank's position. Maybe he was senile. No sane person would have wanted to appear in front of the FDA, asking for early release on a product that was dangerous, not after what Suchard had said, not if there was any risk at all. And as far as Peter was concerned, it had nothing to do with legalities, or liability, it had to do with moral responsibility. Imagine if Vicotec was cleared for sale, and they killed someone. There was no doubt

232

in Peter's mind that in that case he and Frank would be responsible, and not the drug. It was out of the question.

It took him the entire hour of the trip to recover from the meeting with Frank, and when he got home Katie and all three boys were milling around the kitchen. She was trying to organize a barbecue and Mike had promised to help, but he was on the phone setting up a date for later that night, and Paul said he had something else to do. Peter looked at his wife ruefully, took off his jacket, and put on the apron. It was two o'clock in the morning for him, but he hadn't been home all week, and he felt more than a little guilty.

He tried to kiss Kate hello once he had the apron on, but he was surprised by how cool she was, and wondered if she suspected something about Paris. The telepathy of the female race amazed him. He had never cheated on her in eighteen years, and the one time he had, he suspected she knew it. The boys disappeared almost immediately, to pursue their own plans, and she remained chilly with him all through dinner. It was only once the boys were gone that she actually said something to him, and his heart sank when he heard it.

'My father tells me you were very rough on him tonight,' she said quietly, looking daggers at her husband. 'I don't think that's fair. You've been gone all week, and he was all excited about the launch of Vicotec, and you spoiled it.' It wasn't another woman she was upset about, it was her father. As usual, she was defending him without even knowing what had happened.

'I didn't spoil it, Kate, Suchard did,' he said, feeling drained. He couldn't fight both of them. He had barely slept all week, and he wasn't up to it, besides the fact that he had to defend his business decisions to her upset him deeply. 'The laboratory in France detected a serious problem, a flaw in the makeup of Vicotec which could potentially kill someone. We have to change it.' He said it calmly and matter-of-factly, but she still looked suspicious as he explained it to her.

'Dad says you're refusing to take it to the hearings.' Her voice was a plaintive sound in their kitchen.

'Of course I am. Do you think I want to take a product with a serious flaw to the FDA and ask for an early release, to sell it to an un-suspecting public? Don't be ridiculous. I have no idea why your father reacted the way he did. But I assume that, when he reads the reports, he'll come to his senses.'

'Father says you're being childish, that the

234

reports are hysterical, and there's no need to panic.' She was relentless and a muscle tightened in Peter's jaw. He was not going to discuss it with her any further.

'I don't think this is the right time to talk about it. I'm sure your father was upset, so was I. And just like him, I didn't want the results to be what they were. But denial is not the answer.'

'You make him sound stupid,' she said angrily, and this time Peter snapped at her.

'He acted like it, and you're acting like his mother, Kate. This is not between us. This is a serious business matter in the company, and an important life-threatening decision. It's not yours to make, or even to comment on, and I don't think you should be involved here.' It infuriated him that Frank had obviously called her to complain the moment he left the office. And it reminded him suddenly of everything Olivia had said. She was right. Kate did run his life, and so did her father. And what annoyed him was that he had never allowed himself to see that.

'Dad says you don't even want to appear before Congress about pricing.' She sounded wounded as she said it, and Peter sighed, feeling helpless.

'I didn't say that. I said I thought we should

keep a low profile right now, but I haven't made any decision about Congress. I don't know anything about it.' But she did. Frank had told her everything. And as usual, she knew more than he did.

'Why are you being so difficult?' Kate hounded him as he put their plates in the dishwasher, and tried to help her. But he was so exhausted and so jet-lagged he could hardly see straight.

'You don't belong in this, Kate. Let your father run Wilson-Donovan. He knows what he's doing.' And he shouldn't have been whining to his daughter. Peter was livid.

'That's exactly what I was saying to you,' Kate said victoriously. She didn't even look pleased to see him. All she wanted to do was defend her father to him. She didn't even seem to care how tired Peter was, or how disappointed he was himself by the flaw in Vicotec, and their inability to go to the FDA with it, or commence production. Her only thought was for her father. It had never been as obvious to him as it was now, and seeing the look in her eyes hurt him deeply. 'Let my father make the decisions. If he says you can go to the FDA with it, there's no reason not to. And if it makes him happy for you to appear before Congress on pricing issues, why not do that?' Peter wanted to scream as he listened.

'Appearing before Congress is not the issue here, Kate. And going to the FDA too soon on a product that's potentially dangerous is suicide, for all of us in the company, and for the patients who might choose to use it, unaware of potentially lethal complications. Would you take thalidomide knowing what you do now? Of course not. Would you ask for early release by the FDA? Of course you wouldn't. You can't ignore potentially fatal flaws in these products once you're aware of them, Kate. That's insane, and so is going to the FDA prematurely. You can turn the whole country off the drug by exposing it too soon, or unwisely.'

'I think Father's right. You're a coward,' she said bluntly.

'I can't believe this,' he said, staring at her in disbelief. 'Is that what he said to you?' She nodded in answer. 'I think he's overwrought and I'd like you not to get involved in this. I've been gone for nearly two weeks, and I don't want to get in an argument with you about your father.'

'Then don't torment him. He was very upset by the way you behaved this afternoon.

I think that's rotten of you, Peter, and unkind, and disrespectful.'

'When I need a conduct report from you, Kate, I'll ask for one. But until then, I think your father and I can work this out for ourselves. He's a grown man, and he doesn't need you to defend him.'

'Maybe he does. He's almost twice your age, and if you don't have any respect for him, you'll drive him into an early grave, if you ride over him roughshod.'' She was near tears as she berated her husband, and he sat down and took off his tie. He couldn't believe what he was hearing.

'Oh for God's sake, will you stop? This is ridiculous. He's a grown-up. He can take care of himself, and we don't need to fight over him. You're going to put me in an early grave if you don't give me a break. I've hardly slept this week, worrying about the testing at the laboratory,' and then of course there was Olivia, and three nights spent talking to her and driving to and from La Favière. But none of that was mentioned, and it seemed so unreal now that even he could no longer believe it. Kate had catapulted him back into his own world with the subtlety of a nuclear explosion.

'I don't know why you were so cruel to him,' she said, blowing her nose, and Peter stared at her, wondering if she and her father were both crazy. This was a product they were dealing with. It had some problems to work out. It was not personal. His refusal to go to the FDA with it was not a mutiny against Frank, nor was his candor with him meant as an affront to Katie. Were they all nuts? Had it always been like this? Or was it suddenly worse than ever? As tired as he was, it was difficult to make heads or tails of it, and Katie crying over it was the last straw, as he got up and put his arms around her.

'I wasn't cruel to him, Katie, believe me. Maybe he had a bad day. So did I. Let's go to bed, please . . . I'm so tired I feel like I'm dying.' Or was it losing Olivia that made him feel that way? He couldn't figure any of it out now.

Katie went to bed with him reluctantly, and she was still complaining about his injustices to her father. It was so ridiculous he stopped answering her, and in five minutes he was asleep, dreaming of a young girl on a beach. She was laughing and beckoning to him, and he ran toward her thinking it was Olivia, but when he got to her, it was Katie, and she was angry at him. She was shouting at him, and as he listened, he saw Olivia disappearing into the distance.

And when he awoke the next day, he felt leaden again. It was that overwhelming feeling of despair that felt like rocks had been dropped on him. He couldn't remember what it was, or why he felt that way, and then as he looked around and saw the familiar room, he remembered. He remembered another room, another day, a different woman. It was hard to believe it was only two days before. It might as well have been a lifetime. And as he lay in bed, thinking of her, Katie came in and told him they were playing golf that afternoon, with her father.

Olivia was gone, the dream was done. This was the reality he had come home to. It was the same life he had always led, it was just that suddenly it all felt so different.

## Chapter Nine

Things settled down somewhat eventually. Katie's spirits improved, and she stopped defending her father as though he were a child in the sandbox. They saw a lot of him socially, and after the first few days Peter was home, both she and her father were in better humor. And Peter always liked it when the boys were around, though this year they seemed to spend less and less time with their parents. Mike had a driver's license now, and he drove Paul everywhere, which lightened the load on them and also meant they didn't see them. Even Patrick seemed to spend very little time with them. He had a crush on the girl next door, and spent most of his waking hours at her house.

'What is it about us this year? Do we have leprosy?' Peter complained to Kate one morning over breakfast. 'We never see the kids anymore. They're always out somewhere. I thought they were supposed to spend time with us when they came home from boarding school, instead they're out with their friends all the time.' He felt genuinely bereft without them. He liked spending time with his kids, and it made him feel sad somehow when he didn't. They provided a kind of companionship and ease he no longer shared with Katie.

'You'll see them at the Vineyard this summer,' she said calmly. She was more used to their comings and goings and more inured to their busy lives, than he was. And in truth, she didn't enjoy them quite as much as he did. He had always been a terrific father even when they were little.

'Should I make an appointment with them now? I mean hell, August is only five weeks away. I'd hate to miss them. I'll only be there for a month.' He was only half teasing and she laughed at him.

'They're all grown up,' she said matter-of-factly.

'Does that mean I've been fired?' He looked genuinely startled. At fourteen, sixteen, and eighteen, the boys didn't have much use for their parents.

'More or less. You can play golf with my dad on weekends.' The irony was that she still spent more time with her father than her own sons did with their parents. But he didn't point it out to her, or say that their sons' reactions were far more normal.

And things were still more than a little strained between Peter and Frank. Only that week, Frank had approved an enormous research budget for Vicotec, conducted by double teams, working night and day, but he had still not agreed to cancel their appearance before the FDA, although Peter had grudgingly agreed to appear before Congress on pricing issues, to please Katie's father.

He didn't like doing it, but it wasn't worth fighting over, and it was prestigious for the firm for Peter to be seen there. He just didn't like having to defend the high prices they, and others in the industry, charged for products they didn't have to. But as Frank pointed out, they were in the business for profit. They were caring for mankind's ills, but they still expected to make money. But Peter wanted Vicotec to be different, he was hoping to convince Frank to make their profit on volume rather than astronomical prices. And for the beginning at least, there would be no competition for the product. But for the moment, Frank wasn't willing to discuss it. All he wanted was Peter's promise that he would still try to get to the FDA with it by September. It had become an obsession. He wanted to bring Vicotec into the marketplace as fast as he could, at all costs. He wanted to make history, and several million dollars.

He continued to insist that they had plenty of time, and with any luck at all, they'd 'work the kinks out' before September. Peter had finally stopped arguing with him, and knew that, if need be, they'd withdraw from the hearings later. There was a slim chance they could be ready by then, but according to Suchard, it was doubtful. And Peter thought Frank's goals were unrealistic.

'What about bringing Suchard here? That might speed things up a little,' Peter suggested, but Frank didn't think it was a good idea, and when Peter called Paul-Louis to discuss it with him, he was told that Dr Suchard was on vacation. Peter thought that surprising, and was annoyed at his timing. But no one in Paris knew where he had gone for his holiday, and there was nothing Peter could do to find him.

It was the very end of June before things seemed calm again, and by then it was time for

Frank, Kate, and the boys to leave for the Vineyard. Peter was going to spend the Fourth of July weekend with them, and then come back to town and start commuting. He was going to use the company studio in town during the week, and work longer hours at the office. And then go to Martha's Vineyard on the weekends. Monday through Friday, he wanted to be available to the research teams, to help them in any way they wanted. And he liked staying in the city. It was lonely for him in Greenwich anyway, without Kate or the children. It was a great opportunity to get a lot of work done.

But it wasn't only work he had on his mind at the end of June. He had seen the announcement two weeks before that Andy Thatcher would be running for president, first in the primaries, and if he won them, in the national elections a year from November. And Peter had noticed with interest that when Thatcher held his first press conference, and even subsequent ones, Olivia had been standing beside him. They had promised each other not to call, so he could hardly call now to ask her about it. Her sudden high visibility at Andy Thatcher's side was disconcerting to him, and he wondered what it meant in light of her earlier plan to leave him. But they had agreed not to call each other, and as hard as it was, Peter stuck by it. And he decided that her regular appearances at Andy's side in the political arena clearly meant that she had decided not to leave him. He wondered how she felt about it, and if Andy had somehow manipulated that decision. Knowing what he did of her, and their relationship, it seemed unlikely that she had done it out of affection. If anything she had stuck by him out of a sense of duty. He didn't really want to believe it was because she loved him.

It was strange how they had to go on with their lives, after the brief time they'd spent together in France. And he couldn't help wondering if, for her, like for him, suddenly everything was different. At first he had tried desperately to resist it, to tell himself that nothing had changed. But things that had never bothered him before were suddenly major problems. Suddenly everything Kate said or did seemed to have something to do with her father. His work seemed more difficult. The research on Vicotec had wrought no changes yet. And Frank had never been as unreasonable as he was now. Even his sons didn't need him. But worst of all, Peter felt as though there was no joy in his life anymore, no excitement, no mystery, no romance.

There were none of the things he had shared with Olivia in France. But most painful of all, there was no one to talk to. He had never realized over the years how far he and Katie had drifted apart, how busy she was with other things, and how totally preoccupied she was with her own activities and friends, most of which involved committees or women. There seemed to be no room for him anymore, and the only man who mattered to her at all was her father.

He wondered if he was being sensitive, or unreasonable, if he was still overtired, or overwrought after the disappointment over Vicotec, but he didn't think so. And even when he went to the Vineyard with them for the Fourth of July, everything irked him. He felt out of step with their friends, out of synch with her, and even here he felt as though he hardly saw the boys. It was as though, without even realizing it, everything had changed, and his life with her was over. It was incredible as he watched his life unravel. He wondered too if he were somehow forcing things to a showdown with her, without realizing it, as though to justify what he'd done with Olivia in the south of France. Doing that in a defunct marriage would have been more understandable, more easily forgivable, but doing it in a live one was more difficult to live with.

He found himself searching the newspapers for photographs of Olivia, and on the Fourth of July, he saw Andy on TV. He was at a rally on Cape Cod, and there was coverage of him with his enormous sailboat tied up at the dock just behind him. He suspected that Olivia was there somewhere, nearby, but try as he might, he couldn't see her.

'What are you doing, watching television in the middle of the day?' Katie had found him in their room, and when he glanced at her, it was hard not to notice her still trim figure. She was wearing a bright blue bathing suit and the gold bracelet with the heart dangling from it that he had brought her from Paris. But even with her blond hair and her pert face, she didn't have the powerful effect on him that Olivia had on him each time he saw her. It made him feel guilty all over again, and Kate was startled by his worried expression. 'Is something wrong?' she asked. Things had been difficult between them for a while now. He seemed testier than usual, and more irritable, which wasn't like him. He had been that way ever since his last trip to Europe.

'No, everything's fine. I just wanted to see the news.' He looked away from her, aiming the remote control at the TV with a vague expression.

'Why don't you come outside and swim?' she said, smiling. She was always happy there. It was a pleasant place, and their house there was easy to maintain. And she enjoyed being surrounded by her children and their friends. It had always been a good place for her and Peter too. Although this summer everything seemed slightly different. There was a lot of pressure on him, with the research being conducted on Vicotec, and all she could do was hope that it would go well and they'd get the results Peter and her father wanted. But for the moment, Peter seemed unhappy and distant.

It was two full weeks later before he was able to find out the truth at the laboratory, and Peter sat and stared into space after he hung up. He couldn't believe what he'd heard, and he drove all the way to Martha's Vineyard to discuss it in person with Katie's father.

'You *fired* him? Why? How could you do that?' Frank Donovan had shot the messenger that had brought them the bad news. He still didn't understand that in the long run Paul-Louis had saved them.

'He's a fool. He's a nervous old woman seeing demons in the dark. There was no reason to keep him.' For the first time in eighteen years, Peter was beginning to think that his father-in-law was crazy.

'He's one of the foremost scientists in France, Frank, and he's forty-nine years old. What are you doing? We could have used him here to help us speed up our research.'

'Our research is going fine. I discussed it with them yesterday. They tell me they'll be ready to roll by Labor Day. There will be no kinks left in Vicotec by then, no "flaws," no ghosts, no danger.' But Peter didn't believe him.

'Can you prove that? Are you sure? Paul-Louis said it might take a year.'

'That's my point. He didn't know what he was saying.' But Peter was frightened by what Frank had done, and he used company records to locate Paul-Louis, and he called him his first night back in New York to tell him how sorry he was, and talk to him about Vicotec, and their progress.

'You're going to kill someone,' Paul-Louis said in heavily accented English. But he had been touched by the call, and he had always had a great deal of respect for Peter. At first he'd been told that his dismissal had been Peter's idea, but later he had learned that the order actually came all the way from the chairman. 'You cannot take a chance on it yet,' Paul-Louis reiterated. 'You must go through all the tests, and it will take months, even with double teams working around the clock. You must not let them do this.'

'I won't. I promise you that. I appreciate everything you've done. I'm just sorry about the way it happened.' And he genuinely meant it.

'It's all right,' the Frenchman shrugged, smiling philosophically. He had already had another offer from an important German pharmaceutical company with a large factory in France, but he wanted to take some time off to ponder his decision. And he had gone to Brittany to do that. 'I understand. I wish you good luck with this. It could be a wonderful product.'

The two men chatted for a little while, and Paul-Louis promised to keep in touch, and the following week Peter followed their research results even more closely. If Paul-Louis was right, they still had a lot of work to do before they could 'greenlight' the product in good conscience.

But by the end of July, they seemed to be making good progress. And Peter was encouraged when he left for his vacation in Martha's Vineyard. The research department had promised to fax him daily reports from the office. But as a result, he found it harder to relax than usual. He seemed constantly tied by the umbilical cord of his fax machine to both the research on Vicotec, and his office.

'You're not having any fun this year,' his wife complained, but she didn't pay much attention to him either. She had lots of friends to see, gardening to do, and she was spending a lot of time at her father's place, helping him renovate, and deciding whether or not to remodel his summer kitchen. She helped him entertain his friends, and organized several dinner parties for him, which she and Peter attended. But Peter complained about that too. He said she was never around, and every time he saw her, she was rushing off to meet her father.

'What's happening to you? You were never jealous of Daddy before. I feel like I'm being pulled by both of you,' she said, looking annoyed. Peter had always been so good about the things she did with her father, and now he complained constantly. And her father wasn't any better, he was still angry at Peter for his position about Vicotec.

There was a definite tension between the two men that year, and by mid-August, Peter was ready to go back to town, and use work as an excuse. He had had it. He wasn't sure what it was, maybe it was just him, but he had had several arguments with the kids, he thought Katie was being unusually difficult, and he was sick to death of going to Frank's house for dinner. On top of it the weather had been miserable, and they had had a week of storms, and there was the threat of a hurricane coming up from Bermuda. By the third day, he sent everyone to the movies, and he had secured the shutters, and tied down the terrace furniture. Later he was eating lunch in front of the television, watching a ball game, when he switched to the news during a break just to hear about Hurricane Angus. But he was instantly startled when he saw a picture of an enormous sailboat followed by a still photograph of Senator Andy Thatcher. The coverage had already been on for a while, and the anchor was talking about '. . . the tragedy occurred late last night. And the bodies have not, as yet, been recovered. The senator has been unavailable for comment.'

'Oh my God,' Peter said it aloud to himself, and suddenly he was standing there, as he put his sandwich down on the table behind him. He had to know what had happened to her. Was she dead or alive, was it her body they were searching for? He was near tears as he stared at the tube and began frantically changing channels.

'Hi, Dad. What inning?' Mike asked as he drifted through the room, back from the movie. Peter hadn't heard them come in, and he looked like a ghost as he faced him.

'No inning . . . no score . . . I don't know . . . never mind . . .' He looked back at the TV again, as Mike left, but at first Peter couldn't find it. And then he found it on Channel Two, and this time he heard it almost from the beginning. They had been caught in a storm in treacherous waters just outside Gloucester, in Andy's hundred-and-ten-foot sailboat. And in spite of its size and alleged stability, they had hit some rocks in a storm, and the boat had sunk in barely more than ten minutes. There had been roughly a dozen people aboard. The boat was computerized and Thatcher had been sailing it himself with the help of only a single deckhand, and some friends. For the moment, several passengers were missing, but the senator himself had survived. His wife had been aboard, and her brother the junior congressman from Boston, Edwin Douglas. But tragically, the congressman's wife and both young children had been swept over-board. Her body had been found early that morning, but neither of the children had been found yet. And then, in a single breath, the anchor said that the senator's wife, Olivia Douglas Thatcher, had nearly drowned. She was still in critical condition in Addison Gilbert Hospital, and had been rescued late the night before by the Coast Guard. She had been found unconscious, but had been kept afloat in the storm by her life vest.

'Oh my God . . . oh my God . . .' Olivia. And she was so afraid of the ocean. He could only begin to imagine what had happened to her, as he thought frantically of going to her now. But how would he explain it? What would they say on the news? An anonymous businessman appeared at the hospital today, desperate to see Mrs Thatcher, and was turned away. He was put in a straitjacket and sent home to his wife to regain his senses . . . He had no idea how to get to her, or how to see her without causing problems for either of them. And as he sat down again, and stared at the television, he realized that for the moment, while she was still critically ill, there was probably no way to do it. Another channel said she hadn't regained consciousness yet, and was said to be in a deep coma, and they ran all the tabloid pictures of her and indexed every tragedy, just as they had in Paris. The reporters were camped outside her parents' house in

Boston as well, and they showed a few minutes of coverage of her grief-stricken brother leaving the hospital, having just lost his wife and children. It was painful beyond words just seeing him, and Peter felt tears rolling down his cheeks as he watched him.

'Is something wrong, Dad?' Mike had come back in and he was worried when he saw his father.

'No, I'm . . . I'm fine . . . something just happened to some friends. It's terrible. A storm off Cape Cod last night, Senator Thatcher's boat went down. It sounds as though a number of people were lost, and several others were injured.'. . . And she was still in a coma. Why had this happened to her? What if she died? It was beyond thinking.

'Do you know them?' Katie seemed surprised as she walked through the living room on her way to the kitchen. 'There was something about the accident in the paper this morning.'

'I met them in Paris,' he said, afraid to say more to her, as though she would know from the tone of his voice, or worse yet, see him crying.

'They say she's very strange. I hear he's going to run for president,' Katie said through the kitchen doorway, and Peter didn't answer.

He had gone upstairs as quietly as he could, and was calling the hospital from their bedroom.

But he learned nothing from the nurses at Addison Gilbert. He said he was a close friend of the family, and they told him exactly what he had heard on TV. She was in ICU and hadn't regained consciousness since she was rescued. And how long could that go on? He wondered if she would be brain-damaged, if she would die, if he would ever see her again. Just thinking about it made him want to be with her. But all he could do was lie on his bed now, and remember.

'Are you all right?' Katie came upstairs looking for something, and was surprised to see him lying on their bed. He had been behaving strangely for days, as far as she was concerned, actually all summer. But her father had too. From what she could see, Vicotec had been disastrous for both of them, and she was sorry they had ever decided to develop it. It wasn't worth the price that any of them were paying. Katie looked down at Peter then, and she thought his eyes looked damp. She had no idea what he'd been doing. 'Are you feeling all right?' she asked again, concerned. She put a hand on his head. But he didn't have a fever.

'I'm fine,' he said, feeling guilty toward her again, but so desperately frightened for Olivia that he could barely think straight. Even if he never saw her again, he knew the world would be a different place without her gentle face, her eyes that always reminded him of brown velvet. He wanted to go to her now and open them, and kiss her again. He wanted to be there for her. And when he saw Andy on TV again, he wanted to strangle him for not being with her. He was talking about everything they'd done, how quickly the storm had come up, how tragic it had been that the children couldn't be saved. And somehow, without actually saying it, he managed to convey that in spite of the loss of life, and the danger to his wife, he was a hero.

Peter was still quieter than usual that night. The promised hurricane had passed them by and he called the hospital again. But nothing had changed. For him, and for the Douglases waiting at the hospital, it was a nightmarish weekend. But late Sunday night, after Katie had gone to bed, he called again. It was the fourth time that day, and his knees felt weak when the nurse said the words he had prayed for.

'She's awake,' she said, as he felt his throat fill with tears for her. 'She's going to be okay,' she said gently, and when he hung up, he put his face in his hands and cried. He was all alone, and he could let it out now. He had been able to think of nothing else for the past two days. He hadn't even been able to leave a message for her, but he had sent her all his good thoughts and his prayers. He had even surprised Kate by going to church by himself on Sunday morning.

'I don't know what's happened to him,' she'd said to her father that night on the phone. 'I swear, it's all that nonsense with Vicotec. I hate that stuff. It's making him sick, and driving me crazy.'

'He'll get over it,' her father said. 'We'll all be happier once it's on the market.' But Katie was no longer so sure. Their battles over it were just too painful.

And the next morning, Peter called the hospital again, but they wouldn't let him talk to her. He kept leaving false names, and this time said he was a cousin from Boston. There was no way of even sending a coded message to her, because he had no way of knowing who might intercept it. But she was alive, and doing well. Her husband said in a press conference how fortunate they'd been, and that she'd be home in a few days. And he left for the West Coast later that morning. He was on the campaign trail, and she was out of the woods now.

He came back in time for the funeral of Edwin's wife and their children. Peter was mesmerized by all the TV coverage and he was relieved to see that, mercifully, Olivia wasn't there. Peter knew her well enough to know that she couldn't have borne it. It would have reminded her too much of her own child. But her parents were there, and Edwin, grieving visibly and standing close to them, and of course Andy with an arm around Olivia's brother. They were the consummate political family, and every possible newspaper and television channel was there, covering it from a discreet distance.

Olivia watched it on television from ICU, and she cried terribly. The nurses didn't think she should watch, but she had insisted. They were her family, and she couldn't be there, but later when she saw Andy give an interview about how brave they had all been, and what a hero he was, she wanted to kill him.

And afterwards, he didn't even bother to call her to tell her how Edwin was. When she called home, her father sounded as though he were drunk, and said her mother had had to be sedated. It was a terrible time for all of them, and Olivia was sorry she hadn't been able to give her life instead of them. The children were so young, and her sister-in-law had been pregnant again, although no one knew it. And in Olivia's eyes, she herself had nothing to live for. She was living an empty life, as the puppet of an egotist. It wouldn't have mattered to anyone if either of them had died, except maybe her parents. She thought of Peter then, and the hours they had shared, and wished there were some way she could see him. But like other people she had loved, he was part of the past now, and there was no way to include him in her present or future.

She lay in bed afterwards, once the television was turned off, and cried, thinking of how futile life was. Her nephew and niece had died, their mother, her own baby had . . . Andy's brother Tom. So many good people. It was impossible to understand why some were spared and others weren't.

'How's it going, Mrs Thatcher?' one of the nurses asked her gently as she cried. They could see how unhappy she was. And with her whole family in Boston for the funerals, no one had been in to see her. The nurse was worried about her, and then she remembered. 'Someone's been calling you every few hours since you came in. A man. He says he's an old friend,' and then she smiled, 'and this morning he said he was your cousin. But I'm sure it was the same one. He never leaves his name, but he sounded very worried about you.' And without a moment's hesitation, she knew it had to be Peter. Who else would call and why wouldn't he leave his name? It had to be him, and she raised eyes filled with sorrow to the nurse standing near her.

'Can I talk to him next time?' She looked almost like a battered child. She was covered with terrible bruises where she had been hit by debris that was torn off the sailboat. It had been a terrible tragedy, and she knew that she would never again go near the ocean.

'I'll try to connect you if he calls again,' the nurse reassured her and moved on. But when Peter called again early the next morning, she was sleeping. And after that, a different nurse was on duty.

Olivia lay in bed thinking of him constantly after that, wondering how he was, and what had happened to Vicotec and the FDA hearings. She had no way of getting news of him, and they had agreed not to contact each other when they left Paris. But now it seemed so difficult. Especially here, in the hospital. She had so much to think about, there was so much about her life now that she hated. She had promised Andy to stick by him, but it was costing her everything she had to fulfill her promise. And suddenly all she could think of was how brief and unpredictable life was, and how precious. She had sold her soul for the next five years, which seemed like an eternity now. She could only hope he didn't win the election. She knew she'd never survive it. And the wife of a president couldn't simply disappear. For the next five years, she would have to stand and face the music.

She spent another four days in ICU, until her lungs were almost clear, and they could move her to another room, and then Andy flew up from Virginia to see her. He had had some work to do there, but as soon as he arrived at the hospital, there were suddenly reporters everywhere, and a camera crew, and one of them even snuck in to see her. She disappeared under the sheets immediately, and a nurse escorted them off the floor, but Andy attracted press like blood attracted sharks, and Olivia was the little fish they wanted to feed on.

But Andy had a great idea. He had arranged a press conference for her at the hospital the next day, right outside her room. He had a hairdresser coming for her, and a makeup man. It was all set up, and she could talk to the press from a wheelchair. But as he explained it to her, she could feel her heart pound, and her stomach turn over.

'I don't want to do that yet.' It reminded her of when Alex had died, and when the press had hounded her constantly. Now they would want to know if she had seen her niece and nephew die, or her sister-in-law, and how she felt now that they were gone and she had survived, and how could she explain it. She felt strangled just thinking about it, and all she could do was shake her head in panic. 'I can't, Andy . . . I'm sorry . . .' she said, turning away from him, wondering if Peter had ever called again. She hadn't seen the same nurse since she left ICU, and no one had ever told her. And she couldn't ask for him, a man with no name who had been calling for days. She couldn't do anything at all that might draw attention to her.

'Look, Olivia, you have to talk to the press, or they'll think we're hiding something. You were in a coma for four days. You don't want the country to think you're brain damaged, or something.' He spoke to her as though she were, and all she could think of was her tearful conversation with her brother that morning. He was a mess, and she could only imagine how he felt, after all she'd gone through with Alex. But he had lost his entire family, and now Andy wanted her to talk to the press from a wheelchair.

'I don't care what they think, I'm not doing it,' she said firmly.

'You have to,' he snapped at her, 'we have a contract.'

'You make me sick,' she said, turning away from him, and the next day, when they came, she refused to see them. She wouldn't see the hairdresser, or the makeup man, and she never came out of her room in the wheelchair. The press thought they were playing games with them, and Andy held a press conference in the lobby without her. He explained about the trauma she'd been through, and the guilt of being one of the few survivors. He said he was suffering from it too, but it was hard to believe Andy Thatcher was suffering from anything, except an overwhelming desire for the White House, no matter what it cost him. But he wasn't about to lose this opportunity, and the next day, he let three reporters into her room himself. And when she looked up and saw them, Olivia looked pathetically frail, and desperately frightened. She started to cry, and a nurse and two orderlies forced them to leave her. But they'd managed to get half a dozen photographs of her before they left the room, and congregated together back in the hallway where they chatted with Andy. And when he returned, after the reporters left the hospital, she came out of her bed and flailed at him with a vengeance.

'How could you do that to me? Edwin's whole family just died, and I'm not even out of the hospital.' She was sobbing as she pounded her hands against his chest, over-whelmed by a sense of violation. But he had needed to prove to them that she was alive and well, and that she hadn't snapped, as they were beginning to suspect, since she seemed to them to be hiding. What she was trying to preserve was her dignity, but Andy couldn't have cared less. What he was protecting was his political survival.

Peter saw the photographs of her on the news that night, and his heart went out to her. She looked frightened and frail as she lay in bed, and cried. The abandoned look in her eyes tore his heart out. She had a hospital nightgown on, and she had intravenous tubes in both arms, and one of the reporters said she was still suffering from pneumonia. It was a dramatic glimpse of her, and sure to arouse a lot of sympathy, which was exactly what her husband had wanted. And Peter could think only of her after he turned the set off.

But Olivia surprised Andy when the hospital told her they were willing to release her at the end of the week, she said she wasn't going home with him. She had already spoken to her mother about it. She was going home to her parents. They needed her. And she was going to the Douglas house in Boston.

'That's ridiculous, Olivia,' Andy complained when she told him over the phone what she was doing, 'you're not a little girl, you belong in Virginia with me.'

'Why?' she asked him bluntly, 'so you can let reporters into my room every morning? My family has been through a terrible ordeal, and I want to be with them.' She didn't blame him for the accident. The storm hadn't been his fault, but the way it had all been handled since certainly lacked dignity or compassion, or even decency, and she knew she would never forgive him. He had exploited all of them. And he did it again, when she found a fleet of reporters waiting for her in the hospital lobby when she left Addison Gilbert. Andy was the only one who knew when she was getting out, he was the only one who could have told them. And they appeared at her parents' house too, and this time her father put his foot down.

'We need some privacy here,' he explained, and as the governor, people listened. He gave a few select interviews, but he explained that neither his wife, nor his daughter, and certainly not his son, were in any condition to entertain members of the press at the moment. 'I'm sure you understand,' he said graciously, posing for a single picture. And he said he had no further explanation for Mrs Thatcher's presence in his home, except that she wanted to be with her mother, and brother, who was also staying with them. Edwin Douglas couldn't bring himself to stay at his own house yet, let alone begin to sort through it.

'Have the Thatchers been estranged since the accident?' one of the reporters shouted at him and he looked surprised by the question. It hadn't even occurred to him, and he asked his wife the same thing that night, wondering if she knew something he didn't.

'I don't think so.' Janet Douglas frowned at him. 'Olivia hasn't said anything,' but they both knew she kept a lot to herself. She had been through a great deal in the past few years, and she liked to keep her own counsel.

But Andy was quick to complain to her when he heard about the question. He told her that if she didn't come home soon, she would start rumors.

'I'll come home when I'm well enough to leave here,' she said coldly.

'When will that be?' He was going back to California in two weeks, and he wanted her with him.

She was actually planning to go back to Virginia in a few days, but his pushing her only made her want to stay away longer, and after she'd been there a week, her mother finally questioned her about it.

'What's happening?' she asked gently, as Olivia sat in her mother's bedroom. Her mother got migraines regularly, and she was just recovering from one, while wearing an ice pack. 'Is everything all right with you and Andy?'

'That depends on your definition of "all right,"' Olivia said coolly. 'Nothing's any worse than usual. He's just annoyed that I'm not letting the press beat me to death, or re-enacting the accident for them on tabloid TV. But give him a day or two, Mom, I'm sure he'll arrange it.'

'Politics does strange things to men,' her mother said wisely. She knew better than anyone what it was like, and how much it had cost them. Even her recent mastectomy had been announced on TV, with diagrams and an interview with her doctor. But she was the governor's wife, and she knew she had to expect it. She had been in the public eye for most of her adult life, and it had taken a lot from her. And she could see now that it had already taken something from her daughter.

One paid dearly for winning, or even losing, elections.

And then Olivia looked at her quietly, and wondered what her mother would say if she told her the truth. She had been thinking for days. And she knew what she had to do now. 'I'm leaving him, Mom. I can't do this. I tried to leave him in June, but he wanted the presidency so badly, I agreed to do the campaign with him, and stay for the first four years if he won.' She looked at her mother unhappily. The crassness of what she'd done sounded awful in the telling. 'He's paying me a million dollars a year to do it. And the funny thing is I didn't even care. It sounded like play money when he offered it to me. I did it for him because I used to love him. But I guess I didn't love him enough, even way back in the beginning. I really know now I can't do it.' She didn't owe this to anyone, not even Andy.

'Then don't,' Janet Douglas said bluntly. 'Even a million dollars a year wouldn't be enough. Ten wouldn't either. No amount is worth ruining your life for. Get out while you can, Olivia. I should have done it years ago. It's too late now. It drove me to drink, it ruined my health, it destroyed our marriage, it kept me from doing everything I wanted to do, it hurt our family and made life hard for all of you. Olivia, if this isn't what you want, if you yourself don't want this desperately, get out now, while you still can. Please, honey,' her eyes filled with tears as she squeezed her daughter's hand, 'I beg you. And no matter what your father says, I'm one hundred percent behind you.' And then she looked at her even more seriously. It was one thing to abandon politics, another to abandon a marriage that might still be worth saving. 'What about him? What about Andy?'

'It's been over for a long time, Mom.'

Janet nodded again. It didn't really surprise her. 'I thought so. But I wasn't sure.' And then she smiled slowly. 'Your father is going to think I lied to him the other day. He asked me if everything was all right with you, and I said it was. But I wasn't sure then.'

'Thanks, Mom,' Olivia said, putting her arms around her. 'I love you.' Her mother had just given her the greatest gift of all, her blessing.

'I love you too, sweetheart,' she said as she held her daughter. 'Do whatever you have to do, and don't worry about what your father says. He'll be fine. He and Andy will make some noise for a while, but they'll get over it. And Andy's young. He can always get re-married and do it next time. They haven't seen the last of him in Washington. Don't let him bully you into coming back, Olivia, unless you want to.' What she really wanted for her daughter was to be far from here. She wanted her freedom.

'I don't want to go back, Mom. I never will. I should have left him years ago . . . before Alex was born, or at least after he died.'

'You're young, you'll make a life for yourself,' she said wistfully. She never had. She had given up her own life, her career, her friends, her dreams. Every ounce of energy she'd had had gone into her husband's political career, and she wanted something very different for her daughter. 'What are you going to do now?'

'I want to write.' She smiled shyly and her mother laughed.

'It all comes full circle, doesn't it? Do it then, and don't let anyone stop you.'

They sat and talked all afternoon, and they made lunch together in the kitchen. Olivia even thought of telling her about Peter, but in the end she didn't. She did say that she thought she'd probably go back to France, to the fishing village she loved so much. It was a good place to write, a good place to hide, but her mother warned her about that too.

'You cannot hide forever.'

272

'Why not?' She smiled sadly. There was nothing else for her to do now, except disappear, legitimately this time. But she wanted nothing more to do with the press or the public.

Her brother joined them for dinner that night. He was grief stricken and subdued, but at least she made him laugh once or twice, and he kept up with what was happening in Washington by phone and fax every day. It was incredible to Olivia that he could even think about that now, but even in the face of such a major loss, he was still very much like their father. It was obvious that he was consumed by politics in very much the same way as her father and her husband. And late that night she called Andy and told him that she had made an important decision.

'I'm not coming back,' she said simply.

'Not that again.' He sounded annoyed this time. 'Have you forgotten our contract?'

'There's nothing in it that says I have to stay with you, or follow you to the presidency. It only says that if I do, you'll pay me a million dollars a year. Well, I've just saved you a bunch of money.'

'You can't do that,' he said, sounding angrier than she'd ever heard him. She was interfering with the one thing he wanted.

'Yes, I can. And I am. I'm leaving for Europe tomorrow morning.'

She wasn't actually leaving for a few days, but she wanted to be sure he knew it was all over. He showed up in Boston the next day anyway, and as her mother had predicted, her father entered the fray with them. But she was thirty-four years old, she knew her own mind, and she was a grown woman. And she knew that nothing would sway her.

'Do you realize what you're giving up?' her father shouted at her from across the room, as Andy looked gratefully at him. To Olivia, it looked almost like a lynch mob.

'Yes,' she said quietly, looking straight at them, 'heartbreak and lies. I've experienced both of them for quite a while now, and I think I'll manage fine without them. Oh, and I forgot, exploitation.'

'Don't be so grand,' her father said in disgust, he was a politician of the old school, and not quite as lofty as Andy. 'It's a great life, a great opportunity, and you know it.'

'For you maybe,' she said, looking at her father with undisguised sorrow. 'For the rest of us it's a life of loneliness and disappointment, of broken promises along the campaign trail. I want a real life with a real man, or alone if it has to be that way. I don't even care anymore.

I just want to get as far from politics as I can, and never hear the word again.' She cast a sidelong look at her mother, and saw that she was smiling.

'You're a fool,' her father raged at her, but when Andy left their house that night, he was truly venomous, and promised her she'd pay for what she'd just done to him. And he wasn't lying. On the day she left for France, three days later, there was a story in the Boston papers that she knew only he would have planted. It said that after her recent, tragic accident, in which three members of her family had died, she had suffered severe traumatic stress, and she had just been admitted to a hospital with a nervous breakdown. It said that her husband was deeply worried about her, and although the article didn't actually come out and say it, there was the hint of an estrangement, because of her mental state. And the article was entirely slanted to sympathize with Andy for being saddled with a nutcase. He was covering his tracks nicely. If he said she was crazy, then it would be okay to dump her. Round one for Andy . . . or was it round two . . . or ten? Had he knocked her out, or had she simply run away and saved her own life while he wasn't looking? She was no longer sure now.

Peter saw the story too, and suspected that

it had been planted by Andy. It didn't sound like Olivia, even after the short time he knew her. But he couldn't check this time, since it didn't say what hospital she was in. There was no way to find out the truth and it drove him crazy with worry.

Her mother took her to the airport on a Thursday afternoon a few days after she'd told Andy she was leaving. It was late August by then, and Peter and his family were still at the Vineyard. Janet Douglas put her daughter on the plane, and stood there until the plane took off. She wanted to be sure that she was safe, and truly gone. Olivia had escaped a fate worse than death as far as her mother was concerned, and she was relieved as she saw the plane swoop slowly overhead, on its way to Paris.

'Godspeed, Olivia,' she said softly, hoping she wouldn't come back to the States for a long time. There was too much pain waiting for her here, too many memories, too many rotten, selfish men waiting to hurt her. Her mother was happy knowing she had gone back to France. And as the plane flew out of sight, Janet signalled to her bodyguards, and walked slowly out of the airport with a sigh. Olivia was safe now.

## Chapter Ten

As the month of August wore on, and faxes continued to roll in about the research on Vicotec, the tension between Peter and his father-in-law seemed to heighten. By Labor Day weekend, it was almost palpable, and even the boys had begun to feel it.

'What's happening between Granddaddy and Dad?' Paul asked on Saturday afternoon, and Kate frowned at him as she answered.

'Your father is being difficult,' she said quietly, but even her son could see that she blamed Peter for the tension between them.

'Did they have a fight or something?' He was old enough to understand, and his mother was usually pretty candid with him, although 'fights' didn't usually proliferate in their family. But once in a while he knew that his father and his grandfather disagreed about something.

'They're working on a new product,' she said simply, but it was a great deal more complicated than that, and she knew it. She had asked Peter repeatedly to go easy on him. Her father had been worked up about it all summer, and at his age, it wasn't good for him. Although even Kate had to admit that her father looked better than ever. At seventy, he still played tennis for an hour every day, and he swam a mile every morning.

'Oh.' Paul was satisfied with her explanation. 'I guess it's no big deal then.' He brushed off the multimillion-dollar trouble with Vicotec with an easy sixteen-year-old assessment.

They were all going to a big party that night to celebrate the end of the summer. All their friends were going to be there, and in two days they were all leaving. Patrick and Paul were going back to school, and Mike was off to Princeton. And on Monday they were all moving back to Greenwich.

Kate had a lot to do, closing her own house, as well as her father's, at the Vineyard. And she was putting some of her clothes away when Peter wandered in and watched her. The summer had never gotten off the ground for him. The double blow of nearly losing Vicotec and having to give Olivia up only moments after they'd met had been an agony for him straight through August. The worries about Vicotec had put a damper on things to be sure, and Frank's constant pressuring hadn't helped, but neither had Katie's constant clandestine involvement in what should never have been her business. She was too involved with what happened between them, too concerned about protecting her father. And there was no denying that what had happened to Peter in France had changed things. He hadn't wanted it to. He had been so determined to come back and pick up where he had left off, but that just didn't happen. It was like opening a window and seeing a view, and then boarding up the house again. He kept standing in the same place, staring at a blank wall, and remembering what had been there, even if only briefly. The scenery he had seen with Olivia had been unforgettable, and although he had never intended it to, he knew now that it had changed his life forever. He wasn't going to alter anything, and he wasn't going anywhere. He had never contacted her, except to call the hospital after her accident and get reports on her from the nurse in ICU. But he couldn't forget her either. And her accident had terrified him, just knowing she had almost died seemed like terrifying retribution. But why her and not him? Why should Olivia be punished?

'I'm sorry it's been such a lousy summer,' Peter said sadly, sitting down on the bed, as Katie put a stack of sweaters away in a box with mothballs.

'It wasn't that bad,' she said kindly, glancing at him over her shoulder from the top of a short ladder.

'It was for me,' he said honestly. He had been miserable all summer. 'I've had a lot on my mind,' he said in an oversimplified explanation, and Kate smiled at him again, and then her eyes grew serious as she watched him. She was thinking of her father.

'So has my dad. This hasn't been easy on him either.' She was only thinking about Vicotec. Peter was thinking about the extraordinary woman he had met in Paris. Olivia had made coming home to Katie nearly impossible. Kate was so independent and so cool, so willing to function without him. They didn't seem to do anything together anymore, except see their friends at night occasionally, and play tennis with her father. He wanted more than that. He was forty-four years old, and suddenly he wanted romance. He wanted contact with her, he wanted comfort, and friendship, and even some excitement. He wanted to snuggle next to her, and feel her flesh next to his. He wanted her to want him. But he had known Katie for twenty-four years, and there was very little romance left between them. There was intelligence, and respect, and a variety of shared interests, but he didn't stir when he saw her lie next to him, and when he did, she usually had phone calls to make, or a meeting somewhere, or an appointment with her father. They seemed to miss every opportunity to make love, to be alone, just to laugh sometimes, or sit around and talk, and he missed it. Olivia had shown him just exactly what he was missing. And in truth, what he had with her, he had never had with Katie. There was a kind of heady excitement to everything he did with Olivia that took his breath away. Life with Katie had always been more like going to the senior prom. With Olivia, it was more like going to the ball with a fairy princess. It was a silly comparison, and it made him laugh when he thought about it, and then he saw that Katie was staring at him.

'What are you smiling at? I was just saying how hard this has all been on my father.' He hadn't heard a word she was saying. He'd been dreaming of Olivia Thatcher.

'That's the price you pay for running a

business like ours,' Peter said matter-of-factly. 'It's a huge burden, and a tremendous responsibility, and no one said it was going to be easy.' He was tired of hearing about her father. 'But I wasn't thinking about that just then. Why don't you and I go somewhere? We need to get away.' Martha's Vineyard hadn't been the restful vacation it had been in previous years. 'Why don't we go to Italy or someplace else? Maybe the Caribbean, or Hawaii?' It would be different and exciting just being there with her, and he thought maybe a trip like that would put a little life back into their marriage.

'Now? Why? It's September, I have a thousand things to do, and so do you. I have to get the boys into school, and we have to take Mike to Princeton next weekend.' She looked at him like he was crazy, but he was persistent. After all these years, he had to at least try to keep them together.

'After we get the kids settled in school then. I didn't mean today, but maybe sometime in the next few weeks. What do you think?' He looked at her hopefully as she came down the ladder and he wanted to feel more for her than he did. But the agony was that he didn't. Maybe a trip to the Caribbean would change that.

'You have to go to the FDA hearings in September. Don't you have to prepare for that?'

He didn't tell her that no matter what her father said, he had no intention of going, and he wouldn't let her father go either. They couldn't perjure themselves on the remote chance that all the problems would be solved sometime before Vicotec hit the market. 'Let me worry about that,' was all he said to her, 'just tell me when you can get away, and I'll plan it.' The only thing on his schedule were the Congressional hearings on pricing he had finally agreed to appear at. But he knew that, if he had to, he could postpone his appearance. It was more a matter of courtesy and prestige than a life-and-death situation. To him, their marriage was far more important.

'I've got a lot of board meetings this month,' Katie said vaguely, and opened another drawer full of sweaters. And as Peter watched her work, he suddenly wondered what she was really saying.

'Would you rather not go away?' If that was the case, he wanted to know it. Maybe there was something bothering her too, and then he had a sudden thought that hit him like a bolt of lightning. Had she had an affair too? Was she in love with someone else? Was she avoiding him? It could have happened to her too after all, though it had never even occurred to him, and he felt suddenly foolish at the realization that she was just as vulnerable as he was. She was still attractive, and fairly young, and there were a lot of men she would appeal to. But Peter had no idea how to ask her if that had happened. She was always fairly cool, and somewhat prim and asking her if she'd ever had an affair was out of the question. Instead, he narrowed his eyes at her as she threw some more mothballs in another box of sweaters. 'Is there some reason why you don't want to take a trip with me?' he asked as bluntly as he could, and she finally looked up at him, and gave him an answer which annoyed him greatly.

'I just don't think it would be fair to my father right now. He's upset about Vicotec. He has a lot on his mind. I think it would be really selfish of us to go lie on a beach somewhere while he sits in the office and worries.' With difficulty, Peter tried to hide his aggravation. He was sick of worrying about Frank. He had been doing just that for eighteen years now.

'Maybe right now we need to be selfish,' Peter pressed her. 'Doesn't it worry you sometimes that we've been married for eighteen years, and we don't pay much attention to us, or what we need, or our marriage?' He was trying to say something to her, but not set any alarms off while he did it.

'What are you saying to me? That you're bored with me, and you need to see me on a beach somewhere to put a little spice into it again?' She turned around and looked at him and for a moment he wasn't sure how to answer. She was much closer to the truth than he would have dared to tell her.

'I just think it would be nice to get away from your father, and the kids, and our answering machine, and your board meetings, and even Vicotec. Even here, we're hounded constantly by the fax machine, or at least I am, it's like being in the office, with sand. I'd just like to go away with you somewhere, where there are no distractions and we can talk, and remind ourselves of what it was we were crazy about when we first met, or when we got married.'

She smiled at him then. She was beginning to understand. 'I think you're having a midlife crisis. And what I really think is that you're nervous about the FDA hearings, and you want to run away, and you're using me to do it. Well, forget that, young man. You'll be fine. It'll all be over in a day, and we'll all be proud of you.' She was smiling as she said it, and he felt his heart sink. She didn't understand anything, least of all the fact that he needed something from her that he wasn't getting, nor that he had no intention of going to the FDA hearings. The only thing he was going to do was appear before Congress about pricing.

'This has nothing to do with the FDA,' he said firmly, trying to sound calm, and refusing to discuss the hearings with her again. He got enough of that from her father. 'I'm talking about us, Kate. Not the FDA hearings.' But one of the boys interrupted them then. Mike wanted the keys to the car, and Patrick was downstairs with two friends, and needed to know if there were any more frozen pizzas hidden somewhere, they were starving.

'I was just going to the store!' She called down to them, and the opportunity was lost. She turned and looked at her husband over her shoulder as she left their bedroom. 'Don't worry, everything will be fine.' And then she was gone, and he sat on their bed for a long time, feeling empty. At least he had tried. But he had gotten nowhere, which was small consolation. She had no idea what he was talking about, and the only thing she could focus on was her father, and the hearings.

Frank mentioned them to him again at the party. It was like listening to a broken record, and Peter did his best to change the subject. Frank had been telling him to be a 'good guy' and 'go along with things' for a while. He was sure that their research teams would find all the bugs long before Vicotec hit the market, and they would lose face, and important ground, if they backed out now on asking for early release from the FDA. In Frank's mind, it would be a red flag signalling to the industry that their product had serious problems.

'It could take us years to live that down. You know what it's like once that kind of talk gets started. It could taint Vicotec forever.'

'We have to take that chance, Frank,' Peter said, with a drink in his hand. It was a litany he knew by heart now, and the two men remained glued to their polarized positions from each other.

As soon as Peter could, he walked away from him, and a little while later he saw Frank talking to Katie. He could guess what about, and it depressed him watching them. It was obvious to him she was not discussing their proposed vacation. And he knew without a doubt that that little plan would never come to fruition. He didn't say anything more about it to her that night. And for the next two days, they were busy closing up the house. It had never been winterized, and they wouldn't be back until next summer.

On the drive back to town, the boys talked about going back to school. Paul was looking forward to seeing his friends at Andover, Patrick wanted to visit Choate and Groton that fall. And all Mike could talk about was Princeton. His grandfather had gone there, and all his life he had heard about eating clubs and reunions.

'Too bad you didn't go there, Dad. It sounds so great.' But a degree earned at night from the University of Chicago was hardly Princeton.

'I'm sure it is great, son, but if I had gone there, I would never have met your mother,' he said, remembering their first meeting at the University of Michigan.

'That's a point,' Mike said with a smile. He was planning on joining his grandfather's eating club as soon as they would let him. He had to wait a year, but he was going to talk to some fraternities in the meantime. He had everything planned, and everything worked out already. And he talked about it all the way back to New York, which left Peter feeling left out, and somehow lonely. It was strange, he'd been one of them for eighteen years, and yet sometimes he still felt like an outsider, even with his own kids now.

And as they drove south, and the others weren't speaking to him, his thoughts drifted to Olivia. He remembered their talks in Montmartre the first night, and walking on the beach with her in La Favière. There had been so much to say, so much to think about. He almost hit another car as he let himself daydream about her, and everyone in the car shouted as he veered to avoid a collision.

'God, what are you doing, Dad!' Mike couldn't believe what had just happened.

'Sorry!' he said, and drove on more carefully, but she had given him something no one else had. He remembered too her saying that what he had accomplished had been thanks to him, and not the Donovans, but that was hard to believe, especially for Peter. It was so obvious to him that Katie and her father had made it all happen.

But as his thoughts drifted back to Olivia again, he wondered where she was now, if the story about her being in a hospital were true. Everything about it had seemed phony. It sounded like one of those cover-ups for a separation, or an affair, or a face-lift, and he knew that in her case, at least two of those were unlikely. He wondered suddenly if, in spite of Andy's bid for the presidency, she had left him. And it was just like Andy to say she had gone crazy.

And two days later, he realized he'd been right, when he got a postcard from her in the office. It was sitting on his desk when he got back from lunch. There was a drawing of a little fishing boat on it, and the postmark said La Favière.

It was written in her small, careful hand, and was somewhat cryptic. 'I'm back here again. Writing. At last. I'm out of the running for good. I couldn't do it. Hope all is well with you. Don't forget how brave you are. It's all you. You've done it all. It takes more courage to do it, than to run away, as I have. But I'm happy. Take good care. Love always.' And she had signed it simply 'O.' But along with her words, he felt what was between the lines. He could still remember the hoarseness in her voice when she said she loved him. And he knew she still did, just as he loved her. He would always love her. She would live in his heart, and his memories, forever.

He read the postcard again, thinking about it. She was so much stronger than she knew. It was leaving that had taken the real courage, not staying, as he had. He admired her. And he was glad for her that she had escaped the life she led. He hoped she was happy there, and peaceful. And he was sure that whatever she was writing would be brilliant. She was so brave about what she felt, so willing to be who she was, to say what she was thinking. She sliced through the mists like a knife, as she had with him. There was no hiding with her, no falsifying anything. She was a woman who lived by the truth, no matter what it cost her. She had made her compromises too, and she admitted that. But she wasn't now. Olivia was free now, and he envied her, as he put the postcard away, hoping no one else had seen it.

The test results came in on Vicotec the next day, and they were better than he'd hoped, but in terms of an early release of the drug, they were disastrous, and Peter knew it. He was becoming a pro at interpreting them now, and even he knew what these meant, and so did Katie's father. The two men had scheduled a meeting to discuss them at length on Friday, and they met in the conference room next to Frank's office at two o'clock. Frank was waiting for him with a stern expression, already anticipating what Peter would tell him. And they wasted no time on chitchat, except to talk about Mike. Peter and Katie were taking him to Princeton the next morning, and Frank was visibly proud of him. But the moment that subject had been touched on, he turned back to serious business.

'We both know why we're here, don't we?' he said, looking deep into Peter's eyes. 'And I know you don't agree with me,' he said carefully. His whole body seemed to be coiled with anticipated tension, he looked like a cobra about to spring. And Peter felt like his prey, as he prepared to defend himself, and the integrity of the company, but Frank had anticipated him, and he was prepared to pull rank if he had to. 'I think you're just going to have to trust my judgment here. I've been through this before. I've been in this business for nearly fifty years, and you've got to believe me when I tell you I know what I'm doing. It's not wrong to go to them now. By the time we put this product on the market officially, we'll be ready. I wouldn't take a chance on this if I didn't think we can deliver.'

'And if you're wrong? If we kill somebody? Even one person . . . one man, woman, or child . . . what then? What do we say? How do we live with ourselves? How can we take that chance by asking for an early release date?' Peter was like the voice of his conscience, but Frank thought it was the voice of doom, and he accused him of being an old woman like 'that idiot in Paris.' 'Suchard knows these things, Frank. That's why we hired him, to tell us the truth. Even when it's bad news we have to listen. I know he's no longer an issue here, but we opened a Pandora's box we can't just ignore. And you know it.'

'I'd hardly call ten million dollars' worth of additional research in two months "ignoring it," Peter. And we've turned up nothing. Face it, he sent us on a witch-hunt . . . worse than that, it's a wild-goose chase. There's nothing there. We're talking about an element which "could" react, or "might" cause an extraordinarily rare series of circumstances on a million-to-one bet, on the off chance that everything lines up wrong and we wind up with a problem. Now for God's sake, you tell me, does that sound reasonable to you? Hell, you can take two aspirins with a drink and have that go sour on you. So what's the deal here?'

'Two aspirins and a drink won't kill you. Vicotec will if we're not careful.'

'But we *are* careful. That's the whole point. Every drug has its risks, its side effects, its downside. If we weren't willing to live with that, we'd have to close our doors and start selling cotton candy at the state fair. For chrissake, Peter, stop busting my chops on this, be sensible. I want you to understand I'm going to override you on this. I'll go to the FDA myself if I have to, but I want you to know why. I want you to know that I truly believe Vicotec is safe, I'm willing to stake my life on it!' he said, and by the time he finished what he had to say, he was shouting at Peter. He was red in the face, and agitated, and his voice had gotten louder and louder as they sat in the conference room, and as Peter watched him, he suddenly saw that Frank was shaking. Frank was in a complete state over it, he was perspiring, and gray, and he stopped for a moment and had a sip of water.

'Are you all right?' Peter asked quietly, watching him. 'This *isn't* worth staking your life on. That's really the whole point. We have to treat this clinically, and address it calmly. It's a product, Frank, that's all it is. I want it more than anyone, but in the end, it'll either work, or it won't, or it may work, but maybe it'll just take longer than we wanted to get it ready. Nobody wants to get it on the market more than I do. But not "at all costs," not as long as there's a single factor we're not sure of. There's a loose wire in here somewhere. We know that. We've seen signs of it. Until we find it, we can't let anyone use it. It's as simple as that.' He spoke concisely and clearly, and the more agitated Frank got, the calmer he was.

'No, Peter, no . . . it's *not* that simple!' Frank bellowed at him, provoked to even greater fury by his son-in-law's maddening coolness. 'Forty-seven million dollars in four years is not "simple" by any means. Just how much money do you think we're going to pour into this for chrissake? How much money do you think there is?' He was getting nasty, and Peter refused to rise to the bait as he addressed him.

'Enough to do it right, I hope, or kill the product. We always have that option.'

'The hell we do!' Frank was on his feet shouting at him. 'Do you think I'm just going to throw nearly fifty million dollars out the window? Are you crazy! Whose money do you think it is? Yours? Well, think again, it's mine, and the company's, and Katie's, and I'll be goddamned if you're going to tell me anything. You wouldn't even be here today if I hadn't bought you, lock, stock, and barrel for my daughter.' His words hit Peter like a club and took his breath away, and suddenly all he could think of were his father's words eighteen years before when he had told him that he and Katie were getting married. '*You'll never be anything more than a hired hand, son . . . don't do it.*' But he had, and look what had happened. This was what they thought of him eighteen years later.

Peter was on his feet too by then, and if Frank Donovan had been even a few years younger, and a little less crazed, Peter would have hit him. 'I'm not going to listen to this,' Peter said, feeling his whole body shake as he restrained himself from hitting him, but Frank wouldn't give it up. He grabbed Peter by the arm and went on shouting.

'You'll listen to anything I goddamn tell you, and you'll do whatever I want here. And don't give me that holier-than-thou look, you sonofabitch. She could have had anyone, and she wanted you, so I made you what you are today, so she wouldn't have to be embarrassed. But you're nothing, you hear me, you're *nothing*! You start this whole goddamn project here, you cost us millions, you make promises, you see rainbows, and then when there's a little problem that some French prick thinks he sees in a dark room, you stab us in the back and want to squeal like a little pig all the way to the FDA. Well, let me tell you something, I'll see you dead before I'll let you do it!' But as he said the words, he clutched his chest, and began to cough frantically. His face was so red it was almost purple, and it was obvious he couldn't breathe. He clutched both Peter's arms then, and Peter was supporting the older man's full weight as he began to fall, and Peter almost went with him. For an instant, he couldn't believe what had happened, and then he knew. He set him down quickly on the floor, and dialed 911 as fast as he could, and gave them the details. Frank was vomiting by then, and still coughing, and as soon as Peter set down the phone, he knelt next to him, turned him on his side and tried to support his weight, and keep his face out of his own vomit. He was still breathing, though with extreme difficulty, and he was barely conscious, but Peter was still reeling from everything the old man had said to him. He had never known he was capable of so much venom, so much that it may have killed him. And all Peter could think of as he crouched holding him was what Katie would say if he died. She would blame Peter for it, she would say it was his fault for being so difficult and challenging him on Vicotec. But she would never know what Peter had just heard, what her father had said to him, the unforgivable things he had just hurled at Peter. And he knew, just as the paramedics came, that no matter what happened afterwards, it would be impossible to forget, or forgive him. These were not just affronts conjured up in a fit of rage, these were deep, ugly weapons that he had been hiding for years, concealing from him, and keeping to use on him one day. They were hurtful daggers that had run him through, and Peter knew he would never forget them.

The paramedics were working on Frank by then, and Peter stood up and backed away. His own clothes were covered with vomit, and Frank's secretary was standing in the doorway in hysterics. Several people were in the hall, and one of the paramedics looked up at Peter and shook his head. His father-in-law had just stopped breathing. The other two paramedics took the defibrillator out, and ripped his shirt open, just as half a dozen firemen came through the doorway. It looked like a convention, and they all knelt, working on him for half an hour, while Peter watched them, wondering what he was going to tell Katie. He was just beginning to think there was no hope at all when the paramedics told the firemen to get the gurney. His heart was beating again, irregularly, but it was no longer in fibrillation, and he was breathing. Frank looked up at Peter blearily, with an oxygen mask on, but he didn't say anything, and Peter touched his hand as he went by him. They were carrying him to the ambulance, and Peter had had the secretary call his doctor. They were waiting for him at New York Hospital with a team of cardiologists. He had come within a hair of dying.

'I'll meet him there,' Peter told the paramedics and hurried to the men's room to see what he could do with his pants and jacket. He kept a clean shirt in a drawer, but the rest of him was a mess. Even his shoes were covered with what Frank had vomited on him. But even more than that, Peter still felt covered by the ooze of what he'd said to him just before that. The viciousness that he had hurled at him was so vile it had almost killed him.

And five minutes later, Peter emerged from the men's room in a clean shirt, pants that had been cleaned as best he could, a sweater, and clean shoes. He went to his office to call Katie. Luckily, she was still at home, she had been just about to go out and do some errands. And as she answered the phone, Peter almost choked on his own words. He didn't know how to tell her.

'Katie . . . I . . . I'm glad you're home.' She wanted to ask him why, he had been so strange with her lately, clingy in an odd way, and depressed. He had watched television a lot a few weeks before, and then not at all. He had been obsessed with CNN for a few days, and he had been so strange about wanting to take a vacation with her.

'Is something wrong?' She glanced at her watch. She still had a number of things to do for Mike before he left for Princeton in the morning. He needed a rug for his room, and she needed to get him a new bedspread. But she was suddenly caught short by the tone of her husband's voice when he answered.

'Yes . . . there is . . . Katie, he's all right now, but it's your father.' She almost stopped breathing when he said it. 'He had a heart attack in the office.' He didn't tell her how close he'd come, or that his heart had actually stopped beating for a few seconds. The doctors could tell her that later. 'They just took him to New York Hospital and I'm on my way there now. I think you should come in as soon as you can. He's feeling pretty rocky.'

'Is he all right?' She sounded as though the bottom had just fallen out of her world, and it had, and for an ugly moment Peter couldn't help wondering if she would have sounded like that if it had been him instead of her father. Or was Frank right? Was he just a toy they had bought and paid for?

'I think he'll be all right. It looked a little grim there for a minute, but the guys from 911 were great. We had paramedics here and the fire department,' and there was still a policeman outside calming everyone down, and taking a report from Frank's secretary, though even she didn't know exactly what had happened. They were waiting to talk to Peter, but it all seemed pretty straightforward. But as Peter listened to his wife, he realized that she was crying. 'Take it easy, sweetheart. He's fine. I just think you should come in to see him.' But he suddenly wondered if she'd be in any shape to drive. He didn't want her having an accident on the way in from Greenwich. 'Is Mike around?' She sobbed into the phone that he wasn't. He could have driven his mother in if he'd been there. Paul only had a learner's permit, and wasn't a good enough driver to come all the way in from Greenwich. 'Could you get one of the neighbors to drive you?'

'I can drive myself,' she said, still crying. 'What happened? He was fine yesterday. He's always been in such good health.' He had, but there were mitigating factors.

'He's a seventy-year-old man, Kate, and he's under a lot of pressure.'

She stopped crying then, and her tone was hard when she asked the question. 'Were you two having an argument about the hearings again?' She knew they'd been planning to meet about it.

'We were discussing it.' But they were doing more than that. Frank had been hurling abuse at him, but he didn't want to say anything about it to Katie. What her father had said had been too hurtful to repeat, particularly in light of what had happened after. If he died now, Peter didn't want Kate to know that had come between them.

'You must have been doing more than "discussing" if he had a heart attack,' she said, accusing him, but he didn't want to waste time with her on the phone and he said so.

'I think you should come in. We can talk about all this later. He's going to cardiac ICU,' he said bluntly, and she started crying again. Peter hated the thought of her driving. 'I'm going over now, and see what's happening. I'll call you in the car if anything changes. Make sure you leave your phone on.'

'Obviously,' she said with a cutting edge to her voice as she blew her nose. 'Just make sure you don't say anything to upset him.'

But Frank was beyond listening to anyone when Peter got to New York Hospital twenty minutes later. He had to talk to the police first, sign some forms the paramedics had left, and he got caught in endless traffic on his way to the East River. And when he got there, Frank had already been heavily sedated. He was being closely watched, and his face had gone from florid to gray now. His hair was disheveled, there was still dried vomit on his chin, and his bare chest was covered with wires and sensors. He was attached to what looked like half a dozen machines, and he looked both extremely sick and far older than he had an hour before. And the doctor told Peter honestly that Frank was by no means out of the woods yet. He had had a major heart attack, and there was still a risk that his heart would go back into fibrillation. The next twenty-four hours were crucial. And looking at him, it was easy to believe all of it. What was impossible to believe was that two hours before, he had actually looked youthful and healthy when Peter walked into his office.

Peter waited for Kate in the lobby downstairs, and he tried to warn her before she came up. She was wearing jeans and a T-shirt, and her hair was a mess, and she had a wild-eyed look of panic as she rode up in the elevator with her husband.

'How is he?' she asked for the fifth time since she'd arrived. She was completely distraught, and unusually distracted.

'You'll see. Calm down. I think he looks a lot worse than he is.' The machines attached to him were frightening, and he looked like a body they were working on, more than just a patient. But Katie was in no way prepared for what she saw when she went to the CICU and caught a glimpse of her father. She started sobbing the moment she saw him, and had to force herself not to cry when she stood next to him and clutched his hand. But he opened his eyes and recognized her, and then drifted off to a drug-induced sleep again. They wanted him to rest completely for the next few days, in the hope that he'd live through it.

'Oh my God,' she said, nearly collapsing into Peter's arms as she left the room. He had to get her into a chair as quickly as he could, and a nurse brought her a drink of water. 'I just can't believe it.' She couldn't stop crying for the next half hour, and Peter sat with her. And when the doctor finally came back to talk to them, he said that Frank had about a 50-50 chance of surviving.

His words sent Kate into hysterics again, and she spent the rest of the afternoon crying in a chair outside the CICU, and going in to visit him every half hour for five minutes, when they let her. But most of the times she went in, he was unconscious. And by the end of the day, Peter tried to get her to leave to get something to eat, but she absolutely refused. She said she would sleep in the waiting room for as long as she needed to, but she wasn't leaving, not for an instant.

'Kate, you have to,' Peter said gently. 'It won't help anything if you get sick too. He'll be all right for an hour or so. You can go to the apartment and lie down, and they'll call you if they need to.'

'Don't waste your breath,' she said stubbornly with the look of a child who would not be moved. 'I'm staying with him. I'm sleeping here tonight, and for as long as I have to till he's out of danger.' In truth, it was nothing more or less than Peter had expected.

'I should go home and check on the boys at some point,' he said thoughtfully, and she nodded. Her children were the last thing on her mind as she sat in the bleak hallway. 'I'll go out and settle them down, and then I'll come back later tonight,' he said, making a plan while he talked, and she nodded. 'Will you be all right while I'm gone?' he asked her gently, but she scarcely looked at him. She already looked bereft as she stared out the window. She couldn't even imagine a world without her father. For the first twenty years of her life, he had been all she had in the world. And for the next twenty, he had been one of the most important people in her life. Peter thought Frank was a kind of love object to her, a passion of sorts, almost an obsession, and although he would never have said it, she seemed to love him more than her own children. 'He'll be all right,' he said softly, but she only cried and shook her head as he left, and he knew there was nothing more he could do for her. All she wanted was her daddy.

Peter drove home as quickly as he could in the Friday night melee, and fortunately all three boys were home when he got in, and he told them as gently as he could about Frank's heart attack, and all three of them were deeply worried. He reassured them as best he could, and when Mike asked, he said only that they'd been having a business meeting when it happened. Mike wanted to go into town to see his grandfather, but Peter thought it was better to wait. When Frank was feeling up to it, his oldest grandson could come in to see him from Princeton.

'What about tomorrow, Dad?' Mike asked. They were supposed to take him to Princeton the next day, and as far as Peter knew, almost everything was ready except for the rug and bedspread Kate hadn't been able to get that afternoon, but Mike could make do without them.

'I'll take you in the morning. I think your mom is going to want to stay with Granddad.'

Peter took them out to a quick dinner, and by nine o'clock he headed back to town, and called Kate from the car. She said there was no change, although she thought he looked worse than he had a few hours before, but the nurse taking care of him had said that was to be expected.

Peter got back to the hospital at ten, and stayed with her till after midnight, and then he went back to Greenwich to be with the boys. And he took Mike to school with all his trunks and bags and sporting gear at eight o'clock the next morning. He had been assigned a room with two other guys and by noon Peter had done everything that was expected. He gave Mike a hug, wished him well, and headed back to New York to see Kate and her father. He got there just before two, and he was astonished at what he found there. Frank was sitting up in bed, looking weak and tired. He was still pale, but his hair was combed, he had clean pajamas on, and Kate was spooning soup into him like a baby. It was a huge improvement.

'Well, well,' he said as he walked in. 'I'd say it looks like you turned a corner,' he said, and Frank smiled. But Peter was still cautious with him. He couldn't forget the things he'd said, or the tone with which he'd said them. But in spite of that, he didn't begrudge him his survival. 'Where'd you get the fancy pajamas?'

He certainly didn't look like the same man who'd lain on his office floor, covered in his own vomit only the day before, and Kate smiled brightly. She didn't have those memories to contend with, nor the ones of his vicious attack on Peter about having been bought and paid for.

'I had Bergdorf messenger them over,' she said, looking pleased. 'The nurse said they might move Daddy to a private room tomorrow if he keeps improving.' Kate herself looked exhausted, but she didn't falter for a moment. She would have given him all her strength, all her lifeblood, if it would have helped him.

'Well, that's good news,' Peter said, and then told them both about Mike's arrival at Princeton. Frank looked extremely pleased, and a little while later, Kate gently helped him lie down again for a nap, and she and Peter walked out into the hallway. But she didn't look nearly as animated as she had when she was spooning soup into her father. And Peter knew instantly that something had happened.

'Daddy told me about yesterday,' she said with a pointed look as they wandered down the hallway.

'What does that mean?' He was tired himself, and had no interest in playing games with her. He found it hard to believe his father-in-law had confessed how vicious he had been, or repeated what he'd said to and about Peter. Peter had never known him to apologize, or admit a mistake, even when it was blatant.

'You know what it means,' she said, stopping to look at him, wondering if she even knew him. 'He said you threatened him about the hearings, almost to the point of violence.'

'He said *what*?' Peter almost couldn't believe it.

'He said he'd never heard you speak to anyone like that, and you refused to listen to reason. He said it was just too much for him, and . . . and then . . .' She started to cry and couldn't go on speaking for a moment as she looked up at him, her eyes filled with accusations. 'You almost killed my father. You would have, if he weren't basically so strong . . . and so decent . . .' She looked away from him then, unable to face him any longer, but Peter heard what she said very clearly. 'I don't think I can ever forgive you.'

'That makes two of us then,' he said, looking at her with unbridled fury. 'I suggest you ask him what he said to me before he went down. I believe it was something about having bought me years ago, lock, stock, and barrel, and seeing me dead if I didn't go to his goddamn hearings.' He looked down at his wife with clear blue eyes, and she saw something in them she'd never seen before, and then he strode away as fast as he could, and got in the elevator while she watched him. She made no move to follow him, but it didn't matter to him now. There was no question in his mind anymore about her allegiance.

## Chapter Eleven

Frank recovered surprisingly well from his heart attack, and within two weeks he was sent home, and Katie went to stay at his house with him. Peter thought it was just as well, they both needed some time to think, and decide how they felt about each other. She had never apologized to him for what she'd said to him in the hospital, and he'd never brought it up again. But he hadn't forgotten it either. And of course, Frank made no mention again of Peter having been 'bought and paid for.' Peter almost wondered if he even remembered.

He was cordial with his father-in-law when he visited him, which he did regularly, both out of courtesy and to see Kate, but relations between Peter and Frank were visibly cool.

And Katie was keeping her distance from Peter. And she was too busy with her father to even pay much attention to Patrick. Peter was taking care of him, cooking dinner for him every night, and he really was no trouble. The two older boys were away at school, and they had already heard from Mike several times. He was crazy about Princeton.

It was exactly two weeks after his heart attack that Frank brought up the hearings again. Both men knew that in spite of everything, they were still on the FDA agenda. And the hearings were only days away. If they were not asking for early approval from the FDA, their appearance in front of them had to be canceled.

'Well?' Frank asked, leaning back against the pillows Kate had just fluffed for him. He was impeccably shaven and clean, and his barber had just come to give him a haircut. He looked like a magazine ad for pajamas and expensive sheets, not a man returning from death's door, but Peter was nonetheless anxious not to upset him. 'Where do we stand these days? How does the research look?' They both knew what he was asking.

'I don't think we should discuss this.' Katie was downstairs making lunch for him, and Peter had no intention of starting an argument with him, and then having to deal with both Donovans. As far as he was concerned, until the doctors told him otherwise, Vicotec was a taboo subject.

'We have to discuss it,' Frank said staunchly. 'The hearings are only a few days away. I haven't forgotten that,' he said calmly. Nor had Peter forgotten what he had said to him in his office. But Frank made no mention of that as he looked at his son-in-law. He was a man with a mission. It was easy to see now where Kate got her stubbornness and perseverance. 'I spoke to the office yesterday, and according to the research department, we've come up clean on everything.'

'With one exception,' Peter added.

'A minor test, done on laboratory rats in exceptional conditions. I know all about it. But apparently, it's irrelevant, because the conditions represented in those tests could never be reproduced in humans.'

'That's true,' Peter conceded to him, praying that Katie wouldn't come in and catch them in this discussion, 'but technically, in terms of the FDA, that disqualifies us. I still say we don't go to the hearings.' And what's more, they hadn't been able to complete their redo of the French tests yet, and those were crucial. 'We need to check Suchard's material again too. That's where the real flaw lies. The rest of this has all been fairly routine. But we need to go over the same ground he covered.'

'We can do that before Vicotec is ever used clinically, and the FDA doesn't need to know anything about it right now. Technically, we've passed all their requirements with flying colors. They don't want anything more than we have. That should satisfy you,' he said pointedly to Peter.

'It would. If Suchard hadn't come up with a problem, and we'd be lying if we concealed that fact from the FDA.'

'I give you my word,' Frank said, ignoring him, 'if anything . . . anything at all . . . the merest hint of a problem appears on the subsequent tests, I'll pull it. I'm not crazy. I don't want a hundred-million-dollar lawsuit. I'm not trying to kill anyone. But I don't want us killed either. We've got what we need. Let's go with it. If I give you my word to pursue it to the nth degree even if we get approval for early human trials, after all our laboratory tests, will you appear at the hearings? Peter, what harm can it do? . . . Please . . .' But it was wrong, and Peter knew it. It was premature, and it was dangerous. With approval for early clinical trials, they could administer it to humans immediately, and he didn't trust his father-in-law not to do that. It didn't matter to Peter that the clinical trials would involve extremely low doses of Vicotec used on a very small number of people. The whole point, to him, was not taking undue and irresponsible risks with even one single person. They had been warned of potential hazards in using Vicotec, as it was now, and Peter was unwilling to fly in the face of that warning. Other companies had experienced horror stories when they did, and there were even legendary stories of products that had been fully packaged and sitting on trucks, waiting for FDA approval, so they could be delivered moments after they got it. Peter was afraid that his father-in-law had something like that in mind eventually for Vicotec, despite its potential problems. If Frank wasn't prepared to be reasonable, the possibilities for abuse were endless. And the abuse could result in needless loss of life. Peter couldn't endorse it.

'I can't go to the FDA,' Peter said sadly. 'You know that.'

'You're doing this as revenge . . . for what I said . . . for God's sake, you know I didn't mean it.' He did remember then. Had he said it only to be cruel, or because he believed it? Peter would never know now, and he also knew he would never forget it. But he was not vengeful.

'It has nothing to do with that. It's a question of ethics.'

'That's bullshit. What do you want then? A bribe? A guarantee? You have my word that I won't go forward if there's still a problem when we complete all the tests. What more do you need?'

'Time. It's only a matter of time,' Peter said, looking tired. The Donovans had worn him out in the past two weeks, and actually, if he thought about it, long before that.

'It's a matter of money. And pride. And reputation. Can you calculate the loss to us if we back out of those hearings now? It could even hurt our other products.' It was an endless round-robin and neither of them agreed with the other's position. They were both looking grim when Katie came in with Frank's lunch, and suspected they were having forbidden discussions.

'You're not talking business, are you?' she asked both of them, and they both shook their heads, but Peter looked guilty, and she cornered him a little while later. 'I would think you'd want to make it up to him,' she said cryptically, as they stood in her father's kitchen.

'Make what up to him?'

'What you did.' She still thought Peter had nearly killed him, and had caused his heart attack by upsetting him, and nothing anyone could have said would have changed her mind about it. 'In a way, you owe it to him to go to those hearings. There would be no real harm done. It's a question of saving face as far as he's concerned. He stuck his neck out for early trials, and now he doesn't want to admit he's not ready. He's not going to use Vicotec on people if it's dangerous. You know that about him. He's not stupid, or crazy. But he's sick, and he's old, and he has a right not to lose face in front of the entire country. You could give him that if you wanted to, if you gave a damn,' she said accusingly. 'Somehow, it doesn't seem too much to ask. Unless you really don't care about him. He told me he said some pretty rotten stuff to you the other day, because he was upset. But I'm sure he didn't mean it. The question is,' she said pointedly, 'are you big enough to forgive him? Or are you going to make him pay for it by taking away the one thing he wants from you? You're going to Congress at the same time anyway, you could still appear at the FDA. You owe him that much after what you did. And he can't go himself now. You're the only one who can do it.' She made him feel like a real sonofabitch for not doing it, and she was determined to make him feel responsible for her father's heart attack. And she seemed hooked, as her father did, on the idea of his getting revenge on Frank for the things he'd said. It all seemed so petty and twisted.

'It has nothing to do with that, Kate. It's a lot more complicated. It has to do with integrity, and ethics. He has to look beyond just saving face. What would people think, the government for instance, if they ever found out that we went to the hearings prematurely? They'd never trust us again. It could destroy the business.' Worse yet, it would destroy him. It violated all his beliefs, and he knew he couldn't do it.

'He told you he'll pull it, if he has to. All you're giving him is a grace period, and an appearance before the FDA.' She made it sound like so little, and she was far more convincing than her father. She made it sound as though he had to do it, as though it were such a small thing to ask, that she couldn't understand why he wouldn't. And she somehow managed to interject herself into it, as though he owed it to her to prove he still loved her. 'All he's asking you to do is compromise. That's all. Are you so small you can't do that? Just give him that . . . this once. That's all. The man almost died. He deserves it.' She sounded like Joan of Arc as she waved the flag at him, and Peter never knew why, but when he looked at her, he could feel himself slipping. He felt as though his whole life was on the line. She had put it there. And the stakes were too high now for him to resist her. 'Peter?' She looked up at him, seductive suddenly, the temptress she had never been, endowed with superhuman abilities and wisdom, and he didn't even have the strength to answer her, let alone resist her. Without even meaning to, he nodded. And she understood. It was done then. She had won. He would go to the hearings.

# Chapter Twelve

The night before he went to Washington was a nightmare for Peter. He still couldn't believe what he had agreed to do for them. But Kate had been obviously grateful to him ever since he'd agreed, and her father had actually improved by leaps and bounds, and he was overflowing with warmth and praise for Peter. And Peter felt as though he had been catapulted onto another planet where nothing was real, his heart had turned to stone, and his brain was weightless. He could barely fathom what he was doing.

Intellectually, he could still rationalize it to himself, just the way Frank had. Vicotec was almost there, and if there were further wrinkles in it, they would pull it before it ever hit the market. But morally and legally, what they were doing was wrong, and they all knew that. And yet, Peter knew he had no choice now. He had promised Kate and her father he would do it. The only question for him was how he would live with himself after that, or was it simply a matter of chipping away at his ethics gradually? Once he did this, would other slippage occur, other violations of principles he had previously adhered to? It was an interesting philosophical issue, and if he hadn't felt as though his life were at stake, he would have been deeply interested in it. As it was, he couldn't eat, he couldn't sleep. He had lost seven pounds in a matter of days, and he looked dreadful. His secretary asked him if he were ill the day before he was to leave for Washington, and he merely shook his head, and just said he was busy. With Frank gone, and planning to stay at home for another month, there was even more than usual on his shoulders. And he was appearing before Congress on the pricing issues, on the same day as the FDA hearings, in the morning.

He had stayed at his desk late that afternoon, looking at the latest research. It looked good actually, except for one little blip that coordinated perfectly with some of the things Suchard had said in June, but Peter was entirely sure what the latest blip meant. According to the researchers, it dealt with a relatively minor issue, and Peter didn't even bother to call Frank about it. He knew what his take on it would be anyway. 'Don't worry about it. Go to the hearings, and we'll work it all out later.' But Peter took the reports home with him anyway, and read them all again that night, and he was still troubled by them at two o'clock in the morning. Katie was asleep in the bed next to him. She wasn't staying at her father's anymore, and she was actually coming to Washington with him and had bought a new suit for it. She and her father were so pleased that he'd capitulated that they'd both been in high spirits ever since he'd agreed to go to Washington for them. It still felt like a mission from hell to him, and Katie had chided him for overreacting. She tried to pretend he was just nervous about appearing before Congress.

But as he sat in his study in Greenwich at four A.M., he was still thinking about the latest reports, and staring out the window. He wished there were someone knowledgeable he could talk to. He didn't know the men on the German and Swiss research teams personally, and he didn't have a good rapport with the new man in Paris. Frank had obviously hired him because he was malleable and a yes-man, but he was also difficult to understand, and so scientific in his approach to everything that it was like listening to Japanese to Peter. And then he thought of something, and flipped through the Rolodex on his desk. He wondered if he had the number at home and then he found it. It was ten o'clock in the morning in Paris, and with any luck at all he'd be there. He asked for him by name as soon as the switchboard answered. The phone beeped twice, with the sound of a friendly robot, and then the familiar voice was on the phone.

'*Allô?*' It was Paul-Louis. Peter had called him at the new company he worked for.

'Hi, Paul-Louis,' Peter said, sounding tired. It was four A.M. for him, and it had been an endless night. He wondered if Paul-Louis would be able to help him make a decision he could be comfortable with at least. It was the only reason he'd called him. 'This is Benedict Arnold.'

'*Qui? Allô?* Who is this?' he asked, confused, and Peter smiled as he answered.

'He was a traitor who was shot a long time ago. *Salut*, Paul-Louis,' he said then in French, 'it's Peter Haskell.'

'Ah . . . *d'accord*.' He understood instantly. 'You're going to do it then? They forced you?'

He knew the moment he heard him. Peter sounded ghastly.

'I wish I could say they forced me,' he said gallantly, although they had, but he was too gentlemanly to say that. 'I volunteered, more or less, for a variety of reasons. Frank had a near-fatal heart attack nearly three weeks ago. Things haven't been quite the same since then.'

'I see,' he said solemnly. 'What can I do for you?' He was working for a rival company, but he had a real fondness for Peter. 'Is there something you want from me?' he asked bluntly.

'Absolution, I think, although I don't deserve it. I just got some new reports in, and I think they're fairly clean, if I understand them correctly. We substituted two of the materials and everyone seems to think that solved the problem. But there's one odd series of results that I'm not sure I understand, and I thought maybe you could shed some light on it for me. There's no one I can talk to candidly here. What I want to know is if we're going to kill anyone with Vicotec. It boils down to that basically. I want to know if you still think it's dangerous, or if we're well on our way now. Do you have time for me to go over this?' He didn't, but he was willing to make time for Peter. He told his secretary

325

to hold all his calls, and was back on the line in an instant.

'Fax it to me now.' Peter did, and there was a long silence, while Paul-Louis read the memo. For the next hour they went backward and forward over the research, while Peter answered as many questions as he could, and then finally there was yet another long silence, and Peter sensed that Paul-Louis had made his mind up. 'It's very subjective, you understand. At this stage, there is not necessarily a clear-cut interpretation. It is a good thing, of course. It is a wonderful product which will change our ability to cope with cancer. But there are additional elements that must be evaluated. It is that evaluation which is so difficult to give you. Nothing is sure in life. Nothing is without risk, or cost. The question is if you are willing to pay it.' He sounded very French in his philosophy, but Peter understood him.

'The question for us is how great the risk is.'

'I understand that.' He understood it perfectly. It was what had worried him in June while Peter had been in Paris. 'And the new research is good, unquestionably. They're on the right track now . . .' His voice trailed off as he frowned and lit a cigarette. All the scientists Peter had met in Europe were smokers.

'But are we there yet?' Peter asked hesitantly, almost afraid to hear the answer.

'No . . . not yet . . .' Suchard said sadly. 'Perhaps soon, if they continue to work in this direction. But you are not there yet. In my opinion Vicotec is still potentially dangerous, particularly in unskilled hands,' which were precisely the hands it was meant for. It was being made for laymen to use, at home if necessary. It meant staying at home for chemotherapy, and not going to hospitals, or even doctors.

'Is it still a killer, Paul-Louis?' That was what he had called it in June. Peter could still hear him.

'I think so.' The voice on the other end sounded apologetic but clear. 'You're not there yet, Peter. Give it time. You will be.'

'And the hearings?'

'When are they?'

Peter looked at his watch. It was five o'clock in the morning. 'In nine hours. At two o'clock this afternoon. I'm leaving the house in two hours.' He was taking an eight o'clock plane, and planned to appear before Congress at eleven.

'I don't envy you, my friend. There is very little I can say. If you want to be honest, you must tell them that this will be a wonderful drug, but it is not ready yet. You are still in process.'

'You don't go before the FDA to say that. We're asking for permission for early clinical trials, based on our laboratory testing. Frank wants it on the market as soon as we can push it through all the phases of human trials, and get FDA approval.'

Suchard whistled at the other end. 'That's frightening. Why is he pushing so hard?'

'He wants to retire in January. And he wants to know it's well on its way before that. This would have been his farewell gift to mankind. And mine. Instead it feels like a time bomb.'

'It is, Peter. You must know that.'

'I do. But no one else wants to hear it. He says he'll pull the product before the end of the year if we're not ready to use it on humans. But he's still insisting we go to Washington. To tell you the truth, it's a long story.' It had to do with the ego of an old man, and calculated risk in a billion-dollar business. But in this case, Frank's calculations were not good ones, and they were based on his ego. It was a dangerous move that could destroy his whole business, but he still refused to see that. And the odd thing was that Peter saw it so clearly. Frank was being stubborn to the point of insanity. Maybe he was getting senile, or just crazed with his own power. It was impossible to know that.

He thanked Paul-Louis for his help, and the Frenchman wished him luck, and when he hung up, Peter went to make a pot of coffee. He still had the option to back out, but he just couldn't see how to do that. He could also go to the hearings, and then resign from Wilson-Donovan, but that wouldn't protect the people he had tried to help and was being forced to put at risk now. The trouble was he didn't trust Frank to cancel its human trials, if their lab reports didn't improve radically in the immediate future. Something told Peter he was too willing to gamble. There was too much money to be made here, no matter what the risk to human life. The temptation was too great now.

Katie heard him stirring a little while later, and she came out to the kitchen before the alarm went off. She found Peter at the kitchen table with his head in his hands, drinking his second cup of coffee. She had never seen him like that before, he looked almost worse than her father right after his heart attack.

'What are you so worried about?' she said, putting a hand on his shoulder.' But it was too hard to explain it to her, it was obvious she didn't understand it, or want to. 'It'll be over before you know it.' She made it sound like a root canal, instead of the violation of everything he believed in. His ethics, his integrity, his principles were all in jeopardy and she couldn't see that. He looked up at her unhappily as she sat across the table, looking as trim and as cool as ever in her pink nightgown.

'I'm doing this for all the wrong reasons, Kate. Not because it's right, or because we're ready for it. But I'm doing it for you, and your father. I feel like a Mafia hit man.'

'That's a disgusting thing to say,' she said, looking annoyed at him. 'How can you make a comparison like that? You are doing it because you know it is right, and you owe it to my father.'

He sat back in the kitchen chair, and looked at her, wondering what the future held for them, at the rate they were going. Not much, from what he could see lately. And now he knew how Olivia had felt when she said she had sold out to Andy. It was a life built on lies and pretense. And in this case, blackmail.

'What is it that you both seem to think I owe you?' he asked calmly. 'Your father seems to think I owe him a lot. As far as I've known for all these years, it's all been a fair exchange, I work hard for the company and get paid for it. And you and I had a real marriage, or I thought so. But lately this concept of "owing" seems to keep getting into things. Why exactly do either of you think I "owe" it to you to go to these hearings?'

'Because,' she trod very carefully on delicate ground, knowing it was potentially a minefield, 'the company has been good to you for twenty years and this is your way of paying it back, standing up for a product that can make billions for us.'

'Is that what this is all about then? Money?' He looked slightly ill as he asked her. Was that what he had sold out for? Billions. At least he hadn't sold himself cheaply, he thought, wincing.

'Partly. You can't be that much of an innocent, Peter. You share in our profits. You know what we're all here for. And consider the children. What would happen to them? You'd ruin their lives too.' She looked very cold and very calculating, and very hard. And for all her talk about her father, she still cared about the money.

'It's funny. I had this crazy idea that it was for the good of mankind, or at the very least to save lives. I think that's why I did it, why I've pushed it for the last four years. But I wasn't willing to lie for it, even then. And I'm even less inclined to now, "for money."'

'Are you backing out now?' she asked, looking horrified. She would have gone to the hearings herself, if she could. But she wasn't employed by the company, and her father was still too ill to go, so it was up to Peter. 'You know, I'd give it some very serious thought before I backed out of this,' she said, standing up and looking down at him. 'I think it would be fair to say that if you chicken out on us now, your bright future at Wilson-Donovan is about over.'

'And our marriage?' he asked, playing with fire now, and he knew it.

'That remains to be seen,' she said quietly. 'But I would view it as the ultimate betrayal.' And he could see she meant that, but suddenly, just looking at her, he felt better. She was so crisp and so clear, so much what she had always been, although he hadn't always seen it.

'It's good to know where you stand on this, Kate,' Peter said calmly, their eyes meeting over the kitchen table as they stood on either side of it. And before she could answer, Patrick came in for breakfast.

'What are you two doing up so early?' he asked, looking sleepy.

'Your mother and I are going to Washington today,' Peter said firmly.

'Oh, I forgot. Is Granddad going too?'

Patrick yawned and poured himself a glass of milk as he chatted.

'No, the doctor said it was too soon,' Peter explained, and Frank called a few minutes later. He wanted to catch Peter before he left, and remind him what he wanted him to say to Congress about pricing. They had already discussed it a dozen times in the past few days, but Frank wanted to be sure Peter would stand by the party line in front of Congress.

'We're not giving anything away, and certainly not Vicotec, when it comes around. Don't forget that,' he reminded Peter sternly. Even his ideas about pricing Vicotec went against everything Peter believed in. Kate was watching him when he came back to the table.

'Everything all right?' She smiled at him as he nodded. And then they both went to dress, and they drove to the airport half an hour later.

Peter seemed strangely calm on the way there, and he said very little to Kate. He had terrified her for a little while, but she realized he must have been nervous. She had been afraid he would back out, but now she was just as sure he wouldn't. Peter always finished what he started.

It was a short flight from La Guardia to National Airport, and Peter spent most of it going through his papers. He had several files on pricing issues in front of him, and all the new reports on the Vicotec research. He particularly went over the parts Suchard had pointed out to him earlier that morning when Peter called him. The Vicotec material worried him a lot more than his appearance before Congress.

Kate called her father from the plane and assured him that all was going along on schedule. And in Washington, they were met by a limousine, which took them to Congress. And as soon as they got there, Peter felt much calmer. He knew what he was going to say to them more or less, and he wasn't really worried.

Two congressional aides were waiting for him in the staff room, and he was led to a conference room, where he was offered a cup of coffee. Kate was still with him then, but a page came for her shortly after that, and escorted her to a seat in the gallery, where she could watch him. She wished him luck, and touched his hand as she left, but she didn't stop to kiss him. And a few minutes later, he was led into the room himself, and for an instant he looked startled. No matter how well prepared he was, it was still an extraordinary experience to face the men and women who ran the country, and offer them his opinions. It was only the second time he had ever been there, and the first time, Frank had done all the talking. This time was entirely different.

Peter was led to a witness table, and sworn in. The members of the subcommittee sat across from him, with microphones, and after he gave his name, and the name of his company, the questions began without further ado, as the members of Congress listened with interest.

He was asked specifically about certain drugs, and his views about their extraordinarily elevated prices. He tried to give easily comprehensible reasons for it, but in fact, even to his own ears, the explanations sounded hollow and somewhat futile. The truth was that the companies producing these drugs were making a fortune overcharging the public, and the members of Congress knew it. Wilson-Donovan was guilty of some of it, though their practices and their profits were not quite as blatant as some of the others.

They brought up some insurance issues after that, and at the very end, a congresswoman from Idaho said that she understood he was appearing in front of the FDA later that day, to request early human testing for a new product. And just to keep them informed on new developments in the field, she asked him to tell them something about it.

Peter explained it as simply as he could, without going into technicalities, or jeopardizing any secrets, and he told the members of Congress that it was going to change the nature of chemotherapy, and make it accessible to the layman, without need for professional assistance. Mothers could administer it to children, husbands to wives, or with care, one could administer it to oneself. It was going to revolutionize the care of all patients with cancer. It was going to make the common man able to treat himself or his family, in rural or urban areas, anywhere that it was needed.

'And will the "common man," as you say, be able to afford it? I think that's the key here,' another congresswoman asked, as Peter nodded.

'We certainly hope so. It is among our goals for Vicotec, to keep the price down as much as possible, and make it accessible to everyone who needs it.' He looked quiet and strong as he said the words, and several heads nodded approval as they listened. He had been a very knowledgeable, straightforward, and impressive witness. And a short time later they thanked him as he was excused, the entire panel of the subcommittee shook his hand, and they wished him luck at the FDA hearing that afternoon, with his clearly remarkable product. Peter was pleased as he left the room, and walked back to the conference room behind an aide. And a moment later, Katie joined him.

'Why did you say that?' she asked him unhappily under her breath as he gathered up his papers. She had yet to congratulate him or tell him how well he'd done. Even strangers had done that much. But his wife was looking at him with scarcely concealed disapproval. It was like looking at Frank as Peter watched her. 'You made it sound like we're going to give Vicotec away. You know that isn't the impression Dad wanted you to create here. It's going to be an expensive drug. It's got to be if we're going to make our money back, and make the kind of profit we deserve to on it.' Her eyes looked calculating and hard as he watched her.

'Let's not talk about it,' Peter said as he picked up his briefcase, thanked the aides and walked out of the building with Katie right behind him. He had nothing left to say to her. She didn't understand any of it. She understood the profit in the drugs they sold, but not the heart, she understood the words, but not the meaning. But she also didn't dare push him now. He had successfully overcome one obstacle, but now he had his biggest hurdle in front of him, at the FDA hearings. They had a little over an hour left before he had to appear, as they got into the limo.

Kate suggested they go somewhere for lunch, but Peter only shook his head. He was thinking of what she had just said to him after the congressional hearings. He had blown it, as far as she was concerned. He had failed, he had not upheld the party line, promising to keep Vicotec, and all their other drugs, as expensive as possible, so they could make a huge profit on them, and please her father. He was glad he had said what he had, and he was going to fight like a dog in the next months, to keep Vicotec's price down. Frank had no idea how relentless Peter planned to be about it.

In the end, they ate roast beef sandwiches in the limousine, with coffee in paper cups. And Peter looked nervous to Kate as the car stopped at the FDA at 5600 Fishers Lane in Rockville, Maryland. It had taken them half an hour to get there from Capitol Hill, and when they arrived, Peter could see easily it was not a pretty building, but important things happened here, and that was all Peter could think of. He kept thinking of what was going to happen here today. What he had come here to do. What he had promised Frank and Katie. The promise he'd made them hadn't come easily, but being there was far worse, knowing that he was hiding a dangerous flaw from the FDA, and promising them the drug was ready to be unleashed on an unsuspecting public. He just prayed that Frank held up his end of the deal, and would pull the product if they had to.

Peter's palms were damp as he walked into the hearing room, and he was too nervous to notice the people attending the hearing. He said not a word to Katie as she left him and took her seat. In fact, he forgot all about her. He had important work to do, he had ideals to sacrifice, and principles to relinquish. And yet, if the product worked, they would save lives, or at the very least extend them. It was still a terrible quandary for him, knowing what he did, and also how badly the drug was needed.

At the FDA, Peter was not sworn in, but here truth was even more crucial. And as he looked around, he felt light-headed. But at least he knew what he had to do now. And it would be over soon. He hoped that his betrayal of the very people he had hoped to

339

help would take only a few minutes, though he feared it might take considerably longer.

He felt his hands shake as he waited for the advisory committee to begin asking him questions. It was the most terrifying experience of his life, and nothing like his appearance before Congress only that morning. That had been so harmless and so simple compared to this. His appearance at the FDA seemed so ominous in comparison, there was so much more at stake, so much resting on his shoulders. But he kept telling himself that all he had to do was get through it. He couldn't allow himself to think of anyone, not Kate, not Frank, not Suchard, not even the reports he had read. He had to stand up and speak about Vicotec, and he knew everything about it, as he, sat, waiting nervously at the long narrow table.

He thought suddenly of Katie then, and all he had sacrificed for her, and her father. He had given them the gift of his integrity, and his courage. It was more than he 'owed' anyone, her or her father.

But once again, he forced her from his mind, and tried to gather his wits, as the head of the committee began speaking. Peter could feel his head spinning as they asked him a series of very specific and technical questions, and the reason he had come here. He explained clearly and succinctly, and in a strong voice that he had come before them for approval of human trials for a product which he believed would change the lives of the segment of the American public afflicted with cancer. There was a small stirring among the committee members, a shuffling of papers, and a look of interest, as he began describing Vicotec and how it could be used by cancer patients everywhere. He told them essentially the same thing he had told Congress only that morning. The difference here was that these people were not going to be impressed by a flashy medicine show. They wanted, and were able to understand, all the most complicated details. And Peter was stunned to realize after a while, as he glanced up at the clock on the wall, that he had been talking for an hour, when they asked him the final question.

'And do you in fact believe, Mr Haskell, that Vicotec is ready to be tested on humans, even in small doses on a limited number of people who understand the risk they are taking? Do you truly feel that you have in fact assessed the nature of all its properties, and any risk that could be involved? Do you give us your word, sir, that you feel without any hesitation that this product is ready for human trials at this moment?'

Peter heard the question clearly in his head and he saw the man's face and knew what he had to answer. He had come here to do this. It was a matter of a single word, of assuring them that Vicotec was indeed everything he said, and everything they had thought it would be. All he had to do was promise them, as keepers of the American public's safety, that Vicotec would not harm them. And as he looked around the room at them, and thought of the people there, their husbands and wives, their mothers and their children, and the infinite number of people Vicotec would reach, he knew he couldn't do that. Not for Frank, or for Kate, or for anyone. But most of all, not for himself. And he knew without a moment's doubt, that he should never have come here. Whatever it cost him, whatever they said, whatever the Donovans took from him or did to him now, he knew he could not do it. He could not lie to these people about Vicotec, or about anything. That was not who he was. And it was absolutely clear to him what he was doing when he did it. He knew with absolute certainty that his whole life was gone at that single moment, his job, his wife, maybe even his sons, or not, if he was lucky. They were almost grown, and they had to understand what their father stood for. And if they couldn't accept that, or understand that integrity was worth paying a price for, then he had done his job wrong with them. But whatever it took now, he was willing to pay whatever price he had to, to be fair to the American public.

'No, sir, I cannot,' Peter said firmly. 'I cannot give you my word yet. I hope I will one day very soon. I think we have developed one of the finest pharmaceutical products that the world has yet to see, and one desperately needed by cancer patients the world over. But I do not believe we are sufficiently risk-free yet.'

'Then you can't expect us to grant you permission for Phase One Human Trials at this time, can you, Mr Haskell?' the senior member of the advisory committee asked him, looking confused, as a slight furor spread throughout the rest of the committee, as they asked each other why Peter had come here. FDA hearings were not usually used as a forum to tout unfinished products. But they admired his honesty at least, though none of them knew it had ever been in question. There was only one face in the room that was convulsed with fury. And there would be another at home when she told him that he had betrayed them.

'Would you like another date to come

before us again, Mr Haskell? That might be more appropriate than taking up more time now.' They had a full calendar before them. Peter had been the first of the afternoon, and there were several others after.

'I would like another date, sir. I believe six months is a realistic figure.' Even that would be tight, but from what Paul-Louis had just said, Peter thought they could make it.

'Thank you for coming.' And with that, they dismissed him and it was over. He walked out of the room on legs that were trembling, but his back was straight, his head was held high, and he felt like a decent human being. It was the only thing left to him now and he knew that. He saw Kate waiting for him in the distance, and he walked over to her. He couldn't imagine that she'd forgive him. There were tears on her cheeks when he walked up to her, and he wasn't sure if they were tears of rage or disappointment, probably both, but he didn't offer her any comfort.

'I'm sorry, Kate. I didn't plan to do that. I didn't realize what it would feel like, literally standing up before them and lying to them. They're an impressive bunch in there. I couldn't do it.'

'I never asked you to,' she lied, 'I just wanted you not to betray my father.' And then

344

she looked at him sadly. It was over and she knew it. For both of them. He wasn't willing to compromise for her anymore, to give up what he believed in. He had never realized how far it had gone, until that single moment. 'You realize what you just did in there?' she said unkindly, prepared to defend her father to the death, but not her husband.

'I can figure it out.' But she had already made herself clear that morning across their kitchen table in Greenwich. And he didn't flinch now. In an odd way, this was what he wanted. Freedom.

'You're an honest man,' she said, looking at him. But on her lips it sounded like an accusation. 'But not a very smart one.'

He nodded, and she turned and walked away, without even looking back at him, and he didn't follow her. It had been over for a long time, and neither of them had known it. He almost wondered if she'd ever been married to him, or maybe only to her father.

He had a lot to think about as he walked out of the FDA building in Rockville. Kate had just disappeared in the limo, leaving him stranded in Maryland, half an hour from Washington. But he didn't care. Not at all. It was one of the most important days of his life, and he felt as though he could fly now. He had been put to the test, and in his own mind, he had passed with flying colors. . . . Do you, sir, give us your word . . . no I don't. He still couldn't believe he had done it, and he didn't know why he didn't feel worse about Kate, but he didn't. He had just lost his wife, his job, his home. He had appeared before Congress that morning, and before the FDA that afternoon, as the president of an international company, and he had walked out empty-handed, unemployed, and alone. He had nothing but his integrity, and the knowledge that he hadn't sold out. He had done it!

And as he stood smiling to himself, looking up at the September sky, he heard a voice just behind him. It was familiar but strange, and there was a husky quality to it that came from another time, another place, and as he turned with a look of astonishment, he saw Olivia standing just behind him.

'What are you doing here?' he asked, desperate to put his arms around her, but afraid to do it. 'I thought you were in France, writing.' His eyes drank her in like wine, and she looked up at him with a small smile. She was wearing black slacks and a black sweater, and she had a red jacket slung over her shoulder. She looked like an ad for something very French, and all he could think of was the night he had followed her out of the Place Vendôme, and all that had happened in the five days he'd been in Paris, five days that had changed their lives forever. She was even more beautiful now, and he realized as he looked at her, how desperately he had missed her.

'That was pretty good in there,' she said, smiling at him more broadly. She was obviously proud of him, but she hadn't answered his question. She had come to support him, even if invisibly, at the hearings. She had read about the hearings in the *Herald Tribune* in Europe. And she wasn't sure why, but she knew she had to be there. She knew how much Vicotec meant to him, and the trouble he'd been having with it when she last saw him. And she wanted to be there. Her brother had told her where the hearings would be, and arranged for her to attend them. And she was grateful now that she had followed her instincts. Edwin had told her about the congressional hearings too, and she had seen Peter in Congress that morning. She had been sitting quietly next to Edwin. And although he'd wondered about her sudden interest in the pharmaceutical industry, he hadn't asked her any questions.

'You're braver than you think,' Olivia reminded Peter as she looked up at him, and he pulled her slowly close to him, wondering how he had survived the last three and a half months without her. He couldn't imagine leaving her again, not for a single moment.

'No, you're brave,' he said softly, his eyes filled with admiration. She had given up everything, walked out on all of it, and compromised nothing. And then suddenly he realized that he had just done the same thing. He had given up his wife, his job, everything, for what he believed in. They were both free now. At a huge price, admittedly, but to both of them it had been worth it. 'What are you doing this afternoon?' he asked with a grin. He could think of a thousand things, the Washington Monument . . . the Lincoln Memorial . . . a walk along the Potomac . . . a hotel room somewhere, or just standing there, looking at her forever . . . or a plane back to Paris.

'I'm not doing anything,' she smiled. 'I came here to see you,' she said softly. She hadn't expected to talk to him, just to see him from the distance. 'I'm going back tomorrow morning.' She hadn't even told her parents she was coming, just Edwin, and he had promised not to tell them. All she had hoped for was a glimpse of Peter, to see him again for a minute or two, even if he never knew it.

'Can I buy you a cup of coffee?' he asked, and they both smiled at the memory of the Place de la Concorde, and that first night in Montmartre, as he took her hand, and they walked down the steps to freedom.

**THE END**

**LIGHTNING**
**by Danielle Steel**

As a partner in one of New York's most prestigious law firms, Alexandra Parker barely manages to juggle husband, career, and the three-year-old child she gave birth to at forty. Then lightning strikes – a routine medical check-up turns her world upside down when tests reveal shattering news. Her husband Sam, a Wall Street whiz-kid, is as proud of his long-time marriage to Alex as he is of his successful career – until he is caught off guard by Alex's illness. Terrified of losing his wife and family, Sam fails to provide any kind of emotional support for Alex or his daughter.

Almost overnight, Sam takes his distance from Alex, and they become strangers. As lightning strikes them again, Sam's promising career suddenly explodes into disaster, and his very life and identity are challenged. With his future hanging in the balance, Alex must decide what she feels for Sam, if life will ever be the same for them again, or if she must move on without him.

*Lightning* tells the story of a family thrust into uncertainty. In this significant novel Danielle Steel explores whether the bonds of love and marriage can withstand life's most unexpected bolts of lightning.

0 552 13749 9

## WINGS
### by Danielle Steel

From her family's dusty farmland airstrip near Chicago, the child Cassie O'Malley would look at the planes sitting shimmering in the moonlight. Her First World War veteran father Pat wanted his son to be a pilot, not his reckless red-haired daughter. But ever since she could remember, Cassie had felt the pull of taking to the skies, and her father's partner Nick, fellow air ace and airborne daredevil, was willing to break all the rules to teach her to fly.

When Cassie was invited to California to become a test pilot, her record-breaking flights soon made her a media darling. Risking her life, pushing herself to her limits, in a world preparing for the Second World War, she decided to chart her own course and pursue her own destiny, whatever it cost her.

*Wings* is set in a time of constant change, when the world was on the brink of a war and the skies were filled with adventurers, a time when courage and daring forever changed modern-day aviation.

0 552 13748 0

# A LIST OF OTHER DANIELLE STEEL TITLES
## AVAILABLE FROM CORGI BOOKS

| | | | |
|---|---|---|---|
| ☐ | 13523 2 | **NO GREATER LOVE** | £5.99 |
| ☐ | 13525 9 | **HEARTBEAT** | £5.99 |
| ☐ | 13522 4 | **DADDY** | £5.99 |
| ☐ | 13524 0 | **MESSAGE FROM NAM** | £5.99 |
| ☐ | 13745 6 | **JEWELS** | £5.99 |
| ☐ | 13746 4 | **MIXED BLESSINGS** | £5.99 |
| ☐ | 13526 7 | **VANISHED** | £5.99 |
| ☐ | 13747 2 | **ACCIDENT** | £5.99 |
| ☐ | 14245 X | **THE GIFT** | £5.99 |
| ☐ | 13748 0 | **WINGS** | £5.99 |
| ☐ | 13749 9 | **LIGHTNING** | £5.99 |
| ☐ | 14131 3 | **MALICE** | £5.99 |
| ☐ | 14132 1 | **SILENT HONOUR** | £5.99 |
| ☐ | 14133 X | **THE RANCH** | £5.99 |
| ☐ | 14507 6 | **SPECIAL DELIVERY** | £5.99 |
| ☐ | 14504 1 | **THE GHOST** | £5.99 |
| ☐ | 14502 5 | **THE LONG ROAD HOME** | £5.99 |
| ☐ | 14637 4 | **THE KLONE AND I** | £5.99 |
| ☐ | 14134 8 | **MIRROR IMAGE** | £5.99 |
| ☐ | 54654 2 | **HIS BRIGHT LIGHT:** The story of my son, Nick Traina | £5.99 |
| ☐ | 14503 3 | **BITTERSWEET** | £5.99 |
| ☐ | 14508 4 | **GRANNY DAN** | £5.99 |
| ☐ | 04072 4 | **IRRESISTIBLE FORCES** (Hardback) | £16.99 |
| ☐ | 04362 6 | **THE HOUSE ON HOPE STREET** (Hardback) | £9.99 |
| ☐ | 03442 2 | **THE WEDDING** (Hardback) | £16.99 |